TEMPT ME

TEMPT ME

MASQUERADE CLUB
BOOK TWO

LILITH DARVILLE

eBook ISBN: 978-1-998127-02-3
Paperback ISBN: 978-1-998127-03-0
Hardcover ISBN: 978-1-998127-04-7
Audiobook ISBN: 978-1-998127-05-4

Cover Design by Atra Luna Design (www.atraluna.de)
Editing by Maggie Morris, The Indie Editor (www.indieeditor.ca)
Formatting by Kate Tilton's Author Services, LLC (www.katetilton.com)

For my Neo. There is no more than most! 😉
Thank you for joining me on this journey.

PROLOGUE

I loved Meredith Kincaid with every fiber of my being. She was the one I was meant to spend my life with.

Then the accident changed my life and everything I believed in.

I gave her some flimsy excuse—I can't remember what—for needing to borrow the Porsche 914-6 to shop for a ring.

"You just want to go for a joyride." She laughed. "Take all the time you need. I'm going to bike down to the public beach. I need some exercise if I'm going to keep up with you." She dangled the keys and pulled me in as I reached for them, wrapping herself around me and kissing me deeply.

Several long, breathless minutes later, she cupped my butt and guided me out the door. I paused and took another look at her as she stood framed by the bright afternoon sun.

My God, she's beautiful! Yes, this was the woman I was going to spend the rest of my life loving.

I was thrilled to find the perfect ring in the beach town of Bayfield and eager to get back to Meredith. I cranked up the volume on the sound system and sang at the top of my lungs to my favorite Eagles tunes. Meredith was *my* sweet darling, and she was going to get the best of *my* love. Unsure of how I was going to do it, I was equally sure I'd propose that very night. Meredith was my world.

I came back to reality with a jolt when I neared Kincardine and saw a cluster of cars and people ahead. I pulled to the side and walked over to one of the bystanders.

"What happened?"

"Someone got hit."

"Are they badly hurt?"

"She's not moving."

"I don't think she's breathing."

"Has anyone gone for help?" I asked.

"Yeah. Some guy said he'd go to the nearest house and call an ambulance."

I pushed through the crowd to see whether I could help. The crushed remains of a bicycle lay beside the mangled front end of a van. For a split second, my brain refused to process the sight of Meredith lying curled on her side on the pavement.

I strode forward, pushing someone out of my way, knelt beside her, and gathered her in my arms.

She's only fainted. That's it. She passed out. She'll come to in a minute.

But her utter stillness and the trickle of blood oozing from the corner of her mouth told a different story.

I cradled her and screamed and screamed and screamed without making a sound. I remained frozen with her until the emergency crew took her from me. There were no tears and never would be again. My pain hardened into rage.

"Who did this?"

The woman crouched beside me shrank back at the quiet intensity of my voice. She stood and pointed to a man sitting on the curb holding his head in his hands, rocking and mumbling. I stood and walked toward him. The smell of alcohol fumes overwhelmed me. The man's mumbles became a chant: "It's not my fault. I didn't mean to." I looked at him, and the beginnings of a white-hot fury threatened to consume me.

I bent and whispered, "Even prison is too good for you. I'll make sure you pay for this the rest of your miserable life."

Tormented by the pain of my loss, I shut down and walled off the world. For just over a week, the only action I took was what I needed to keep me alive. At night, I lay on the bunkhouse bed and stared at the ceiling. My chest constricted and my heart tore, again and again and again. I stared at the unpainted planks adorning the far wall and saw nothing but my own tortured thoughts. During the day, I moved to the picnic-table bench in the tiny kitchen.

I couldn't function; at times, I couldn't breathe. Inch by inch, my emotions crawled a little closer to the room in the corner of my mind where I would lock them up and throw away the key. If loving someone hurt this much, it would be better not to love at all.

Over time, I accepted the fact life would never be the same for me. Any emotion I may have known reminded me of how pathetic and weak I'd become. That was about to change. I vowed I'd never allow myself to feel this kind of pain again, to believe in a world that callously tears you apart, seemingly without reason or the slightest hint of compassion.

At the end of ten days, I emerged, unshaven, ragged, and a little beaten down. I was determined to attain the wealth and power I needed to assure me complete control over all aspects of my future. Brett Sandvine, media mogul and my beloved Meredith's mentor, was just the man to help me. He made me his protégé. Under his tutelage, I transferred from medical school and completed a master's in business administration.

I'm not sure whether Brett saw potential in me or whether he took me under his wing knowing how much I'd loved Meredith, but together we built the media empire that was Magnum International. I became the son he never had. He taught me everything I needed to know.

Magnum grew into a powerful consortium beyond expectations. In time, Brett turned over control of the company to me and assumed the position of chair of the board. We were unstoppable. Being busy and successful filled the void. I had my work and my Masquerade Clubs. I had companionship at the snap of my fingers. It was easy to convince myself I needed nothing I couldn't control. All was right in my world, except . . .

KATHERINE

I hadn't thought about Connor in years. There were times the feel of his hand smacking my ass consumed my dreams. I had pushed those dreams aside. Oh yeah, no time for that nonsense. Yup, everything was tickety-boo, that is until my boss, Vice President of Editorial, Kevin Jordan, introduced me to the new Senior Vice President of Operations as one of Magnum International's star performers. I went rigid with shock.

Standing right in front of me was the drop-dead gorgeous Connor McClane, impeccable in what had to be a custom-made suit with a gray shirt and black tie setting off his striking, angular features—*trés chic*. I yearned to reach out and stroke that suit.

Forget the suit, stroke him.

Seriously, my heart went into arrhythmia. Cardiac arrest was imminent, and I wasn't sure whether it was seeing him again after all these years or how gorgeous he looked.

His left eyebrow shot up, and a charming smile spread from a pair of exquisite lips right through the rich velvet of his gray-green eyes.

"Star performer, eh? I'll have to keep my eye on you."

He shook my hand. His gaze caressed my body briefly before he turned his attention to the others in the group.

I saw a flash of recognition and longing jolt through him, but perhaps I read into it. Speechless, I stood and stared after the man I'd loved, and left, in our youth. He hadn't changed. Yes, there were subtle differences, but the fine hair on his arms still started in the same place on his wrist. His hair still had the silky curls I wanted to run through my fingers, and the sound of his voice still made me feel as if I were taking a bath in warm toffee.

I couldn't tear my eyes from him. I was fascinated by the way he motivated and managed the executive group and painted his vision for future growth with fluid grace and ease. He wasn't outgoing even if he could be quite animated when in the spotlight, but he was absolutely stunning with a magnetic personality.

The women on the team each tried their hand at engaging his attention, and I worked hard to control the annoyance shooting through me when they fawned over him. He stood back and watched. Although never impolite, it was evident he rejected their advances. He still seemed to prefer his own company. I relaxed a little; I had no right to be tense.

Looks like he's still as hard to get to know as he ever was.

Red-hot lust shot through my core every time I glanced his way, and I found it hard to focus. My attraction to him was as strong as it had been twenty years ago—maybe stronger, and it scared me. I took care to match his professional courtesy during any interaction.

Note to self: watch it, Katherine.

Exhausted from the effort of trying to appear nonchalant all day, I opted out of dinner and dancing with the group—a political *faux pas*, no doubt, but necessary. I'm an introvert at heart, and I detested having someone dictate how I spend my social time. I needed a few minutes away from the social roller coaster of the executive team meetings, so I grabbed a drink at the hotel bar. I ordered a long island iced tea instead of my usual red wine—not the smartest thing to do, but I needed a release from the pent-up energy driving me, source unknown.

Okay, yes, that's a big fat whopper. Connor was the source, as much as I hated to admit it, and seeing him again had sent me for a major loop. I sat at a small table in a dark corner of the room where I could watch the dancers unobserved.

A bolt of electricity raced up my spine as if the ions rearranged themselves in the wake of a shooting star. I looked up and recognized Connor's cat-like grace as he strolled over to the bar.

As he ordered a drink, I struggled to keep the intensity from my gaze so I wouldn't attract his attention. Then a stunning blonde approached him, stood on tiptoe, and whispered in his ear. His smile was a mixture of humor and cynicism, but he bent to listen. The old irrational possessiveness came flooding back as if it were yesterday. *If he's going to be with anybody, it should be me.*

His reply made the blonde tip back her head and toss her hair. She said something else to him, and he shook his head. I almost heard Blondie's "humph" before she flounced off. He smiled to himself, scanning the room before settling on one of the barstools. I quickly looked down at my table and sank further into the darkness of the corner booth, watching him out of the corner of my eye.

I signaled the server and ordered another "tea," intentionally oblivious to the effect the blend of triple sec, light rum, gin, vodka and tequila was having on me. When I reached for my wallet to pay for the drink, the server said, "It's already taken care of."

"By whom?"

"By me." Connor gestured toward the chair opposite me. "May I?"

"I guess so. I mean, sure."

I took another mouthful of my drink. *Jeez, Katherine, could you be any more articulate?* I blushed at my inability to think of something witty or clever to say. Try as I might, witty repartee always occurred to me after-the-fact.

"It's been a long time." I wanted to kick myself.

Connor held my eyes for a long moment and smiled.

"You left me without a word," he said.

Intense. Always to the point. *My turn.*

"And you never came after me," I retorted. *Came after me? Where did that come from?*

"If you'd wanted to be there, you would have stayed."

"Maybe." *Stalemate.*

I couldn't stop staring. He was exquisite. Those mercurial eyes gazed steadily back. The half smile that made a flutter of sunshine spread throughout my loins came and went. He undressed me with those penetrating eyes. I took another gulp of my drink.

More staring. It would appear he was still comfortable with silence. I most definitely was not, at least not with him. After what seemed like a lifetime, one in which I had more to drink, I looked at my watch and gasped.

"Oh my God. I've got to go. I'm giving a presentation in the morning."

As we got up to leave, I stumbled. *Oh shit, I'm drunk.* And there sat Mister Calm-Cool-and-Collected acting as if he'd been drinking his beloved Pepsi.

Connor smiled, cupped my elbow, and walked with me to my room. As we rode up the elevator, I fought the desire to reach up and kiss those luscious lips, afraid of rejection. I fumbled with the key card. He reached over, took the card, and slid it through the lock.

I froze. Every nerve in my body tingled. He pushed open the door and gave me the key. Those intense eyes undressed me. But I broke eye contact and walked into the room. When the door closed behind me, I released the breath I'd been holding. When I turned to bolt the door, Connor leaned against it, watching me.

"Let me see you." He spoke in a voice quiet with command.

Ignoring the dampness between my legs, I made a pact with myself—I was *not* going to allow this to happen.

"Connor, I'm not . . . We're not . . . I mean . . . It's been years since . . ."

I took a deep, calming breath. *Twit.* Here I was acting like the young woman I'd been on our first date, right down to the wetness spreading between my legs.

"Let me see you," he repeated.

"Um, give me a minute." I fled to the bathroom. *Get it together, girlfriend.*

I splashed cold water over my burning face in a vain attempt to sober up. I looked at the wide, brown eyes staring back at me in the mirror until calm settled over me. What to do? Should I send him packing? Did I even want to? *Wow, wait a minute. Give your head a shake.* Of course, I should stand up to him.

"Let me see you." The words brushed through me, washing away logical thought.

I kicked off my sandals and took an eternity washing my face and brushing my teeth, my mind at war with the sexual hunger burning through me. Part of me hoped Connor would get sick of waiting and leave. Part of me raced with excitement at the certainty of his command of himself and the situation. I straightened up with new resolve. If Connor was still there, I'd ask him to leave.

He sat in the corner, hands steepled under his chin, and looked at me. Under his scrutiny, I instantly became a schoolgirl again, a child who had disobeyed. He shook his head slightly and, with effortless grace, stood facing me.

"Come here." His voice was quiet yet full of command.

As if hypnotized, I moved in front of him. The tips of his fingers traced my bare arms. Goose bumps immediately sprang to the surface, and sexual electricity jolted through me. I lowered my head. He reached under my chin and forced me to look up, challenging me to react. He edged down the zipper of my little black dress and let it fall to the floor. Suddenly, nothing else existed outside my need to give myself to him, to have him take me, *now*.

The heat emanated from him as his fingers outlined the curve of my breasts. I shivered. I loved his hands. His touch reminded me of the thing I craved. Thoughts that filled so many sleepless nights. Thoughts that I avoided admitting to myself—to surrender to his will.

He hooked his index fingers in the band of my bikini briefs and drew them down my legs, waiting until I stepped out of them. I did, like an obedient child wanting to please him.

Now I was naked and more than a bit self-conscious. Needing to do something with my hands, I reached out to unbutton his shirt, but he pushed my arms down to my sides, encouraging a passive acceptance of his control. I complied, allowing him to focus his attention on my breasts while I tried not to think about how I looked standing there. He played with each, first with nimble fingers and then with his lips. I couldn't stop the moan of pleasure escaping as more moisture built between my legs.

"Lie down and spread your legs wide for me. Don't move. Don't speak."

I started to protest. He put a finger over my lips and led me to the bed. I should have objected but couldn't. I closed my eyes and waited. That was the moment I surrendered myself to him, and I liked it.

"Watch me," he said. Again, his voice insisted he be obeyed.

I watched him undress. He had a splendid body, all smooth lines and sinew. I swear Michelangelo used him as the model for David, right down to the brown curls framing the sculpted lines of his face. His engorged cock sprang to attention when it escaped from the prison of his pants.

Naked, he straddled me and pushed my arms up over my head. I closed my eyes.

"Look at me. I want you to watch me watching you," he said.

Holding both hands above my head with one hand, he reached down with the other and pulled my nether lips apart and thrust his cock in straight to the hilt and rode me. He took his time, gliding his heat out inch by inch to the tip before burying it deep within me again and again. With each stroke, my clit brushed against his pubis, fanning the flames of my passion.

Each time my eyes started to close, he reminded me to watch him. Each command, like each thrust, drove me nearer to a frenzy so powerful I wanted to scream. His cock glistened with my essence, exciting me more. Nothing else existed except his body moving in mine. For what seemed like an eternity, he fucked me. I lay spread and captive to his will.

When I struggled with the need to come, he tightened his grip and continued his languid ride. He seemed to take pleasure in teasing me to distraction. Finally, he increased the tempo of his thrusts, and together our bodies convulsed in explosive orgasms.

"Alley Kat." His whisper was so soft I might have imagined it. Without another word, he slid out of me, got dressed, and left.

Some things never change.

I lay alone, relaxing in the afterglow except for a few unexpected quivers running through me. That was the Connor I remembered. Not so much the way he dominated sexually, but the obvious control and emotional distance he maintained. He was a man women wouldn't or couldn't say no to. It wasn't that you ever felt forced or intimidated. It was more the realization that if you resisted, he would only smile and walk away, leaving you wondering about what could have been.

He never kissed me.

He sparked an overwhelming sexual need that exposed every dark fantasy I tried so hard to hide. If I was honest with myself, it was a need I knew too well. One I avoided my whole life. My feelings for Connor threatened to break down my defenses, and that scared me more than I cared to admit. Sex was not the problem. It was those same secret fantasies, late at night, touching myself, that both tortured and excited me beyond reason.

I stumbled to the bathroom. The disarray of loose black curls framing my face mirrored my chaotic thoughts.

I can't believe I did it again. Yet if there were a next time, I would do anything he asked of me. *What on earth is wrong with me?* I was usually so decisive, so in control of my world.

I'd sworn I'd never be anyone's plaything again. Yet Connor drew me to him, like the proverbial moth to a flame. Just the thought of him brought a warm flush of desire to my core. I shook my head and put the evening's events down to the stupidity of an alcohol-fueled moment of weakness.

After all, it's only sex, right?

Wrong. I hadn't experienced such intensity since the first and last time I'd been with Connor.

I'd met Connor at university. Even then, he was cold, dark, brooding, smart, and one of the best-looking guys I'd ever laid eyes on. We started hanging out together. I hid the burning desire growing in my belly, convincing myself I wanted nothing more than a casual relationship. As much as he tried to hide it, my friendship was breaking through the emotional barrier he maintained with the conviction of a religious zealot. When I asked him to talk about what he was looking for in a relationship, he always passed it off saying, "Love isn't on my agenda."

Maybe it wasn't, but there was deep-seated hurt in his eyes when he said it, and I'd loved him all the more because of it.

In the ensuing months, to my growing frustration, he never attempted to sleep with me. Sure, he'd played with me, and there'd been some heavy petting sessions, but he never went beyond that. It was as if he was afraid to, which defied reason because his reputation for sleeping with almost every girl on campus was legendary. Our bond and our friendship deepened.

After graduation, everyone was celebrating at the local pub. Connor worked the room to the delight of the women vying for his attention. They reminded me of a pack of wild dogs fighting over the best piece of fresh meat. Okay, maybe that was a little harsh, but subtlety was never one of my strongest attributes. I wanted to kill every one of them, but all I'd allow myself to do was sit and watch him in action. So, no one was more surprised than I was when Connor walked me home. Just being near Connor excited me, not that I'd ever tell him that.

I was delighted when he accepted my offer for a nightcap.

Of course, I chattered incessantly, hoping I wasn't coming off like a love-struck twit. During one of my tirades, Connor held up his hand, stopping me midsentence.

"Take your clothes off," he said.

I can't explain it, but the next thing I knew, I was standing naked and trembling at the foot of the bed. I didn't resist when he placed me facedown, extended my arms, and bound them to the metal headboard with a couple of scarves he pulled from my dresser. Pulling my legs apart, he knelt between them.

I was exposed and vulnerable. If it had been anyone else, I would have resisted. But it was Connor, and by this time, I'd have done anything he asked. My excitement showed as the wetness oozed from me.

His cupped hand slid under me and captured the full mound of my sex. I pushed down, sliding through the wetness saturating the palm of his hand. My mind and body raged with need when he closed his hand in a vicelike grip, capturing my throbbing clit between the engorged lips of my cunt. In one quick motion, he removed his hand, grabbed my hips, lifted me to my knees, and buried his cock deep within me.

With each stroke, he slapped the cheeks of my buttocks, hard. His hand molded the round globes of my ass perfectly. My flesh shuddered under the impact, and I was sure he'd left his brand with a red-tinged imprint of his hand. I gasped as each slap enhanced the pleasure of his hard cock. I lost control, completely overwhelmed by the unrelenting waves of pleasure pulling me to a climax of uninhibited abandon.

I came, for the first time in my life. Connor clutched the stinging cheeks of my buttocks, arched back, and pulled out of me, painting the cheeks of my ass with the outcome of his climax. He leaned over me for a brief second, and I'm sure he whispered, "My Alley Kat."

Without another word, he untied my arms, dressed, and left.

And there I was, a young, inexperienced woman wrapped in a torrent of unresolved anguish threatening to tear me apart. *Only a slut would let a man tie her down and take her from behind.*

Every bit of my moralistic upbringing rose to the surface, and the emotions overwhelmed me. I couldn't admit how much I'd liked it. My desire for Connor battled with my guilt and shame. Without experience or the perception that comes with age, my shame won out.

Damn my Victorian upbringing. How can I ever look him in the face again?

Left with no choice, I packed up my car and headed to anywhere else, and ended up where? Full circle, right back where I'd started with him. Except I was stronger now. This time, I had a choice. At least that's what I told myself, knowing if he had told me to beg, I'd have done so, and willingly.

He called me Alley Kat. He remembered.

The next morning, to my great relief, he acted as if nothing had ever happened. If not for the soreness between my legs, I could almost convince myself it hadn't. In truth, I wanted him even more than I cared to admit to myself, and I had no idea what to do about it.

2

CONNOR

When you have to remind yourself to breathe, you know you're in serious trouble. I'd avoided trouble for twenty years, and now it was standing right in front of me, and her name was Katherine Aleia King, my Alley Kat.

Seeing the familiar, cocky tilt of her head made me smile. If the definition of beauty was symmetry, she was a perfect symbol. Curves now replaced angles on her five-foot, three-inch petite frame. Loose, black curls framed a round face with large, wide-set, gold-streaked brown eyes.

I'd vowed to forget this woman, but as much as I tried, she was never far from my thoughts. My Alley Kat looked very much the same as she had twenty years ago, all cuddly and warm with tiny, sharp claws ready to pierce at any given moment. A jolt of electricity stirred my cock in a way I'd only ever experienced with two women, and she was one of them.

I should have turned and run as fast as I could. If you've ever stood on the edge of a tall cliff, you know what I mean. The view was intoxicating. The fear was paralyzing. I'd fallen once and barely survived. It wouldn't happen again.

Kat was the only woman besides Meredith who'd inched her way underneath the cage encasing my heart. When I'd realized I cared for her, she'd up and left. The loss was too much to bear. I'd taken those emotions and tucked them into a box, wrapped securely with a ribbon of chain, locked, and hidden away into the farthest corner of the closet. Feelings I swore would never again see the light of day. And now, despite my resolve, I couldn't stop thinking of her.

Against my better judgment, I had to see her again. Her sexuality couldn't be denied. My only thought was to make her submit to her deepest need until she begged for release. It wasn't the pursuit of love; it was pure lust. If she so much as hinted at more, it would be my turn to walk away.

Others saw me as cold, calculated, and emotionally unavailable, the consummate business type. They were right. Yet some unrelenting force drew me. The sight of her lithe, youthful body at the boardroom table during the conference consumed me with thoughts of her writhing beneath me. The tension would build in my cock until it was near bursting, and nothing would bring release. Finally, I relented and sent her a text message, convincing myself our connection would end when the conference ended.

Meet me at the Old Mill Inn. Room 514 C.

And so I began a series of encounters, assuring myself this would be another fuckfest with a willing partner of like mind.

As an executive, Kat was confident, analytical, driven, and often brutally honest. As a lover, she acquiesced and submitted. I liked that. When I opened the door of the suite to greet her, she shed one persona for the other. Was she aware how compelling this was for me, or, for that matter, did she even know she did it?

We sat on the couch, unwinding after a particularly taxing day.

"Are you finding it difficult to keep our work and personal relationships separate?"

"What makes you ask that? Did I say something I shouldn't have?" She looked at me, intensity reflecting in those beautiful eyes.

"Not at all, Kat. In fact, it would be the exact opposite. When you take a position counter to the one I've taken, you usually preface your case with, "Connor, I respectfully submit . . .""

"And how does that make you feel? Do you want me to stop?"

There's that psych degree of hers in action again. I laughed.

"I can't say it makes me feel one way or the other, and no, I don't want you to stop. I do find that your arguments often influence me to change where I stand on an issue, and that's a good thing. I just want you to know I'm pleased that sharing a bed with you doesn't affect our working relationship."

She kept our dinner conversation light, although she discussed current events and occasionally threw in a sexual tidbit about one of her colleagues. If I asked her a personal question, she answered succinctly before changing the subject or challenging me with a personal question of her own.

I learned she preferred to ply me for information about my sexual likes and dislikes and fantasies. She seemed to be searching for something through me as if I had the answers. I didn't know if she was testing herself or me, but I was willing to find out as long as we left my heart out of it.

"It's time you choose a safe word."

There never seemed to be a right time to have this type of conversation, but during one of the sumptuous meals she preferred before sex seemed opportune.

"What do you mean, C? A safe word for what?"

"You know I like to dominate sexually, and my sense is you like it when I do. There's so much more I want to show you if you're open to it. The safe word is for you, to let me know if things are too intense and you wish to stop."

"You're the one who needs to be in control, so why do I need to choose a safe word?" Kat kept her gaze trained on me and took a bite of her salad.

"Alley Kat, a submissive, which I believe you are, is always the one in the driver's seat. If you're ever uncomfortable, all you need to do is say the safe word, and I'll immediately stop all activity."

"Huh." She took a sip of her wine. "I've got one. How about *Rasputin*?"

I coughed, almost choking.

"*Rasputin*? Isn't that a little over the top?"

She smiled. "What do you suggest?"

"How about *red light* if you want things to stop?"

"Okay, but what if I don't want you to stop but need you to back off on the pressure? Can *enough* be the signal for that?"

She was such a playful tease.

"Why don't we keep it simple and use *yellow light* in that instance."

"Sounds good to me. So *green light* would be full steam ahead, right? Shall we try it out?" She grinned at me and lifted her glass in salute.

"By all means. I look forward to it."

So far, she'd said *yellow light* once, leaving me with the distinct feeling it was more of a test than her unwillingness to comply. If there was a limit to her submissive desires, we hadn't found it. We had just scratched the surface, but I began to wonder who was leading whom.

We graduated to using beginner restraints and dildos, and I increased the duration and intensity of our sex until exhaustion overcame her. Surprisingly, she took to rolling over, snuggling her butt against my stomach, and falling into a deep sleep, giving me the opportunity to watch and stroke her before I drifted off. If I wished her to service me with a blowjob or a handjob, I had to catch her before this languid state set in. When I did, she was nothing less than enthusiastic; she was the perfect lover.

I loved the feel and smell of her, especially when she was pungent with the aroma of our sex. With each encounter, my desire to explore and probe the depths of her emerging depravity grew. I suspected my own lasciviousness knew no bounds, and I started to wonder where she would draw the line. She was overcoming the guilt of exploring those dark fantasies that had haunted her. It was the first step for her, not only to accept but also to embrace the truth of her sexuality.

A plan formed in my mind and working out the details to ensure success consumed me.

As the conference week drew to a close, I experienced emotions I had long since forgotten, and they were tearing me apart. Usually, I walked away. No regrets, no looking back. But here was a woman exploring her sexuality, and her enthusiasm was infectious. She openly embraced her mounting passion each time we came together, and the excitement of her lust became an addiction.

I ordered room service with her favorite foods. She preferred to eat in the privacy of the suite. As her confidence increased, she grew bolder. Tonight, she arrived wearing nothing but a coat and shoes. I closed the door. She spread the coat on the floor in front of the fireplace, lay down, and opened her legs for me. Dinner was cold by the time we were ready to eat, and I laughed as she tore into her steak, too ravenous to wait for me to reheat it.

We chatted about inane things as we ate, and I waited until I was sure she was relaxed and eager. As she got up to head for the bedroom, I stopped her.

"Just a minute, Kat, I have something I want to talk with you about."

"Okay, let's talk in bed," she said, smiling.

I almost caved. Perhaps we could wait. *God, this woman is challenging.*

"Let's sit here on the couch and enjoy another glass of wine while we talk."

She hesitated, frowned a little, and then gazed at me with bottomless lust in her eyes and finally complied. She sat quietly while I refilled our glasses.

"Okay, what's up?" she asked.

"I'd like to take our relationship to the next level."

The frown returned, deeper this time, and I hesitated a moment.

"Relationship? Connor, in the past week, you've helped me discover a part of who I am, and you probably have no idea how important that is for me. When I think about what I want you to do to me, it scares me. And yes, we have a lot of fun together. But you're still too emotionally distant, too guarded for me. Let's just enjoy what we have. That way, no one gets hurt."

Damn, she mistakes me. I'm losing her . . .

"I understand, Kat, but I'm not talking about a personal commitment. This has to do with our sexual relationship."

She seemed to relax a bit and sank back on the couch.

"I'm listening."

"I think you'll admit we've discovered a rare compatibility in our sex. I like to dominate, and you like to be dominated. Is that an accurate statement?"

"Yes. It's hard for me to admit, but you're showing me things about myself that I used to hide from."

She isn't making this easy.

"Well, I'd like to take things to the next level."

"But—"

"Hear me out, okay? I've never made a secret of the fact I like to dominate. This has been a serious part of my life for a long time. It has everything to do with control. I want—no, that's not it—I need someone who is not just willing to submit but must submit. It has to be an integral part of her sexuality. Someone who needs to be dominated sexually yet is her own person. Someone who finds true satisfaction by submitting to a master who pushes her to the point that breaks down her inhibitions, allowing her to give in to her darkest needs.

What are you thinking? Was I getting through to her? I couldn't read the cauldron of emotion bubbling behind that piercing stare. I waited a beat. She said nothing.

"It's not just about me. It's about you and what you want. I think you are that woman. Or, am I deluding myself?"

"Con—"

"Before you answer, Kat, know that if this is what you're looking for, you will do what I want, when I want, how I want, no questions asked. You can stop any time you wish, and that will be the end of our relationship. Yes, I said rela-tionship. I'm offering you a chance to submit to me, and, in turn, find yourself. Nothing more.

"I will never do anything to cause any real pain, and you can use the safe words to stop at any time you feel the need. The choice is yours."

I watched her carefully. At one point, she winced, but the interest in her expression encouraged me. I decided to take it one step further.

"The game may also involve you submitting to other

people of my choosing and under my direction. Again, at any time, you may choose not to play, but that will be the end of our relationship."

"You're not leaving me with much choice here." Her expression was inscrutable.

What are you thinking?

"You have complete choice. I believe we both thought this wouldn't continue after this week. However, I'm ready to take the next step. Or we can say our goodbyes and move on."

Was I too forward? What if she ran as she did twenty years ago? Could I accept that?

She sat quietly for a while. When she got up and walked around, my guts started to churn, afraid she might decide to walk out of my life for good. She gazed into the night, her body rigid with concentration. It was not easy to find a woman with her combination of innocence and depravity. I shut out the doubts leaking into my consciousness.

After what seemed a millennium but was only about five minutes, she came back, sat on the edge of the sofa, and looked me in the eyes.

"I have some conditions," she said.

"But, Kat—"

She placed a finger on my lips.

"Now it's my turn. I have a few conditions," she repeated. "This relationship, as you call it, is about sex and only sex."

"Of course. I didn't mean to imply—"

"These terms are nonnegotiable, Connor. I'm not inclined toward group sex or gang bangs. If you decide on bringing other people into the equation, it can be only one at any given time and one of my choosing."

"What else?"

"I'm not into pain. Slaps and a little stinging are one thing, but I'm not into anything that causes real hurt, bruising, or in any other way physically mutilates me. I'm not into sex involving bodily excretions such as urine or feces, either."

Humor tugged at my lips, but she was very serious, so I restrained myself and said, "What else?

"This one is most important—never, ever humiliate me. I can no longer deny I thrive on being controlled, but the thought of being humiliated makes me want to throw up and will definitely end our relationship."

Excellent. She's interested. Now I knew she was willing to proceed with the game; in business, they called her conditions *buying signals.* I looked at her, trying to get inside of her head.

"What would constitute humiliation in your book? After all, I've had you beg during our sex on several occasions. Was that humiliating?"

Her ears turned a deep crimson. "No," she said softly. "That wasn't humiliating. It was controlling. Doing something like leading me around by a leash would be humiliating to me."

"I can give you my word that will never happen unless you want it to. I have no desire to humiliate you nor do I wish to play or have you play with bodily excretions as you call them, although I may want to pee between your legs during my toilet fantasy."

Her spine snapped to attention, and this time I did laugh. "Kidding."

"This isn't a joke." She used her best boardroom voice. I forced myself to match her mood.

"I promise you I will never humiliate you nor will I subject you to group sex. Is that better? How's this—we can tweak our hard limits any time we feel the need. Will that work for you?"

She studied me for a minute and smiled.

"Hard limits, I like that. Yes, that will work for me. Now what are your hard limits?"

"Nothing you haven't covered." I took hold of her chin, pulled her face to mine, and kissed her long and hard.

"Now we can finalize our agreement with a little fun. I want you on the bed, naked, on your hands and knees. Do you want to play?"

Without a moment's hesitation, she walked to the bed, dropping her robe on the way, and knelt over the pillows I'd placed. I knelt behind her and grabbed the soft cheeks of her ass before ramming my hard cock deep inside her. She gasped, and I smiled inwardly with the knowledge I'd surprised her with my seeming lack of care about her state of readiness. But oh, she was ready.

I thrust into her fast and hard, relishing the tremors of her orgasm. I continued to ride her to more of those orgasms, acutely aware each one left her craving the intense clitoral orgasm more and more. I slammed into her until she panted with exhaustion, and then I allowed myself to come. The spasms of a powerful orgasm jerked through me again and again until all I wanted was to sink down beside her and hold her tight as we slept. But I needed to push her even further to ensure she understood the rules. She rolled over and started to curl onto her side in her favorite post-coital position.

"Not yet, my love. First, I want you to play with yourself until you come."

She opened her mouth to protest, and I asserted my dominance, leaving no room to question. "Now."

Her movements were slow, and I reached over and slapped her ass hard enough to sting and give her the message.

"I said now. Touch yourself."

She rolled on her back and used her fingers to rub herself.

Her eyes were closed tight, perhaps to lose herself in self-pleasure or to avoid the awkwardness of someone watching her. Either way, I didn't care. I took great pleasure in seeing her struggle to make herself come and played with myself as my cock jerked back to life.

I loved to watch her whether I played with her or she played with herself. During the conference meetings, I had to stop myself from imagining her writhing in agitation with her need to come or risk exposing obvious excitement when I stood up.

Finally, when I wondered whether she was over the brink of exhaustion, she came with a scream so loud I feared it would bring security, and she collapsed her legs. This time, as she started to curl, I said, "My turn." She seemed ready to succumb to her need to rest. Would she defy me?

"Choose." I lay back on the bed and put my hands behind my head.

She knelt, took my cock into her mouth, and sucked me dry. The game was on . . .

3

KATHERINE

I was sitting in my car, parked in my driveway, and I didn't remember how I got there. I was stone-cold sober, staring out the window into the inky darkness. I couldn't find the answer, but the question kept running through my mind.

What have I done? What have I done?

The last thing I remembered was the Zeppelin song I played on the drive home—"What Is and What Should Never Be."

I'm a smart, organized, rational career woman, and I took pride in all I'd accomplished. I had a good life, a nice home, and someday might share my world with a good husband. Cliché?

Yes, but I believe most people want a safe, secure life for the most part. That's the "what is". "What should never be" was the unpredictable temptation of a man like Connor McClane. Gorgeous? Oh my God—to die for, but too sure of himself, dark, brooding, and dangerous.

When he looked at me, it was as if he could see right through me. Dark secrets I had trouble admitting to myself were quickly becoming the playground for his sexual gratification. What scared me even more was the realization that to know myself, I needed him.

How many times had I explored those twisted fantasies to satisfy myself as I tortured my swollen clit to distraction? My fantasies revealed a side of me I could never talk about. Connor's proposal gave me permission to open that door, and if I did, I might never be able to close it again. I've always believed life is the pursuit of knowing yourself. On the other hand, there's an old saying that is equally true: "Be careful what you wish for, you might get it."

I got out of the car, focused on getting in the door and into a hot bath. I needed sleep. The door swung open as I turned my key in the lock, and I fell into Tim.

Tim? What the hell was he doing here?

"Why didn't you let me know you were coming back?" I pulled my suitcase in and closed the door.

"Hello to you, too. Don't I get a welcome back kiss?" Tim asked. He leaned in to kiss me. I turned my head to the side, allowing his lips to brush my cheek. A split second of guilt washed over me; after all, he was my best friend and one-time lover. *Dammit all, it never rains but it pours.* Now I had two men to contend with.

"When did you get here?" I pushed past him. "Never mind, it's been a long day. We'll talk in the morning."

"You're kidding me, right? I just got here, and you're blowing me off?"

I grimaced at the hard tone in his voice but figured he could smell the sex wrapping me like expensive perfume. It was just like Tim to be naïve enough to think we could pick up where we'd left off.

I put down my suitcase and turned to face him. His light-brown hair feathered over his forehead not quite covering chocolate brown eyes. The tucked and polished preppy look fit his slight frame as if made for it, and he could easily be the model for the academic of the year award.

"Let me get this straight. You fuck off for almost a year to find yourself, send the odd postcard, and then you reappear with no warning and expect me to cater to your needs?"

Tim opened his mouth to respond, but I put up my hand.

"I don't want to hear it, Tim. I'm too exhausted to talk right now. You'll find your room just the way you left it. I'll see you in the morning."

I picked up my bag and struggled upstairs, cursing Tim for not helping. Yes, I know, I was a strong independent woman who didn't need a man's help, but a little chivalry was nice occasionally.

I ran myself a hot bath, but not even the sound of the running water could drown out the slamming of the cupboards below.

Bastard. I should be the one pissed.

He had no right to just show up and then expect me to jump. Anger welled from deep inside with a fierceness that shocked me. I was overreacting, but it felt good to vent my feelings toward Tim. I wanted to run downstairs and shake him until he admitted he'd been a jerk for the way he'd treated me.

Long after I'd settled into bed, self-pity and a myriad of other emotions followed rage. How could he do this to me? What was it about men anyway that made them believe they could just march back into your life and take over? What made him think we could pick up where we'd left off when he returned from his sabbatical?

I'd met Tim Bancroft shortly after I'd settled in Toronto. After graduation from the University of Waterloo and that unexpected, not to mention disturbing, night with Connor, I'd headed for the big city and a future without him. Why choose the city where Connor would be working, you ask?

Well, I'd convinced myself Toronto was a big enough city I'd never run into him. *Yeah right.*

I'd found a job in publishing as a higher education sales rep, and Tim was one of the authors in my territory. Part of my job was to make sure he felt special and well cared for so he'd continue to write for Winston-Smith Publishing. So, I'd invited him to lunch.

We'd spent the afternoon talking, and that led to one date followed by another. Tim was the antithesis of Connor—caring, talkative, articulate, and funny. He didn't have an intense bone in his body—well, maybe the one he'd just shown with the tone at the door, but that was new.

With Tim, I'd felt special, and his solicitous care was just the balm I needed to heal the tear in my heart. The first time we'd made love, it was—um—well, nice. It was really quite lovely in a vanilla sort of way and had been that way ever since—nice and predictably safe. *And boring.*

When we'd both been without a place to stay, we'd found a place and started living together. No strings attached, just roomies. I'd been very clear about that. We'd become friends with benefits, and we'd lived that way for almost twenty years. Tim was a safe place to hide, one I needed. And a handy escort when needed.

Then Tim told me he'd accepted a one-year contract at the University of Edinburgh and asked me to go with him. I'd refused. I had my own life here in Toronto. By that time, Magnum International had acquired Winston-Smith, and I'd progressed up the ladder to the position of Director of Acquisitions. Also, if I'd gone with him, I would have had to make a commitment I wasn't prepared to make.

"Will you wait for me then?"

"A lot can happen in a year that we can't predict. Making a promise we probably won't keep would be wrong."

"You know you mean the world to me. Please, Katie. I've kept my word and never pushed, but now it's time. Come with me. Be with me. Let's move our relationship to the next level."

He'd been heartbroken and continued to plead. The best I could do was offer to agree to discuss how we felt about each other when he came back. We'd spent hours discussing our relationship, and now his words would come back to haunt him.

After all, hadn't he been the one who advocated sex for its own sake? We were both attractive people, and he'd been convinced we could maintain our relationship while befriending others. I thought he'd lost his mind, and the sentiment was proof positive he wasn't the one for me. I should have been the only one he ever wanted.

"I'm not sure that's possible, Tim. Or if it is, it's rare. I mean, as soon as you engage in conversation with someone, you've started a relationship."

He'd guffawed at what he called my naïve sentiment. Yes, he did actually guffaw. He'd said, "Maybe it's that way for women, but a man can have many conversations and indeed multiple sexual encounters without any emotional attachment at all."

"Several times? How is that possible? I couldn't screw a guy more than once without emotional involvement."

"That's because women often are looking for something deeper, like a lifelong relationship."

Hypocrite! Who's the one looking for deeper now?

"I don't think that's necessarily the case. It's just I wouldn't have sex with someone unless I liked the way he looked and I felt safe with him. How would I know if I felt safe with him unless I talked to him? So, what would you do if I were the one to fool around?"

"Well, I guess I'd have to kill you."

"I'm serious, Tim." My don't-mess-with-me tone was out in full force. This was not a trivial matter for me.

"Okay, I'm sorry. I guess that would depend."

"On what?"

"On whether you had feelings for him. Sex for sex's sake wouldn't be worth ruining our relationship."

"So let's say I met some guy at a conference, got drunk, and ended up having sex with him. You'd be okay with that?"

"I don't know if okay is the way I'd put it. Sure, I'd be hurt, but if it was just sex, then I'd get over it. Our relationship is more important to me than some meaningless sexual encounter."

Tim had struggled to keep from laughing as he watched me try to get my head around this. He had been so confident, so cocksure, and so certain I would never be capable of a meaningless sexual encounter.

But that's not how he'd behaved when I walked through the door earlier. Maybe he hadn't smelled the sex on me. Maybe it was just my imagination. Maybe the change in our relationship had everything to do with me and nothing to do with Tim.

Despite the conflicting emotions, I slept well and woke refreshed. My first thoughts were of Connor—what was he doing? Would he call? *Get it together, Katherine. You have Tim to deal with.*

I tried to find a sense of calm I could bring to our conversation. I thought back to our early days. I couldn't help but smile as I remembered how inexperienced and curious I had been. Although somewhat damaged by men who had used me badly, I was still eager to explore.

But Tim was into vanilla. An exciting encounter for him was getting a blowjob. And I'd convinced myself that was enough. I'd tried *really* hard.

Yet, if I was honest with myself, I'd always wanted more.

Yearned for more. I'd just refused to dwell on it except in my secret world of masturbation. Living together without commitment, we'd had the best of both worlds, although I wasn't one for playing around. I focused on my career, and Tim was always handy when I needed a warm body.

I laughed out loud as I recalled how I'd responded to his encounters with other women. In the very early days, it wasn't that nasty trait of jealousy driving my fury, but a deep sense of possessiveness—if he was going to have sex, then it should be with me. He always said I had the strongest sex drive he'd ever seen in a woman. I wasn't sure about that, but I did know I wasn't getting it often enough for him to be having a little on the side. I reached my ping point when he screwed one of his *friends*.

"Tim, you and I need to talk."

He sat on the couch looking all satiated and cozy while I fumed.

"Sure. What would you like to talk about?" He patted the couch beside him.

I threw up a little in my mouth at the thought of sitting next to him while the smell of his little slut wafted from him. I sat in the armchair opposite.

"Um, I know that we've agreed that we're just friends with no strings attached."

Tim laughed and looked entirely too smug for words. I wanted to take that limp little dick and tie it into a couple of knots.

"Get to the point, Katie. It's obvious something is bothering you."

I took a deep breath. "Okay, I need you to promise you won't bring any of your women here anymore."

"Do you mean to tell me I can't have friends visit anymore? Didn't we agree we wouldn't make demands on each other?"

"Well, not visit exactly . . ." I got up and paced the floor. The bastard. He knew exactly what I was getting at, but he was going to make me work for it. I was a fiery little twenty-five-year-old and unwilling to back down from a fight. I stopped wearing a hole in the living room rug and faced him down, arms akimbo.

"Look, Tim, I need you to give me your word you won't have sex with any of your little hookups here in the apartment. If you can't do that, then I'll move. It's as simple as that."

At first, he simply stared at me, and I started thinking about whom I could stay with. Why I was so angry with him? I danced around the long story and realized I was just as mad at myself as I was with him. Before she'd come over and screwed his ass off, this *friend* asked me to meet for a drink. She'd gone on at length about how important her marriage was to her and how she and Tim were strictly friends. I couldn't believe I'd fallen for that load of crap.

Anyway, he'd given me his word. He broke that word only once while I was in the apartment, but that is a story for another time. Other than that once, I never made demands or ultimatums, which was one of the many reasons he said he loved me. *As a friend.*

As the years moved on and our relationship grew, he battled with his jealousy as his physical possessiveness turned to emotional yearning. He was always up front about his love for me, but something kept me from making a commitment to him. I couldn't recall Tim ever complaining, and that was part of his attraction. He'd seemed quite content with our relationship. And then he'd, as I so eloquently put it, pissed off for a year. He may have been trying to make a point, but if so, that little plan had backfired on him.

I ruminated for a few more minutes, planning how I

would manage the conversation about resuming our relationship. I took my time getting ready, but the smell of fresh coffee pulled me downstairs. Tim sat at the table reading the newspaper.

"Good morning." I poured myself a cup of coffee. "Did you get any sleep?"

"I'm not into small talk this morning. We've got a lot to talk about, Katie."

As my eyebrows shot toward the ceiling, I fixed my eyes on his.

You show up unexpectedly after a frigging year, and it's all about what you want? Take a deep breath, Kat.

I took my own sweet time adding cream to my coffee before sitting down across from him.

"So, what brings you back so soon?"

"We'd better talk about the elephant in the room. How about starting with his name?"

I was shocked by the vehemence in his voice, but I had bigger issues to worry about. Would I break our vow of honesty and lie to him? Should I try to hide the truth? His eyes burned into mine as he studied my face.

"Connor."

"The Connor you were with before me?"

"Yes."

"Do you love him?"

"No."

In truth, I had no idea of my feelings except I thrived on the intensity Connor brought to my life.

Tim relaxed just a titch. "Are you having an affair with him?"

"I have no idea what you mean by that, nor is it any of your business."

"You're being deliberately obtuse, Katie, and I haven't the patience for it. We agreed we'd continue our relationship when I returned, so it's my business if you're involved with someone else."

My eyes widened at his tone, but I continued to return his gaze without flinching. My nerves were so bad I was ready to vomit, and he acted as if he couldn't care less about how I was feeling.

"No, I'm not being deliberately obtuse, Tim." I enunciated every word. "I just can't fathom how you think you can drop back into my life and pick up as if you'd never left. And, I'm not sure what you're asking me. If you mean am I emotionally involved with him, then the answer is no. If you're asking if I'll have sex with him again, then the answer is probably, and you'll just have to deal with it."

"I'll just have to deal with it?" Sarcasm dripped off his tongue. *"Deal with it?"*

I said nothing. He took a deep breath. I could tell this talk was not going the way he'd imagined.

"Okay. Sorry. I thought we had something special. I thought our sex was the best you'd ever had. I thought you were happy and satisfied with me. Have you been living a lie?"

I sighed. How did I let him down without destroying his ego and hurting him badly?

"No, Tim, it wasn't a lie, but things have changed." I kept my voice gentle and full of caring. His eyes filled with tears, and I could imagine his pain. Bursting his bubble would hurt him.

"No," I said again, "it's not about us. It's about me. I don't even know how to explain it, but I'll try. While you've been gone, I've had a lot of time to think about us. I do love you. You're my best friend . . . *Time to drop the f-bomb* . . . And I hope we can still be friends. I was satisfied with our lovemaking, but I wasn't passionate about it.

"Connor makes me feel something I've never felt before. I

didn't go looking for this—it just happened. I'm trying to figure it out myself. Sometimes I get this itch for a certain kind of sex, an itch you can't satisfy because you love me."

O-M-G, I said that out loud. Connor is getting to me.

"Itch! Isn't our love more important than some itch?"

"Give me a break here, Tim. If you want to hear how I feel, then let me explain, okay?"

He stared at me for a beat. "Okay, continue. What itch?"

"Okay, here goes." I took a deep breath. "Remember when I asked you to role play being a Dom with me in the sub role? I told you how much I thought I'd like it. I wanted to try more, and we had some great sessions. But you weren't dominant, and after each one, I needed more."

"More what?"

You would ask that. I sighed. "That's what's hard to explain. More force. To be controlled without being humiliated. Just more. Part of it is an attitude thing, and I've discovered you probably can't be the one to fill this need."

I looked down into my mug of coffee for a beat. He waited. I was certain he didn't want to hear what was coming next.

"And, I don't love you the way you think you love me, Tim. It's time for us both to be honest with each other."

"What the hell is that supposed to mean? You don't love me the way I *think* I love you?" His shout had a hysterical quality to it. *If only he'd brought that passion to the bedroom.*

"It means you're my best friend, and the love I feel for you is that for a very dear, very close friend."

"Do you sleep with all of your friends?"

I winced as the rawness of his hurt washed over me. He couldn't stop himself from lashing out.

"Like some—"

The hardness in my voice cut into the film of his fury. If he called me the s-word, I'd grab hold of his balls and twist—

hard. No, I'm not into violence, but let's be honest. Hasn't everyone dreamed of putting a hurt on someone being bitchy if pesky little laws didn't hold them back?

"Be very sure you want to say what you're going to say, Tim. Once said, you won't be able to take it back." I stood up and took his mug for a refill, giving him the space he needed to regain some semblance of control. I handed over his mug and took my seat.

"Better?"

"Yes. I'm sorry. This isn't easy, you know. First, let me be very clear about something. I don't think I love you. I do love you. If there's one thing my time away proved to me, it's that you're the one for me."

I opened my mouth, and this time it was Tim who put up his hand.

"And if I understand you correctly, you love me, but you're not in love with me. Have I got that right?"

He gave a ghost of a smile, and I almost gave my usual quip: I love it when you get professorial on me. But this wasn't the time.

"I confused my need for your safe haven, your acceptance, and your friendship with love. This time with Connor has helped me realize I need more than our relationship can give me. I'm no longer the frightened young woman. More importantly, it's time I found out who I am."

"So some other guy comes along who says he loves you to get into your pants, and you're willing to give up everything we've had?"

"Really, Tim, you're not doing yourself any favors with these snide remarks. Connor doesn't love me, and he's about dominance and control. Each time we meet, I feel like he's scratched the itch. I want to—no I need to see how far this will go."

"Is he married?"

"No, he never married."

"Why ever not, if he's such a prize?"

I ignored his childishness. "I haven't asked him why. For me, this really is about the sex."

"And you're willing to throw away the love of a good man for sex? How often do you want to see him?"

"Why does that matter?"

"If we decide to go ahead with this . . ."

"There's no *we* about it. If you can handle this, you're welcome to stay here while we figure things out. If not . . ." I shrugged my shoulders.

I gave Tim a moment, although it was everything I could do to stop from drumming my fingers while I waited. I told myself he needed time. He was probably too emotionally fragile to think clearly.

I sipped my coffee and waited. I could feel the tension and worry radiating from him.

"Okay, here's the deal," he said. "I need to meet him."

"Meet him? You can't be serious."

"I'm dead serious. I want to see what I think for myself."

"Seeing us together won't—"

"I didn't say I wanted the three of us to get together. I said I wanted to meet him. Alone. Just the two of us."

"But—"

"This is not negotiable, Katie. If there's any hope of me getting past this, I need to do this. Don't worry. You can tell him I'm not interested in any kind of sordid confrontation. I just need to take his measure and satisfy myself he's right for you. It's not just about how you feel. Regardless how this turns out, you matter to me, and I don't want to see you get hurt."

"But I told you—"

"I repeat, this is not negotiable. Are you going to give me the number, or do we take this discussion to another level?"

Fire flashed in the golden-brown eyes challenging me. Finally, I said, "Okay. I'll get it for you."

Considering the years spent with Tim, I owed him that much. I left to get the number. I wasn't sure I was doing the right thing, but time would tell. Time would most certainly tell.

4

KATHERINE

He's going to meet him. O-M-G, Tim's going to confront Connor. Oh well, I warned him. He's a big boy.

I pushed the thoughts out of my head and started the car. I loved my bronzed black BMW 340i. It drove like a rocket, and it looked sexy with its tinted windows and black leather interior. Rush-hour traffic was a bitch, but I looked forward to the drive to the Don Mills office of Magnum. It gave me time to clear my head and ready myself for the workday ahead.

I snapped my cell phone in the audio console, set the cruise control at one hundred and nineteen kilometers per hour, and let the car purr along the highway. I turned up the volume of Whitney Houston's greatest hits and sang along, enjoying the quiet power of the 330 hp 6-cylinder engine.

The British media giant, Magnum International, purchased Winston-Smith Publishing a month ago and merged it with the smaller Anaconda Press. As Director of Acquisitions at W-S, I played an essential role in working with the executive management team on the integration of the three distinct corporate cultures.

They'd scheduled yet another three-day management meeting while they worked through the logistics of the merger, so Connor would be there. I couldn't help thinking of his hands and mouth exploring every crevice of my body. I tingled with excitement.

Just the thought of Connor made me lightheaded, and I had to remind myself to breathe. The rational part of me told me to run far and fast once again, but the truth was I'd been running away from myself for much too long. I didn't know if I was ready to find out how far I was willing to let Connor take me. *You mean how far you're willing to go.*

When he touched me, I never wanted him to stop. I was becoming insatiable, and I liked it. Yes, whispers from the ghosts of childhood admonitions reminded me only bad girls liked sex, but when I was with Connor, a new voice banished those whispers with shouts of ecstasy.

On the first day of the meeting, Connor passed me a cryptic note that said, "Be prepared for your first test." Excitement and fear rippled through me. I found it hard to focus on the business at hand.

How will I know it's the test? What will he make me do? What if . . .

"Katherine . . ."

What if I can't go through with it?

"Katherine!"

I jolted to attention. Everyone in the room was looking at me. I wasn't even sure who had spoken.

"I'm sorry. What did you say?"

"This is most unusual for you, Katherine. What do you estimate the earnings for your department will be for the next fiscal year?"

There was a slight edge to Connor's voice as he spoke, yet I saw the trace of a smile at the edges of his mouth. I pulled myself together. After all, I had the great gift of being able to live in the moment. Now I just had to put it to use.

"Sixteen point eight million." I looked him straight in the eye. "Seventeen point two if we go ahead with the new product launch."

"Aren't you being a little optimistic?" my boss Kevin asked. He preferred his directors to lowball our estimates for future revenues. That way, when we exceeded their targets, he could play the champion who had led the team to victory. Connor cut him off and moved the meeting forward. I had the distinct feeling it took tremendous willpower for him to avoid winking at me. Connor detested Kevin Jordan.

I made myself stay focused throughout the remaining three days of continuous meetings. On Friday morning, it took every ounce of my strength to get out of bed after the six o'clock wake-up call. I took a tepid shower in an attempt to shock my system into alertness before dressing and packing for checkout.

Coffee, a lot of it, helped me stifle the yawns overcoming me after too much rich food and drink and too little sleep. Connor said very little to me during the three days and nothing unrelated to work. Surely, that wasn't the test?

Somehow, I got through the customer service presentation a colleague and I gave to our fellow directors while the executive management team looked on. Kevin gave the wrap-up, rah-rah speech and let us leave early so we could beat rush-hour traffic. With a swift goodbye and take care, I was out the door and headed for my car. I couldn't wait to get home to my own bed. Would Tim be waiting to renew his efforts at salvaging our relationship? I certainly hoped not. I was too tired to deal with him.

I threw my briefcase and purse into the back seat and was just about to sit behind the wheel when a flash of white on the driver's seat caught my eye. *What the hell?*

I stared at the envelope. How the hell had it gotten there? I'd locked the car after I'd stowed my luggage this morning. I'd checked twice to be sure; that's how tired I'd been. So who could have gotten into my car? I checked the door for damage but found none. Perplexed, I opened the envelope and took out a card with a handwritten message on beautiful linen stationery.

For your pleasure and mine, proceed to the InterContinental Toronto Yorkville at Bloor and Avenue Road for an evening of adventure and delight. Once there, go to the Proof Bar and await instruction. There'll be an empty seat in the right-hand corner just for you.

I was exhausted, and the thought of the drive home was almost too much to bear, never mind an evening out. Yet, a bead of excitement pulsed through me, pushing my fatigue to the background. *Oh my God, it's the test.* Was I up for this? I'd better give Tim the courtesy of letting him know I'd be late.

"Babe." He sounded so happy to hear my voice.

"Hi."

"You sound exhausted. When will you be home? I'll have a hot bath and a glass of your favorite wine waiting for you."

The throbbing between my legs did battle with the sting of tears in my eyes. *Damn you, Tim.* Was he forcing me to hurt him or just plain oblivious?

"That's a nice thought, but not necessary. I'm going to be a bit longer than I expected. Connor asked me to meet with him."

The silence at the other end was palpable. I waited, one beat, then two, then three.

"Tim, are you there?"

"Yes, I'm here. Okay. Try not to be too late. I'll be waiting for you."

I could hear the disappointment in his voice as I signed off. What would it take to get through to him?

Before starting the car, I crossed my arms over the steering wheel and rested my head. Maybe I should settle for my stable and secure life with Tim. Was Connor worth this? My brain said no, but my body screamed yes.

Who was I kidding? I would go, I was that excited. With a sigh, I set the GPS and headed for the hotel.

The bar was packed, and the strong bass of "Dr. Feelgood" jolted every nerve in my body. Maybe a drink would help me regain control. I made my way to the bar as instructed. Sure enough, the far right-hand seat was empty, which was surprising with this crowd.

There were several young and very attractive men and women working the long white granite bar. Their fluid movements reminded me of what I called the dance of the seasoned bartender. I sat down and waited for one of them to notice me. Soon, a very cute young man approached and slid what looked like a red martini in front of me. He winked and turned away.

"Excuse me," I said. When he didn't respond, I raised my voice and yelled, "Excuse me."

He turned and faced me. He was exquisite. He reminded me of Connor when he was that age. Of course, Connor was still exquisite, but now he carried the distinction of the mature man.

"I didn't order this drink. Do you have red wine by the glass?"

"Your Master would prefer you drink these tonight. It's our signature ice sphere martini," he said.

He gave me a smile that lit up his face and my crotch. Would he be the test? If he was, I could think of worse things. He was very young, but oh, what a ride he would be.

Get a grip, girlfriend.

I shook myself back to reality and eyed the red concoction in front of me. I rarely drank liquor, and I detested martinis, especially those with gin or vermouth. I took a tentative sip and found I liked it. It tasted like cranberry juice and vodka. Before I realized it, I'd finished it, and my hunk of a bartender refilled the empty glass.

"Your Master will be pleased," he said.

My Master! Who the *fuck* was my Master? It had to be Connor. Was he here? Did he own this place? Too many unanswered questions. I'd have to change that.

Lightheaded, I needed something to eat. Another of the beautiful bartenders served the man sitting beside me, and I leaned over to get her attention.

"Excuse me. Am I able to order food here?"

A pair of brilliant blue eyes turned my way, and the woman said, "Your Master has taken care of that."

Your Master. Your Master? There it was again, reference to this mysterious man. What if it wasn't Connor. What if it was one of those random strangers. *Quit fussing. You know you like the attention.*

The drink tasted better with each sip, and I felt very mellow. He wouldn't drug me, would he? Whoever *he* was. *Stop being such an alarmist, Kat.* I tried to figure out how I would get home but could focus only on the warm excitement rippling through me. Even my hunger subsided.

I sat back on the stool and let my thoughts drift to the feel of Connor's skin as my hands slid over his taut stomach and through the trimmed hair at the base of his rigid cock. He rarely allowed me the pleasure of exploring his body, although I dreamed of spending all day discovering his nooks and crannies and the effect my touch had on them. But I learned early on that, within minutes, he would push my hands toward his engorged penis.

Unlike Tim's cock, which always seemed to spring to attention and strain for release at the very sight of me, Connor could control every aspect of his sexuality. Pleasure washed through me at the thought. Connor adored my body, but he controlled when and where he would get an erection.

I wished many times that just once he would give some external demonstration of raw sexual desire for me. Connor's control combined <u>with his desire for me was the strongest aphrodisiac I had ever experienced. A ripple of pleasure passed through me as I imagined him shoving me against the hotel door</u>, ripping off my panties, and riding me through a series of never-ending orgasms.

Someone tapped my shoulder. I turned and faced a woman who looked exactly like Elizabeth Taylor, with violet eyes and closely-trimmed hair, too perfect to be real. I scanned the woman's perfectly proportioned body. Was I dreaming? I couldn't remember falling asleep.

"Come with me," the woman said. She turned and walked through the bodies gyrating on a dance floor I could barely feel as I scrambled to follow. Liz, as I thought of her, led me through the marble and rosewood lobby and up the elevator to the penthouse floor. She paid no attention to me while we took the short ride up and walked out ahead of me as the doors slid open. I stepped out into a long hall with two doors recessed in the rich wood-paneled walls. Liz held one of them open as I caught up with her, gesturing me into the room before closing the door, leaving me on my own.

That's a relief. For a minute I— I shook the thought away. *He wouldn't . . .*

I dropped my purse on the side table and turned around, awestruck at the opulence of the suite. A large fireplace held a crackling fire and a table set for one stood in front of it. The aroma of fresh-cut fries drifted by me, awakening the hunger I'd forgotten. I checked the room to ensure I was alone and found a steaming bath. But not even the invitation of the fragrant bubbles could distract me from my hunger. I rushed to check out the sideboard standing against the wall.

A magnificent buffet was spread before me with so many of my favorite foods I didn't know where to begin.

Crisp, fresh Greek and pasta salads, pâté, cheeses, fruit, and rolls stood on one side and led to a series of covered dishes revealing poutine, tenderloin, crab legs, corn on the cob drenched in butter, and a platter of sliders with home-made patties. I moved from dish to dish, taking a serving for the plate and then a forkful for my mouth. Who cared whether I was acting like a piglet; after all, no one was watching.

I paused with my fork halfway to my mouth—or was he? I turned in place and looked for hidden cameras or peep-holes, then gave my head a shake and went back to stuffing my face.

When I couldn't eat one more bite, I sighed, stretched, and walked over to the huge bed standing in an alcove in the massive room. A beautiful lapis-blue silk robe with an ornate dragon embroidered on the back lay on the satin duvet. *Ah, he remembered my favorite color.*

The bath called to me, and I hurried to it, carrying the robe with me. A small dressing room stood at the entrance to the marble bath. I folded my clothes over the chair in the corner before getting into the bubble-filled water. For just a moment, I wondered how the water could still be warm, and then I sank down with relief and let the suds cover me. *More of Connor's magic.*

Connor liked me pristine when I came to him. How thoughtful of him to remember I loved hot bubble baths. He detested them and much preferred to wash away his debauchery with a tepid shower. I let myself soak and drift until the water started to cool. When I opened my eyes, another of the cranberry martinis sat beside me on the marble edge of the tub.

I sat up with a jolt. How did that get there? I looked

around again and listened intently for noise from the other room. Then I smiled to myself and relaxed. Of course, he was waiting for me. I stepped out of the tub, dried off, and applied the *L'Air du Temps* skin cream lying open on the counter. *That Connor doesn't miss a trick.*

Once anointed, I donned the robe, grabbed the martini, and strode out eager to see him. I stood stock still as I saw a naked Liz standing at the foot of the bed.

"What are you doing here?"

I couldn't keep the edge from my voice. Needing to hide my shaking hands, I walked over and placed the martini on the bedside table. I was careful to take a wide arc around the bed as I moved to stand behind the chair on the other side of the room.

"The Master says you're mine until I make you come, so I'll be taking my time." Liz's smile sent shivers up my spine.

Heat bloomed in the wake of Liz's gaze as it roamed where my robe fell open revealing my small breasts and the shadow of dark pubic hair.

I shook my head frantically. *He wouldn't.* Yes, he could, and would obviously.

"Uh-uh. I don't do women. And who the hell is this Master anyway? Where is he?" I took a step back and looked around. Liz laughed.

"Connor said you'd say that, and he said to remind you that you do have a choice. What will it be?"

I stepped over to the martini sitting on the bedside table and took a large gulp.

"How do you know Connor?" I stalled for time.

"I'm not here for chitchat." Liz gazed at me with those deep violet eyes. "In fact, I'd prefer you not talk at all. Moans of pleasure are the only sound I want to hear from you. If you're staying, remove the robe and lie on the bed with your legs spread."

"But—"

"Or get dressed and leave. No one will stop you. Those are your choices. Of course, I'll pass along your choice to Connor."

I finished off the martini and glared. I suppressed the excitement coursing through me when I let my eyes stray to Liz's large breasts and firm buttocks. She didn't carry any extra weight, but every ounce of what she had was distributed to form a curvaceous body. She had the body I dreamed of having and seemed perfectly comfortable displaying it.

Liz gazed back at me with expressionless eyes, waiting for me to decide. I stood rooted to the spot, unsure of what to do. As my confused emotions played through my mind, Liz pointed to an envelope lying on the pillow.

"He left this for you. I'll leave for a minute while you decide." Liz put on an emerald-green robe with the same dragon embroidered on the back and left the room.

I sank back on the bed with relief—at least I had a moment's reprieve. The note was written on the same paper as the card I'd found in my car.

I hope you will not let fear keep you from the world of pleasure that is ours to explore. This is the first step on that journey. Stay or leave, I'll respect your choice. But first, answer one question—are you wet?

I stared down at the note. Parting my thighs slightly, I slid my hand down between them. I wasn't just wet, I was soaking. He knew me too well. I often fantasized about what it would be like to have a woman make love to me, but I'd never had the desire to explore the reality. *Or is it because I've never had the opportunity?*

Calm settled over me. *Why not?* If I was honest with myself—and Lord knows I tried to be—I wanted and needed to explore this side of my nature. *Didn't I?* I prayed I was right. After all, once I took this step, there was no going back.

I inched my robe off and lay back on the bed. On cue, Liz entered the room and walked over to me. She slid the robe from her shoulders and let it drop to the floor.

"Now for the ground rules," Liz said. "You're not to speak unless I ask you to. You are to do exactly what I say, and no matter what happens, you're to keep your legs spread. Do you understand?"

I nodded as I tried hard to control my breathing. *Oh my God, what have I done?*

"Do you understand?" Liz's voice demanded a response.

"Yes."

"Well then?"

Although she spoke softly, the command was implicit in Liz's question. I sighed and opened my legs. Liz took hold of my ankles and raised my feet toward my thighs as she spread my knees as far apart as they would extend. I closed my eyes, hiding from the emotional conflict of being exposed, vulnerable, yet unable to resist.

She traced her fingers over my mound, pressing briefly on the shaft of my clit and then swirling in the moisture pulsing from my vagina. My core awakened as it did with Connor, and I gasped. I could not stop every muscle, every fiber from straining, reaching, begging for release. Like Connor, Liz spent some time running concentric circles around my outer lips, never touching the pulsing point no matter how I strained. All thought centered on the small pain that came as my clit fully engorged. Each time Liz came within reach of it, my body arched into a spasm curving toward the moving hand. I was acting like a shameless plaything begging for attention, but I was beyond caring.

When Liz's hand slid up toward my breast, painting my stomach with the excess of my juices, I panted, seeking air.

For a fleeting moment, I wondered at the raw lust I seemed unable to control. Then Liz sucked on my hard, protruding nipples, and sensation obliterated logical thought.

After an eternity of playing with each breast and nipple, each flick of her tongue taking me closer to the edge than the last, Liz moved back between my legs and spread my vulva. She dipped her index finger in the well of juice and then moved it back and forth, slowly, over my clit. Without altering the pressure, Liz worked me to the edge but wouldn't let me come. Sweat dripped off me, and unable to help myself, I started to beg.

"That's it, moan for me, baby," Liz said.

"Please, please."

One thought repeated in my head, like a mantra. *My Master will be well pleased.*

"Please," I screamed.

Liz increased the intensity, and I went rigid as every muscle clenched and then released, riding the wave of pent-up sensation. She thrust her fingers into my vagina and massaged the internal button that was as sensitive as my clitoris. Within seconds, I rode the new wave of orgasm ripping through me. Liz continued finger fucking me until I screamed from the explosive impact of the continuous orgasms. When she stopped at long last, I curled into a fetal position, my chest heaving.

I awoke with a start and looked around frantically. I was sure someone had touched me, but I was alone. A third note lay beside me.

I am well pleased. My driver will take you home and arrange for your car to follow. Until next time . . .

A note. He left a note? I needed to see him. I picked up my cell and punched in the private number he'd shared with me.

"McClane." His voice was several shades of liquid ice and stopped me cold.

"What is it, Katherine? I haven't got time for this right now."

Katherine?

"Connor, I—" I couldn't get past the chill in his tone. After what I'd just done for him, this was the reception I got?

"Look, I've got to go. We'll talk later." And with that, he hung up the phone.

I choked back the threatening tears. *Well fuck you, too, mister.*

5

TIM

Tim put off calling Connor for a few weeks; he wasn't sure why. Maybe it was the fear of hearing something he didn't want to know. Maybe it was the fear that Connor would reject his proposal. His guts were in constant turmoil, and he was having trouble focusing on the business at hand. This was not a good thing. He was starting a new position as Provost at Royal University so had networks to forge and teams to build now that he was no longer faculty.

The phone rang while his thoughts roamed between the presentation he was giving to the Senate the following week and what he would say to Connor when they spoke.

"Tim Bancroft."

"Shouldn't that be *Doctor* Tim Bancroft?"

The saccharine sweet voice of Sophia Drake, the Vice President of Development, came through with her usual razor-sharp edge. Sophia was beautiful, but Tim had been warned her reputation as a barracuda made it difficult for her to bond with the management team. Her appointment as VPD was unusual in the world of academia, but by all reports, she would work the miracles required to bring in the corporate dollars the university needed. However, there was something about her that made him wary.

"To whom am I speaking?" He wanted to knock her down a peg or two by refusing to take the bait.

"Come off it, Tim," she said. "You know full well who this is."

He waited a few beats. This was one fish she was not going to hook. He heard her long nails drum against a hard surface followed by a heavy sigh. A satisfied smile spread over his face. Hell, he was as catty as Katie. Her influence must have rubbed off on him. He could hear her voice in his head. *"Meow."*

"Tim, it's Sophia."

He waited another beat, still smiling. Another heavy sigh.

"Sophia Drake from Development."

"Oh Sophia, I'm sorry. I didn't recognize your voice."

Tim could feel the tension radiating from her. She was not accustomed to being less than the center of attention, and he was happy to disavow her self-importance. His smile broadened.

"How may I help you, Sophia?"

He was playing with the tiger, but he couldn't help himself. He could feel her smug grin. Maybe he was reading too much into a simple phone call, but his colleagues had him on alert about Sophia.

"Actually, Tim, you have no idea what I can do to help you." Her obvious attempt at seductive innuendo made the hair on the back of his neck stand up.

"In this case," she said, "you might like someone to bounce your presentation off, and since I'm an old hand at managing the Senate Committee, I thought I'd offer."

Oh my God. They were right about her. Cougar alert.

"How nice, Sophia. Thank you, but I'm good for now. I'll keep it in mind and let you know if I need any help."

"Now don't let your male ego get in the way. After all, you'll have only one chance to make a good first impression. Let's have dinner tomorrow night so I can make sure you're hitting the major points you'll need to cover. Then if time permits, we'll talk about what else I can do for you. You'll find I can be very accommodating in ways that will benefit both of us." She gave that wicked laugh again.

Yikes. Straight for the kill.

"What a nice offer, Sophia. I have plans tomorrow night, and the president has reviewed the expectations with me. I do thank you, though."

"Are you sure? I'm happy to help, and I'm not used to taking no for an answer. I think you should reconsider before you blow me off."

Goosebumps broke out on his arms. *Double yikes.*

"Thanks again, Sophia. That's very thoughtful. I'll keep your offer in mind and let you know if I run into any snags. Thanks for calling." He hung up the phone before she could think of any other reasons for them to meet outside the office.

He shouldn't delay the phone call with Connor any longer.

"McClane." The abruptness of his tone threw Tim for a second. The academics he dealt with generally did not have the hard edge to their voices characteristic of many business people.

"This is Tim Bancroft. I am—"

"I know who you are. Katherine told me to expect your call a few weeks ago."

"Yes, well I'm wondering if we could meet," Tim said. "I have a proposal to make."

"A proposal? That sounds intriguing. Sure, why not. I have some time on Friday. Will that work for you?"

They agreed to meet at three p.m. in the Library Bar at

the Fairmont Royal York. Smiling, Tim thought of Katie, who wanted to try their afternoon tea. She'd be so envious when he told her. Connor offered to make the reservation, and Tim thanked him as they disconnected.

Tim spent the next three days running through the dialogue of possible conversations. He resolved to control this meeting. Did he dare go through with his plan? By the time he left to meet Connor, he was still undecided.

Tim arrived early and asked for the McClane reservation.

"Ah yes. Mr. McClane is waiting for you. Right this way, please." *Advantage Connor. And Mr. McClane. How chichi.*

Connor stood, extending his hand as Tim approached the table.

"Hello Tim. I'm pleased to meet you." His warm smile and firm handshake put Tim at ease.

Watch yourself, Tim.

His appearance surprised Tim. He wasn't what he'd expected. He wasn't Katie's type. Too tall, too dark, too Justin Theroux. She much preferred the pretty boy, Brad Pitt type. As she often reminded him, Tim had barely passed the looks test. Too tall for her at five-foot, eight-inches and borderline coloring with his light brown hair and eyes.

"But you were just so damn cute," she always said. "There was something about you that drew me to you. You were such a nice guy." *And you know what they say about nice guys.*

Tim mentally shook off thoughts of her and turned his attention back to the business at hand. After shaking hands, he sat in the chair the *maître d'* pulled out opposite Connor.

"Stewart will be your server for the afternoon," the *maître d'* said. "Would you like a drink in the meantime?"

"What would you like?" Connor asked.

"Rum and coke on ice, please."

"And the usual for me, please, John. Thank you."

"Coming right up."

Tim watched John leave before turning his gaze back to Connor, who was looking at him through eyes intense with a blend of curiosity and wariness.

"Shall we skip the small talk and get right to the point?"

"So you're fucking my woman," Tim blurted out.

"And I gather you have a problem with that?" Connor threw back without a moment's hesitation.

"Well, wouldn't you?"

"I'd have to think about that, but my gut feeling is no, I don't think I would. Not if that's where she chose to be." He paused a moment while he took a drink. "If she were willing, I'd love to see her get off with someone else."

"I don't know whether to take you seriously or whether you're delusional. Even if I found the idea of watching Katie with another man appealing, I'd also find it threatening, as I do now."

"Why? After all, it's only sex. I say that not to downplay the importance, but I have learned not to complicate the issue."

Is this guy for real, or is he playing with me?

"So you say, but one day it's sex and the next she's leaving you for the other guy. I've seen it happen before."

"Sounds like it happened to you."

"No, not me," Tim snapped. "Besides, we're not here to talk about my history."

Connor arched an *"aren't we now"* eyebrow.

"And I'd wager there were already serious problems in those relationships that had everything to do with why she, or he, for that matter, left the marriage.

"Katherine says you went away on sabbatical over a year ago, and you haven't been together since. And now you're back hoping to reunite, but she's not interested. Is that right?"

"That remains to be seen. I only want what's right for Katie. Do you love her?"

The server arrived with their drinks and introduced himself while Connor continued to look at Tim with those unfathomable gray-green eyes. Tim was holding his breath and let it out.

"Are you ready to place your order, sir?" Stewart asked.

"Would you like anything?" Connor asked.

"Why not? Please go ahead and order whatever you like. I'm sure it will be fine."

"We'll start with the antipasto platter. That should hold us for a while. Thank you, Stewart."

Tim took a slug of his rum and coke and settled back to watch Connor. He was curious to see how Connor would handle his question.

After another moment's pause, Connor said, "Do I love her? No, not in the way you mean. Did she tell you anything of our history?"

"A little, but to be fair I didn't give her a chance. I needed some time to absorb the shock before hearing details." *It's not every day you hear your girlfriend fucked around on you.*

"Katherine and I hung out for a couple of years while I was in graduate school. We were very good friends, so I guess you could say I love her as a friend."

A couple of years? She'd told him about Connor and several other guys she'd been with before she met him, but none of them had sounded serious.

"I flirted with the idea of getting together, but by the time I made up my mind to say something, she'd left me."

Tim took another gulp of his drink. Was this the truth?

"So you haven't seen her in years? Is that what you're telling me?"

Tim's throat closed over the words, but he kept his gaze

on Connor. He refused to let Connor see how upset he was getting.

"That's exactly what I'm telling you. We ran into each other a month or so ago at a conference, and that's the first time we'd seen each other since university."

Compassion with a touch of humor lurked in his eyes. *Damn him.* He was starting to like Connor. They took another pause to nibble and let Stewart refresh their drinks.

"Well, we're here to discuss my proposal, not to rehash ancient history. First, let me apologize if I get into too much detail about the terms of it. We academics can get carried away sometimes."

"Go ahead. As I indicated on the phone, I'm intrigued."

"Katie seems to feel she needs to spend time with you to explore this dominance thing you two have happening. I love her, and I want her back. If that means I have to learn more about this submission need she has, so be it."

Connor's left eyebrow shot toward the ceiling, but he stayed silent.

"I'm a bit of a voyeur. It's just something that interests me. I'm thinking somehow I could be involved and learn what it is she needs exactly."

"I'm a *lot* of a voyeur, but I'm not certain your intent is to support Katherine's need. I've just met you, and already I have my doubts, Tim. Reality is not the same as fantasy."

"Well, that kind of contradicts what you said earlier, doesn't it?"

Tim held up his hand as Connor started to protest.

"Please, let me clarify. I don't want to watch Katie with someone—I want to watch people who do this sort of thing. There must be some sort of club or place where this type of thing goes on. I thought maybe you could take me to one of them."

Connor took a sip of what looked like scotch on the rocks while never taking his eyes off Tim.

"Is Katherine aware of what you're asking?"

"No, and I'll be the one to tell her in my own good time."

Connor took another drink and said nothing. Although it was only a couple of minutes, it felt more like ten. Tim ate some more of the appetizer to keep from squirming under Connor's steady gaze. When Tim couldn't stand it anymore, he said, "Well?"

"Maybe. Let me give it some thought and get back to you. What's your cell number?"

"I'm old-school and don't use my cell. It's best to get a hold of me at the office."

Tim took out one of his new business cards and slid it across the table to Connor. As if by magic, Stewart materialized with the bill and handed it to Connor. Tim started to take out his wallet, but Connor gestured for him to put it away. Then he signed the check and stood with his hand outstretched.

"It was nice meeting you, Tim. I'll be in touch." And with that, he walked away.

Unexpectedly, Tim had a hard-on, and not just of the semi-erect variety. He was almost rupturing the zipper of his suit pants, and it was damned painful. As much as he tried to reflect on the conversation with Connor, he was imagining Katie writhing under Connor as he rode her hard and slow. Tim wanted her, and he wanted her badly. He'd do what it took to get her back. To hell with the rest of it; they'd figure it out.

6

CONNOR

For the first time in the weeks that had flown by since Kat walked back into my life, I was optimistic. I'd taken great pains to give her the space she needed, but tonight, I needed her. I was eager to get home to see her, which made the rush-hour traffic more annoying than usual. And I was eager to hear how she felt about her first test.

I stopped at the liquor store and chose a nice bottle of Amarone in the hope of celebrating new beginnings. I refused to examine my reasons for this newfound happiness and put it down to having time with a partner who satisfied my sexual predilections. But I suspected Kat was much more than just another sexual conquest. She was the breath of air missing from my life for the past twenty years. Admitting that, even to myself, wasn't something I was willing to pursue. It would only lead to anguish; I'd learned that the hard way.

Yet, it was always at the back of my mind, and that concerned me. It was so much easier to tell myself, "Don't go there, Connor."

I figured I had just enough time before she got to the

condo to order her favorite Chinese food and set the table. I smiled in anticipation as I pulled into the garage.

I was so focused I didn't notice her standing in the hallway as I opened the door, and her voice startled me.

"We need to talk."

I was looking forward to talking with Kat—hoping to hear her first test was what I imagined. Finding her like this wasn't what I expected. She was upset. She was more than upset. Her eyes were red-rimmed and swollen. My guts clenched. *Was she going back to Tim?* The thought, like a punch to the gut, took my breath away. I wanted to say something, but what could I say? I needed her to want me, but I could hardly tell her that, so I just stood there, taking deep breaths.

Willing my heart to slow down, I managed to relax enough to say, "Okay, we should talk. May I get in the door first?"

"I'll be waiting in the living room." Tension radiated from her every pore.

I slipped the wine into a kitchen cabinet, hoping she hadn't noticed it. The food order would just have to wait. I joined her in the living room.

"What's the wine for? What could you possibly have to celebrate right now?"

"To answer your question, I was hoping to celebrate our — um — arrangement."

She just stared at me, cold and hard.

"Arrangement? That's what you call it? This isn't a business deal, Connor. I'd have thought it meant a great deal more. I'm opening myself up to you, exposing myself so you can help me discover who I am. Do you know how hard that is for me?

"I guess you *arranged*, as you call it, my first test, thinking that would keep me happy. Then you ignore me and don't have the time or the inclination to even take a phone call. Why couldn't you have at least talked to me?"

She slumped back on the sofa, the tension leaving her, but her eyes burned with challenge. I couldn't help but admire her spirit. This was a woman unafraid to explore her deepest emotions when others just hid. One small tear rolled down her cheek, and it shook me to the core. I wanted to hold her in my arms and take away the hurt, but this was not the time. She deserved more than some patronizing soothing.

She wanted answers. I must admit I was relieved this wasn't about Tim, but now I was more worried because it was about me. Tonight wasn't supposed to be this way.

"You're right, Kat. Will you accept my apology? I can see now that I've been insensitive, but that wasn't my intention. I didn't talk to you when you called because I was in the middle of an intense negotiation with an important client. I also thought I should give you some space to figure e out what's going on with Tim. It's not my place to butt in. But most importantly, and believe me I take this very seriously, I wanted you to take the time to consider the full experience of your first test."

"Even more reason for you to take my call."

"It was your first step to understanding the nature of your feelings as a submissive. I need you to honestly know what it meant for you and not because of any influence I may have on our arrange—um, relationship.

"I've made no secret about where I stand on this and how much I want to explore this with you. But you're right. I should've been there for you. My excuse is I've been living this lifestyle so long I forgot how I felt when I started my journey."

I paused a beat and stared down at my hand. She said nothing. I looked up, and the light in her eyes encouraged me to continue.

"I came here tonight to see if your first test was everything I'd hoped it would be because there is so much more I want to show you. Believe me, Kat, there's no other woman who excites me the way you do. Please don't ask me to explain it because I don't know myself. All I know is that I want you, and in time maybe we can find some answers together."

I was relieved to see her facial expression soften, and there was even a small hint of a smile at the corners of her mouth.

"So you were worried this was about Tim, were you?"

Perceptive little thing. "Not worried, concerned."

She laughed. "Okay, let's not split hairs, C. You don't need to worry about Tim."

"That's good to hear. By the way, I met him today."

"You did?" Alertness leaped into her eyes. "What happened?"

"Nothing, really. We met, we talked, we had a drink. It was most civilized."

Her eyes narrowed. She was going for the kill. "What . . . did . . . you . . . talk . . . about?"

How did I give her what she needed without committing the cardinal sin of omission?

"It wasn't very interesting, Kat. He asked me if I love you, and I said I loved you as a friend. I told him about our relationship in university. He assured me of his intentions, and as you said, he's bound and determined to get you back. That's about it."

"And?"

"And there isn't really much more. He asked me if I knew of any good clubs in the area."

"Clubs? It isn't like him to want to go out drinking. That's something else that must have changed while he was away."

"Kat, I'm really not interested in Tim and his motivations.

Let's get back to talking about what's bothering you. I think it must be more than my abruptness on the phone. If that's all there was to it, you'd rip me a new one and move on." I smiled, trying to put her at ease.

"So what are your feelings for me? Am I just another conquest?"

I grimaced at her bluntness but knew this wasn't the time to react.

"I don't quite know what I'm feeling, Kat, but you're more than a conquest to me. At the very least, I consider you a friend, and that may be all I have to give. You once called me emotionally unavailable, and that hasn't changed."

I rubbed the back of my neck. I hated opening the door to my feelings even a crack. Yet that's what I seemed to be doing around this woman.

"How come you run so hot and cold, Connor? One minute you act like you adore me and can't get enough of me, and the next minute it's like you don't even know me. What's up with that? I mean, I know you're moody, but really?"

How the hell could I respond to that? There was no way in hell I was going to get into the real reason now. I'd spent years avoiding the emotional pitfalls people casually attribute to love. I knew too well about being a victim of love, and it was anything but casual.

"I don't know why I'm so moody, Kat, but I'm working on it. I do know being with you makes me happy, and I love exploring our sexuality together. And that's all I have to give right now. I was under the impression that's what you wanted as well."

She continued to look steadily at me while she tucked her feet up and settled comfortably in her chair. It was a good time to take the plunge. I wanted to clear the air.

"I have a request," I said. "It's something I think will help us feel more comfortable about things. I hope you'll give it serious consideration."

I paused, considering the best way to ask without putting pressure on her.

"Okay," she said. "What is it?"

"I want you to quit your job and go work for another publisher."

The look on her face was priceless and almost made me laugh.

"What on earth for? What has my job got to do with having sex with you?"

"I know if you think about it, Kat, you'll see where I'm coming from. Kevin reports to me. That means you work for me, and as long as you do, there's danger of our personal relationship spilling into our working relationship. It's asking for trouble. I've always made a point of not mixing business with pleasure. I want us to be open and honest with each other, and business is sometimes anything but that."

"Actually, I've been giving the situation some thought. Oh, not because of you, but because I'm sick and tired of the politics at Magnum. I got another call from the Canadian Division of Harvard University Press yesterday asking me to consider a position as Editor in Chief of the Higher Education Division. The more I think about it, the more intrigued I am. I wanted to talk to you about it last night but . . ."

My shoulders dropped back to their normal resting position. "Well, I'm here now. How about you get cleaned up while I order some dinner for us. Are you in the mood for Chinese from Lucky's?"

That brought a smile to her face, and I was gratified to see the energy flow back into her as she got up and headed toward the stairs. She paused on the first step and turned to look at me.

"Oh, and Connor, I'm glad we're friends."

Me too.

She sang as she ran the tub. I smiled and ordered the food before setting the table with all the trimmings—linens, candles, china, the works. Maybe, just maybe . . .

When Kat came back down, she was wearing a pair of ornate silk pajamas. Last week I'd given her a hard time for wearing pajamas—I preferred easier access. She'd confessed they were the hedge-the-bet outfit she wore when she wasn't sure whether I was in the mood for sex. As I handed her a glass of the Amarone, I caught a hint of her signature perfume, *L'Air du Temps*. That was another good sign.

The food had arrived a few minutes earlier giving me just enough time to get it on the table.

"Oh my God," she said, "this is wonderful. I'm starving. I haven't eaten all day."

"Dig in then, and tell me about this editor position."

For the next few minutes, we ate and drank, and I watched her with pleasure while she devoured her meal. It never ceased to amaze me such a small woman could consume such large quantities and look so sexy while she was doing it. Usually the two images didn't fit together for me. My hard-on returned with a vengeance.

As her hunger abated, she started to tell me about the recent calls from Harvard U Press. Then she asked me to fill her in on what I'd been doing for the past week. As if by silent agreement, we steered clear of any topics that might spoil the mood. We finished eating and moved to the living room. I sat on the couch as she went toward her chair.

"Come here," I said.

She turned and looked at me uncertainly.

"Come and sit beside me. It's time for you to meet one of my conditions."

As she sat down, I drew her back against my chest and started stroking her face.

"Tell me about your first test."

She tensed for a minute and then relaxed. I could see her thinking, *"In for a penny, in for a pound"*.

"I wasn't keeping it from you, you know. You were right. I did need time to think about how I feel about the encounter with Liz."

Liz? Interesting.

I didn't want to push, but just the thought of Kat with another woman sent shivers up my spine.

"So what did you think about—er—Liz?"

The tips of her ears went beet red.

"You're blushing. This ought to be good."

My hands moved down her face to her neck, and I kept stroking her as she began the story of the Liz episode somewhat hesitantly.

I made very sure to stay relaxed but visibly eager to hear the details. As the story unfolded, I was more than eager to hear the details; I was rock hard visualizing the scene. As she continued to talk—I'm sure the wine helped her along—I slid my hand under her shirt and stroked her breasts. Her breath caught each time I rolled her nipples between my fingers.

She loved having her nipples played with, one of the many things that would throw her to the heights of excitement where she would strain for more. I took great pleasure watching her struggle to talk as her excitement kept pace with her hardening nipples. When she arched forward, I moved my hands and stroked another part of her soft, smooth skin until she calmed. This drove her crazy. There were times I let her needs guide me; however, tonight it was my turn. This time would be on my terms.

"And how did you feel about having sex with a woman?"

"Fine, but I wish it had been you." She took a gulp of her wine.

"Just fine?"

She took another sip before sighing.

"You're not going to rest until I confess, are you?"

"No, I'm not. I'm not going to let it go. So?"

"Okay, okay. I liked it, okay. Happy now?"

"Not even close. Did you come?"

She paused a beat.

"Yes."

It was patently obvious she was uncomfortable exploring these feelings, and I needed to push her a little further. "And?"

"I've never been with another woman, or, I should say, until Liz. I wouldn't seek one out, but I'm willing if it's another one of your tests."

"Did you touch her in return?"

"No. Like I told you, she made me come, and then she left."

"Do you wish you had touched her?"

"No. Yes. I don't know, Connor." She struggled to sit up. I pulled her back.

"What is this, twenty questions?"

"Would you like to see *me* with another woman?"

"No, absolutely not. No. No way."

"Well that's definite, that's for sure. I'm curious as to why not."

I was a little surprised at her vehemence. She didn't seem like the possessive type.

She took a few minutes as if deciding how much to tell me. I waited. She leaned her head back against my chest, her breathing slow and even. For a minute, I thought she might have fallen asleep.

"Quite frankly, the thought of you with another woman makes me feel sick. I think on one level, it excites me, but deep down I think if you want sex, you should have it with me."

"Why, Kat, I wouldn't have taken you for the jealous type." I teased.

"I'm not jealous, C. Jealousy implies I'm resentful toward your partner. I wouldn't resent the woman—okay maybe I would a little, but mostly I just want you for myself. Hard to admit and not my most attractive feature." She sighed.

Works for me. I waited for her to demand I be exclusive with her, but she didn't. She just lay relaxed in my arms, nipples hard as stone.

I continued to play with her breasts, occasionally slipping my hand into her pants to the soft mound between her legs. She wasn't just wet; she was dripping. This went on for at least fifteen minutes before she tried to wiggle out of my arms. I knew exactly what was coming next, pun intended, and I smiled.

"Please C, let's go to bed," she pleaded.

"Not this time, Kat. I want you to stand up and take off your pants. It's my turn to play now."

"Here?"

Her eyes darted to the window. She didn't like feeling so exposed, and yet that's exactly what excited me about it. The idea someone might be watching fueled my enthusiasm.

"It's here or nowhere, Kat. You can always go back to vanilla. You decide."

I deliberately kept my tone low and controlled, knowing this was something else that drove her wild. What she perceived as my lack of excitement or involvement would challenge her to let go and submerge herself in the depths of her sexual longing.

"I know what I like, Kat. Stand in front of me."

She stood facing me. She was anxious, and it may have been concern for what I would ask or being exposed to the window. I didn't know or care. I wanted her to submit to me, and I relished the look of vulnerability a submissive exhibits.

"Shut your eyes."

She complied, probably hoping to avoid the embarrassment of being on display. She would soon learn it enhances the feeling of helplessness trying to anticipate the unknown. I didn't move or speak, prolonging her discomfort, letting her imagination override any level of comfort she knew. Her face twitched, and she opened her mouth to speak.

"Don't talk."

Still I waited for what must have seemed like an eternity. The only sound was my breath tickling her neck.

"Take your pants off, slowly."

She eased the pants over her slim hips, and then slid them off each leg.

"Now, the panties."

I smiled as she revealed a well-groomed swatch of hair outlining the soft swell of her nether lips. I loved that she wore her pubic hair with pride. God, she was beautiful. It would have been so easy to take her right then, right where she stood, but I wanted her to explore the nature of her submissiveness.

"Now, remove your top."

She projected such a blend of raw sexual hunger and innocence. She had no idea how those two qualities drove most men wild. But I liked to play, and play I was determined to do.

I stood to face her, exploring her breasts, stomach, and inner thighs, ensuring I paused on some of her many trigger points—that's what she called those places that, like her nipples, drove her to a lustful frenzy. I slid a finger over her rock-hard clit. She moaned and writhed. I stopped.

"Shhh."

I blew into her ear, causing her to moan and wriggle again. I cupped my hand and grabbed her vulva, exerting a little force.

"Be quiet. Understood?"

I left my hand, now slick with her juices, in place as I stepped back to look at her.

"Understood?"

She nodded her head in assent. This would be a real challenge. Kat needed to make noise in order to relax and release. I'd just put a cap on the volcano. This would be fun.

I slipped two fingers into her and felt her G-spot. She shuddered with pleasure and managed to suppress the instinctive moan. I slid my fingers from her cunt and did the finger dance around her vulva, driving her to impatiently insist on more. Right on cue, she put her hand over mine and tried to move my fingers to her clit.

Not this time, babe. I walked her across the room and turned her to face the wall. I arranged her arms above her head, palms on the wall, and spread her legs. The only sound was her hard breathing.

"Don't move unless I tell you to. Agreed?" I put more firmness into my voice.

Again, after a moment's hesitation, she nodded and then bowed her head, and I went to work. Starting at her shoulder blades, I played her body like a musical instrument, taking my time with every note. I stroked and caressed and licked and nipped and kneaded every square inch from her shoulder blades to her knees.

As her tension grew, I took malicious pleasure in breathing gently in her ear, something that always pushed her to the edge. Each time she moaned, I froze until she quieted. Each time she moved, I gripped her buttocks until she stopped. I lost track of time as I pushed her to the limit.

Her skin flushed a deep red and perspiration beaded on her, and still I continued. I was fascinated by her reaction; I'd never seen her break a sweat no matter how athletic our sex.

At least another half hour, if not more, went by before she finally screamed.

"Now, C, now. I can't take it anymore. Please C, please . . ."

So you think you're ready, do you? Well let's see.

Kat couldn't orgasm unless she was lying down. It was one of her quirks, her sexual signatures as I called them. Now was as good a time as any to see if that had changed. I flipped her around and pushed her back against the wall, then nudged her legs farther apart. I slipped my fingers between her lips and rhythmically worked her clit.

"No, I need to lie down," she moaned.

I gripped her again and reminded her of the rules of engagement before going back to work. She shook and writhed with the tension and started making low guttural sounds. I played her clit like a harp string, and still she didn't come. I altered the rhythm, and a new, raw, guttural sound came forth, and still she didn't come. I was about to take pity on her when her body tensed and her breath caught. I kept up the steady, insistent rhythm for another second or two.

She arched her back, and tremors rippled throughout her body. I continued to play. She screamed and arched until she started to slide down the wall. I let her go, and she curled into her usual post-coital ball, panting from exertion. I gave her a minute to recover while I took my clothes off and admired the gentle curves of her petite frame.

I considered just how to take her. Every way had its advantages. Should I take her as she straddled my lap so I could admire the look and feel of her breasts again? Or maybe have her kneel in front of the chair for rear entry? Or maybe . . . I rolled each image over in my mind's eye. She started to unwind and stretch. One look into her magnetic eyes decided me.

"Wow," she murmured. "Incredible."

"And we're not done yet, my love," I whispered in her ear, causing another shudder.

Taking her hand, I pulled her to her feet, led her to the middle of the plush Oriental rug, and gestured for her to lie down. She adjusted herself on her back, her legs demurely stretched in front of her. There it was again, that distinctly Kat blend of innocence and passion that made my cock convulse.

I knelt, grasped both ankles, and slid her feet toward her ass before lifting them into the air. She reached for me, but that wasn't part of my plan. I grabbed her hands midair and positioned them on each thigh, supporting each leg above her. She whimpered in protest. She loved the feel of my muscles rippling as I fucked her and hated it when I restricted her.

"Spread them wide for me and keep them spread."

I pulled open her swollen lips, revealing the deep rose blush of her quiescent clit. The sight of it tempted me to nuzzle it back to attention, but my cock demanded its due. With one hand braced on the floor, I used the other to guide my hardness toward the open invitation and slid in to the hilt. She moaned and arched her pelvis toward me.

It was all I could do not to moan in return, but I refused to let her read me so easily. I kept my breathing slow and even, matched to the rhythm of my thrusts. My cock strained to explode with each downward stroke. Though self-control was my forte, I was struggling to keep an unhurried pace. When I was sure I was back in control, I increased the rate, enjoying the spasms as her vagina contracted each time I filled her.

She moaned and groaned and panted. Her eyes flew open

as she begged for release. How I loved when she fixed those rich brown eyes, now gold with lust, on me. How I loved knowing there was nothing else except me in her world at that moment. I sped up just the little bit she needed to tip her over the edge, and her vagina convulsed around my pulsing cock.

Whenever I reached the precipice, I slowed, gasping internally as my mind gripped down hard to stop the beginnings of my own contractions. I kept this up until she came, not one, not two, but three times.

Kat's ability to have multiple orgasms when she let go never ceased to amaze me. By this time, we were both bathed in sweat, and she was hoarse from her loud, unrestrained expressions of ecstasy. I slowed until her breath returned to a semblance of normality. Only then did I relinquish my control as I fully embraced the moment to take her hard and fast.

"Now," she screamed. "Now, now, now."

And the damn broke. I arched my back, threw back my head, and roared my release before collapsing, covering her body with mine. She wrapped her arms and legs around me, and we lay luxuriating in the pleasure of sexual exhaustion. If I'd had any doubts, her absolute surrender assured me she was mine for now, but would I be able to keep her?

7

CONNOR

I stared out of the window overlooking Lake Ontario that made up the back wall of my office. Usually, the large expanse of blue water was a calming influence helping me keep my life in perspective. Not today. Ever since my session with Tim, I'd had trouble focusing on the business at hand, which was unusual for me. No matter how involved the task, I found my thoughts straying to images of Kat's beautiful brown eyes, pouting lips, smooth skin, legs spread wide, wet, open, and ready for my command. But there was far more to my Alley Kat than sex.

She was a study in contradictions. Understated elegance or casual clothing were her signature styles. Her smile brought sunlight to even the darkest mood, yet few survived the razor edge of her temper when it ignited. She could champion the underdog with intense conviction and then turn around and ruthlessly cut a business deal.

But there was Magnum to deal with, and with considerable effort, I focused on the reports piled on my desk.

I hid my status as one of the world's preeminent billionaires by divesting my controlling shares in several holding companies, making it virtually impossible to trace my ownership. With the help of my mentor, Brett Sandvine, I used my influence to ensure the Magnum board elected renowned businesswoman, Margaret Scarpetta, as president of the British media giant. She was one of a handful of people who knew I was the majority shareholder in the company. An incontrovertible nondisclosure agreement assured my privacy.

As instructed, Margaret appointed me Senior Vice President of Operations, and the role gave me the clout and freedom I needed to monitor my vast global holdings while protecting the anonymity I craved.

Rumblings of a takeover bid for the publishing arm of my North American holdings raised my antennae, so I'd set up shop in Magnum International's Canadian headquarters in Toronto. It was one of my favorite cities and gave me easy access to Magnum's Canadian and U.S. holdings while I investigated. I suspected the threats might be one of several maneuvers that could lead to losing control of Magnum. I found mingling with the frontline staff the best way to get to the root of corporate politics, and the editorial conference seemed like a good place to start.

Shock rocked the foundation of my world when I met Kat at the conference. A confident and thoughtful woman replaced the brash young woman who needed to prove herself. When the soft scent of her perfume drifted over me as I shook her hand, a jolt of electricity shot through me. I wasn't prepared for the effect she had on me.

I hadn't felt this way since those days in university when she walked away from me. Now I was letting my heart and an overwhelming lust overrule the red flag my brain waved frantically. It was a cardinal rule never to get intimately involved with an employee. Never. *Run. Don't walk. Run away,* my mind chanted. But instead, I'd run right into her arms.

And now I found myself part of a threesome, one that could be my undoing.

Of course, I'd known Kat worked for Magnum, but it was a big company with offices abroad where I'd spent most of my time. I'd periodically tracked her progress over the years, secure in the knowledge that although she would never be mine, she was still a part of my world in some small measure.

Not that it made up for what I lost all those years ago. Twenty years ago, she'd been right to leave. I couldn't give her what she needed then, and I still couldn't. When she'd left, the fissure caused by Meredith's death reopened. Unable to bear strong emotion of any kind, I'd shut the door on my growing love.

But someone picked the lock, and my feelings were waiting on the other side. Now, as I had then, I closed the door firmly. This time I used a deadbolt as additional protection. Or so I told myself.

I had mixed feelings when she called to let me know Harvard University Press made her a formal job offer. It was the right thing for her, for us, but I couldn't help thinking I could lose her. So much for the cardinal rule.

I'd been so stunned at the conflicting emotions racing through me, I'd put the phone on speaker and started to pace.

"Connor, are you still there?"

"I've been thinking about you leaving, and I'm not sure it's a good idea, Kat. You know you're on the fast track to the executive management team. We need you here."

"What on earth are you saying? You're the one who asked me to consider changing jobs."

She took a quick breath. I could visualize her silently counting to ten.

"I've been thinking about this for some time now. It's time for a change. Look, Connor, this is too much to go into on the phone. And to answer your question, it has nothing to do with you, now does it? It would look really strange if you got involved in the day-to-day at the office, wouldn't it? Besides, our working relationship has nothing to do with our—um—get-togethers."

"But, it does make it easier."

"I don't know why it should make any difference. We can still text each other."

"It sounds like you've already made up your mind."

"Connor, what I'm about to tell you has to be off the record and just between the two of us. Agreed?"

"Kat, I—"

"Agreed? Otherwise, I won't say another word."

The phone went silent for a few moments while I paced and considered. The senior management team had just finished working out the plans for the corporate restructure and planned to announce the changes in a few weeks. As much as it was against my better judgment, I was pleased when they'd proposed Kat as Associate Vice President in charge of the Higher Education Division. She was particularly well suited for the position.

As a Senior VP, I should be doing everything in my power to convince her to stay. I'd always been scathing about my colleagues who did more thinking with their dicks instead of their heads, and here I was doing just that. I shook my head and sighed.

"Okay, agreed. I don't want to argue about this. What are they offering?"

"The offer is quite a good one."

Her voice was brimming with excitement, and I could imagine the light in her eyes and the blush in her cheeks. Damn, even the little things excited me.

"You know whatever the offer is, we'll make a better one, Kat. I don't think you realize the significance of the contribution you've made to the organization. Your efforts have been recognized."

"Well, that's not what I hear. But nevertheless, I think it's time for me to make a change. I don't think I want to continue working there. I'm tired of the battles and political maneuvers."

"Have you mentioned any of this to Kevin?"

"Yes, I've alerted him several times as have others on the team. I get the feeling he doesn't want to hear any more about it." She laughed.

"Okay, tell me more."

"It really is a great offer, C, and I'm excited. It's Editor in Chief at Harvard University Press, and I'll be running the entire Higher Ed Division. They've offered me fifty thousand more than I'm making now with all sorts of perks thrown in like a company car and an expense account and one hell of a bonus plan."

I can't believe it's the same fucking position. Someone's leaked.

"Only fifty thousand? They're obviously expecting you to negotiate. You should be getting at least seventy-five more. You haven't accepted yet, have you?" *Please say no.*

"No way, are you kidding me? No, I haven't accepted yet. I'm so rotten at negotiating salary." She sighed heavily.

"I can't believe I'm going to do this. Okay, here's what you do." I went on with tips about how to negotiate a higher salary and performance bonus.

"Are you sure about this?"

"Yes, I'm sure. Give it a try. What have you got to lose? Did Tim tell you we met?"

"Wow. I'm suffering from whiplash with your abrupt subject change." She laughed. "Yes, he told me. He seems eager to go out clubbing with you."

I smiled at the perfect opportunity she'd just given me. "Actually, he was more effete than I thought he would be, but, then again, those academics are often in touch with their feminine side." *Now I sound like a jealous adolescent.*

"Tim? Effete?" she sputtered. "Are we talking about the same person?"

"I take it you don't agree?"

"Not at all. Tim is the least effeminate man I know, and that includes you. Tim loves women, but he's not like one in any way I can think of. He may have a limited imagination, and our sex could be described as vanilla, but he's always been very considerate in bed."

Ouch! I decided to push the envelope a little further. "Are you sure he's not bisexual?"

She laughed. "I'm positive beyond a shadow of a doubt. I'd have more doubts about you than I would about Tim. Why are you so interested in his sexuality?"

"No big reason. I was just a little surprised by him, that's all. He's not who I imagined you'd end up with."

She laughed again. "He said the same thing about you. I think you're both letting your imagination run away with you."

"Well, we'll have to talk about that another time, Kat. I've got to go but keep an eye on your phone. I'm planning your next test."

"What? When? I've got a lot going on, C. It may be hard to coordinate our schedules."

"I beg your pardon?" I put an edge into my voice. "Do I need to remind you it was you who wanted to explore your sexuality? If you've changed your mind, just say so and I'll respect your decision. But until then, it's nonnegotiable."

"No. No. I'm sorry. I was just thinking out loud. When will I hear from you?"

"I'm not sure yet. Stay tuned." With that, I hung up the phone, smiling as I imagined her holding the receiver with the dial tone echoing in her ear.

I shook my head and brought myself back to the present. It was time to decide one way or the other how I was going to proceed with Tim since I committed to helping him.

My biggest concern centered on my need for control. I wouldn't let myself think about the real reason for my concern—*what if he won Kat back?* Yet I needed to know the truth. *I have to know she wants me and only me.* I shook the thought away. I was getting in too deep. There were reasons why that level of emotional commitment was painful to think about. So, I didn't.

How far would I take things with Tim? I'd never put myself in this position before. Yes, I had my Masquerade Clubs, but I had staff who set up any scenes I was involved in. Some might call a fascination with sex a hobby, but for me it was a calling.

That calling led me to open a few very private, very elite BDSM clubs where carefully screened members could practice their activity of choice. Members of the Masquerade Clubs included some of the richest and most powerful people in the world. In return, they would be hard pressed to ignore any favors I requested to further my influence on the international scene. Money and power were at my disposal with sex as the great equalizer.

My security chief and best friend, Brian Patrick Farrell, screened any participants I allowed to be involved in the club's activities with me, and they agreed to the rules of my game. I called the shots. If I wanted to indulge my voyeuristic tendencies, I instructed them about my desires, which always included their immediate departure when the act was finished. Watching post-coital repartee and aftercare was not one of my appetites.

I was living the perfect lifestyle, devoid of any unnecessary emotional attachment to complicate my life. Then Kat came back into my so-called perfect world, and I no longer knew the face in the mirror staring back at me. I shook my head in an attempt to refocus on the very problem I had created.

If this dangerous little game moved along as I imagined, it could give Tim a way to win Kat back. If I was to have her, it had to be because she wanted to be with me. I was curious to see whether the dynamics would change if Tim embraced the D/s lifestyle. Yes, this was an emotionally dangerous game, but Kat was worth it.

I tried telling myself that it was totally irrational. It could be the worst decision I would ever make, but I was like an obsessed game show contestant. I had to know what was behind door number three.

It was time to stop vacillating. Maybe I should just admit it wasn't just curiosity about how far Kat would go intriguing me. I wasn't sure how far I was willing to go, either. Oh well, as my little queen of clichés would say: in for a penny, in for a pound. I picked up the phone and dialed Tim's number.

Tim picked up after one ring. "It's not that easy, is it?"

"Hello to you, too. Do you have any idea who you're talking to?"

"Yes, Connor. That's the beauty of caller ID. What did you decide?"

"You're right, Tim, it's been a hard call to make. Let's give it a try. I'm planning on being out of town for a few days. How about next Saturday when I get back? That should give me enough time to set something up for you."

"You mean your little surprise. Remember as far as Katie's concerned, I'm not part of the equation. I'll wait to hear the details."

"We'll meet at the Amber Star Hotel. Go to the front desk shortly after seven. I'll meet you there." *No need to let him know I own the hotel.* I hung up the phone, picked up my cell, and sent a message to Brian. It read: *Next Saturday. Details to follow. Set up the play with Cecile.*

A few minutes later, I sent a message to Kat: *Old Mill Inn. Room 514 at 8 p.m. sharp. Naked. C.*

The game was on, and there was no turning back.

8

KATHERINE

I arrived a few minutes before eight o'clock and made my way to the suite as instructed, pumped and ready to find out what Connor had in store for me. I liked the freedom and release that came from surrendering to his ministrations. Every now and then, those Victorian ghosts from childhood past whispered their disapproval at this wanton behavior. However, I was getting better at shooing them back to where they belonged. *What was I turning into?*

I wasn't surprised to find a cosmopolitan waiting on the coffee table beside a single, exquisite purple orchid. Connor did think of everything. I downed the contents of the martini hoping to rid myself of some of my nervousness. I was enjoying being the bad girl.

I knew the drill. Bathe, eat, drink, and be ready for whatever Connor fancied on this particular night. What more could a woman ask for? He'd been more cryptic than usual in his last text message if that were possible. Who could figure men? And they said women were complex. Not hardly, in comparison.

I roamed around the living room of the suite, excited to

get a good look at this place Connor kept as his downtown home. The room looked the same as it had last visit with one exception; taped on the bedroom door was a small piece of paper. I put my purse and jacket on a chair before walking over and reading the note.

Enjoy your bath. Enter only when you're ready to submit, not just to me, but to the truth of your hidden sexuality. Are you ready to play? C.

With each word, excitement washed over me. I took a sip of yet another cosmopolitan. As the alcohol warmed me, I started to relax in anticipation of the events ahead. After a quick bath, I slipped into a blue silken gown and chose a selection from the culinary spread on the sideboard. My thoughts wandered as I ate. *Does it get any better than this?*

If there is a heaven on earth, this is surely it—great food, great drinks, and an evening of sexual discovery. *Where did he get the money for this? Does he bring other women here? Did it matter? How far is Connor willing to take this? How had Connor arranged for all of this? What great pie.*

So many questions to which I had few answers. I took my time sipping my drink after eating my fill, letting my mind revel in images of Connor. My excitement grew as I imagined Connor's well-defined buttocks, rock hard, helping to drive his thick, muscular cock into me. *Could cocks be muscular?*

I shook my head—this was not the time to be analytical. A vision of Connor's warm mouth sucking my nipples and working his way down sent a shiver of anticipation through me. *It's time.*

I brushed my teeth, fluffed my hair, loosened the sash on the gown I wore like a second skin, and crossed to the door. The note was gone—when had that happened?

The door opened inward to a candlelit room. A bed stood against the back wall covered with embossed silk the same color as my gown. Lying on the middle of a brocade spread was a black band, which upon closer inspection proved to be a blindfold. I smiled. It was just like Connor to let me know his expectations. Feeling a little self-conscious, I folded my robe and put it on the back of a chair sitting in the corner. I sat on the edge of the bed, slipped the blindfold on, and adjusted it.

I lay luxuriating in the feel of my body contouring to the mattress, tingling with anticipation. I had no idea what to expect; I never did with Connor. He never liked to be predictable. He preferred to prolong the overwhelming emotional thrill and uncontrollable anguish, leaving me breathless.

Every nerve ending awoke as a quiver of excitement in my vulva gained momentum and shot through my abdomen to my nipples. An intoxicating scent lingered like the shadow of an ancient incense used by Aphrodite, and the air stirred around me. I lay still knowing his eyes devoured me. Impatient to begin, I reached out to him.

"I'm ready."

"Are you really?"

He attached the smooth leather restraints he favored around each wrist and fastened them above my head. The feeling of vulnerability excited me, making me more determined to continue exploring the exquisite pleasures of becoming a submissive. Before I had a chance to say more, he grabbed my ankles and pulled my legs apart. The bed gave way as he sat beside me.

His breath brushed my ear. "Tonight you can make all the noise you wish. I plan to make you beg to come. Are you sure you're ready?"

An odd timbre in his voice gave me pause, and a shiver of nervous excitement rolled over me.

"Well?"

It was barely a whisper, yet I felt the question like the crack of a whip and nodded. *God help me, yes, I'm ready.*

"Excellent. Then we begin."

The dampness between my legs spread as I caught a hint of his scent. A soft tickle traced the nape of my neck between my breasts, circled each nipple, and continued its journey over my stomach to my now dripping wet vulva. I arched and moaned as the thin, smooth twig tickled my pulsing clitoris.

Oh my God, it's a feather. He's using a feather.

He knew how much light touch quickly turned to frustrating need that left me shamelessly begging for more. I writhed against the restraints and arched toward him, my body begging him to stop, while knowing my struggle only encouraged him to see how far he could test me. The feather continued fluttering over every exposed surface, forcing me to fight for control, to keep from shouting my need to him.

That's what he wanted, and I'd be damned if I'd let him win that easily. *Two can play this game.* I took a deep breath, long and slow. But my mind screamed. *Breathe in and out. Steady now. You can do this, Katherine. In and out. I can't stand it. Please, Connor. In and out.*

As suddenly as it began, the feather left. Connor shifted his position on the bed. With one hand, he spread my lips wide and one of his long tapered fingers slid over my throbbing clit. I sighed in anticipation of relief for my "little girl in the boat," but hope was short lived.

He slid his finger back and forth a couple of times as if taking the measure of my readiness. Like an artist working a wet canvas, he drew circles around my labia with the occasional foray into my vagina. Moisture rolled down my ass cheeks pooling on the thick silk comforter. Once again, I struggled to control my panting. *In and out. Easy now. Oh God. Oh God. In, out. Now, Connor, now. In and out.*

When I was sure I would pass out from sheer need and the effort to control myself, Connor's weight left the bed. I stretched my legs and took several deep breaths before Connor grabbed my thighs and spread my legs. He traced the pattern left by his fingers with his tongue. In seconds, I was writhing, twisting, panting, and moaning again. It was too much, and I lost any hope of control.

"Suck me," I begged. "Suck." I shoved my pelvis toward his mouth, but his hands held me firmly in place. Wild with want, my head shook from side to side as waves of desire washed over me. "Now, now, now, now, now."

No longer capable of lucid thought, I wasn't sure whether I'd screamed out loud or imagined the words. Connor continued stroking every inch of my vulva slowly and deliberately. I thrashed and whimpered, arched and groaned, writhing and twisting within the confines of the restraints, lost in the agony of my need.

When his lips closed around my engorged nub, I screamed, "Now, oh please God, now, Connor." Yet still he took his time gently sucking, his rhythm just enough to keep me on the edge.

With agonizing deliberateness, Connor increased the pressure and speed, making me teeter on the edge of the cliff yet not allowing me to jump off. A sensation started deep within my core, like a ripple from a pebble making its way to the bottom of a still pond, but release seemed just beyond my reach. I held my breath and arched my back even more as I struggled to take the final leap.

My body went rigid as I reached the point of no return. Every muscle burned, extended to the limit of capability. Then, without warning, the elusive orgasm took hold, turning violent ripples into giant waves crashing through me. Minutes passed as I lay gripped by the spasms of pleasure bursting through me.

Connor gave me no time to recover before mounting me. Like a steed answering the call, he rode me deep and hard. His rigid cock stroked my hungry G-spot, forcing me to come again and again, each time as explosive as the last.

In the midst of my writhing, the blindfold worked its way off, which left me staring into his penetrating eyes. As the power of my orgasms ebbed, I marveled at his ability to control his own. After what seemed an eternity, he threw his head back and found his release.

Connor rested in me a moment before sliding out and getting up from the bed. He removed the straps binding my wrists, then leaned down and kissed me gently on the lips. With his back to me, he put on a robe draped over the chair, walked to the door, and paused, looking back at me.

"You are a wonder," he said. And with that, he was gone.

Disappointment hit me in the gut when the suite door closed behind him. I rested for a few minutes but found I did not feel the usual torpor that overtook me after great sex. The empty bed was a reminder of the mercurial nature of Connor's moods—one minute loving, the next cool and distant. He was an enigma, unpredictable.

If I was honest, it was what made him so exciting; I never knew what to expect. I wanted to explore my feelings while wrapped in the cocoon of his loving embrace, but it was not to be. I wasn't willing to hang around hoping for his return like the needy women who found their satisfaction in what a man could do for them. I took a quick shower, dressed, and was in the car headed for home within fifteen minutes.

I settled back for the half-hour drive. Although tempting, I resisted the urge to check my phone for a text from him, instead focusing on the afterglow of the lingering orgasmic tremors.

When I arrived, Tim's car was gone and the house was wrapped in darkness. Where would he have gone? *Why do you care?* I gave my head a shake. That wasn't fair. I did care for Tim, just not in the way he seemed to hope for.

He'd probably gone out to get something to eat. He was never one to cook and preferred some quick takeout. I hoped he'd be gone long enough for me to have time to think. Connor was never far from my mind, and he was definitely changing my life.

I put on my favorite lounging outfit and opened a bottle of wine when I heard Tim's key in the door. Tim staggered into the kitchen. I could smell the liquor from across the room.

"Tim—"

"So, what did you think of his little sex club?"

"I beg your pardon?"

He shrugged off his jacket. He took the wine from my hand and downed a couple of mouthfuls straight from the bottle. My eyes widened in surprise, but I said nothing—Tim usually drank only when upset.

"I said, what did you think of your Connor's little sex club. You've been one of his acts, haven't you?"

I winced at the sarcasm dripping from his voice and tried not to react to it. It was not good when both of us were upset. Two Scorpios with acerbic tongues spelled a recipe for knives twisting in open wounds that might not heal.

"What's the real issue here, Tim? Are you upset about me being with Connor tonight?"

"Yes. No. I don't know. Let's face it, Katie—Oh, hell. I might as well come right out with it. I love you, and I want you back. Connor's no good for you. Can't you see he's using you, that you're just another notch in his belt?"

His pronouncement stunned me into silence, and the shock froze my expression in place. Now it was my turn to down a glass of wine, giving me precious moments to collect my thoughts. What did he mean, Connor's sex club? Why did he think Connor was using me?

"Is this payback, Tim? Because, if it is . . ."

"No, it's nothing like that. It's just he's not right for you. He's got another woman on the side, maybe more."

"What do you mean?"

"I mean, he's going to hurt you. Look, why don't we sit down. I know this is difficult to hear, believe me, I know. Hear me out while I tell you about my, um, encounter and maybe you'll understand. Deal?"

"Give me a minute."

I walked into the adjoining room, wrapped my arms across my chest, and stared out into the black night. I needed time to sort out my feelings.

Jealousy hit me square between the eyes as did an intense feeling of possessiveness I hadn't felt for years. My own words were coming back to haunt me. "What's good for the gander is good for the goose." *Fuck.*

How could I have been so stupid not to have seen this coming? Was Connor just playing with me? I tried to cope with the deluge of emotions rushing through me. The more I thought about it, the more confused I became. Was I hiding my feelings for Connor even from myself?

One thing I did know, I'd have to hear Tim's story to sort this out. When I returned a few minutes later, I found Tim sitting in the living room with a fresh bottle of wine open on the coffee table.

"Okay, Tim, I want to know everything."

"Where do you want me to start?"

"Let's start at the beginning. Last thing I heard, you and Connor were going to go out for a drink and more talk. Now you're telling me you went to a sex club?"

"I asked Connor to take me to a sex club so I could under-stand what you're looking for, Katie. You keep saying you want to find out what really excites you, and I was hoping we could explore this together. He told me to meet him at the Amber Star."

Tim's eyes were trained on the floor, so he didn't notice the color drain from my face.

"Hard to believe, but there's a sex club on the top floor. I'd had a little too much to drink if that's any excuse."

"I'm having trouble believing this, Tim. It's unlike you."

Tim pursed his lips and was silent for a beat as if contemplating how much, or how little, to tell me.

"Look, none of this is like either of us, so obviously some things have changed. I didn't intend for this to happen. It just did."

"What happened, Tim?"

"He took me to a room where I could watch a couple having sex. That part was okay because that's what I'd asked for. The surprise came when he introduced me to this woman who looked exactly like Elizabeth Taylor."

Tim took a drink while I stared in even more shock. This simply couldn't be true.

"Go on."

"He seemed really comfortable with her, and it was obvious they had an intimate relationship. As I said, I had too much to drink, and when Connor left, she gave me a blowjob. Sorry to be so blunt, and now I'm feeling a little stupid about the whole thing. What can I say? I should have left with Connor."

I was quiet for a beat before asking, "What's her name?"

"I don't know. I just thought of her as Liz."

"You don't know? You never asked her name?" *Neither did you, you silly goose.*

"Why is that so hard to believe? Requiring details is your specialty, not mine. It was one of those mindless moments we've often talked about. She looked good. She smelled good. And she came on to me. Period."

I hesitated, unsure of how much more I wanted to know.

"What makes you think she and Connor are intimate?"

"I don't know. A man just knows these things."

I wasn't sure whether Tim was being deliberately evasive or whether he was choosing his words carefully. It was as if he was lying, but why would he have told me in the first place if he was going to lie about it? I shook my head in confusion.

"They must have done something to make you think they'd slept together."

Tim sighed. I could hear him thinking, *Women.*

"Yes, she did. I guess it was the way she looked at him. She winked and ran her hand down his arm. He didn't seem to mind. They seemed very familiar with each other."

I poured myself another glass of wine and took a deep breath.

"I'm not sure I'm in the mood for this chat, Tim. I think it would be better another time."

"Well, I don't. I think it's important we work through this. How can you stay with a degenerate? Talk to me, Katie. After all, I'm not just your ex-lover, I'm your best friend."

Fear coiled in my belly as the viper readied itself to strike. *Liz?* Was Connor sleeping with Liz? I almost felt like crawling into the comfort of Tim's loving arms and never letting go. *Almost,* but not quite. Tim wasn't Connor.

"That's just it, I don't know how I'm feeling, Tim. Part of me is hurt. Part of me is jealous. Part of me wants to rip his balls off. And part of me wants to kill this Liz of yours. Although, to be honest, I'm just as much at fault here as anyone." My lips felt pinched, but I managed to smile none-theless.

"Why would you want to kill Liz? Both of us are grown

men making our own choices. You can't blame her. Look, I can tell you're hurting. Talk to me. Tell me what you're feeling. I believe it's like you always say—if we're honest about our feelings and keep the lines of communication open, we can grow through this together."

"Oh sure, bring that up now."

My mouth went dry, and I struggled to breathe at the very thought of Connor with Liz. Confusion, hurt, and anger mingled with the overwhelming desire to have these feelings go away.

"Come sit beside me and tell me about your evening, Katie. We could order in, relax, and see how the evening unfolds."

My eyes widened, and I opened my mouth to protest. The warmth radiating from his voice drew me to him.

"No, no," he said, "you've got me all wrong. I don't want to make love right now. I just want to be your friend. Please."

The last word was a whisper, and it was difficult for him to ask this. Tim rarely expressed his emotions and the vulnerability radiating from his eyes penetrated a soft place I thought disappeared a long time ago.

Without another word, I went over to him and gave him a quick hug. For a moment, we stood feeling comfort in the warmth passing between us.

"I just can't talk right now," I said. "I need some time alone."

I picked up my purse and keys and walked out the door. I got in my car and headed toward the center point of the dark moon.

9

CONNOR

The encounter with Katherine rocked me to my core. Emotions I had long since rejected continued to tear down the protective walls I guarded so carefully. I needed to escape to think without distraction, without interruption. I called my executive assistant, and she made the arrangements for a Muskoka retreat.

Stella Sinclair was middle-aged and had worked with me for years. She relocated with me wherever I worked and seemed to have no other life. Extremely competent, her loyalty knew no bounds. Not even Margaret Scarpetta, the president of my media empire, would be able to coerce my location out of Stella when I needed private time; nothing short of a cataclysm would cause her to interrupt me. I turned my cell phone off and told the hotel to hold my calls unless the caller was Stella.

I relaxed in my suite at The Rosseau Muskoka Resort. The hotel was quiet in the off-season, and the large luxury suite had every amenity I could ask for. *Everything except for Kat.* I gave my head a shake, poured myself a Glenlivet 30 from a bottle I'd reserved for just such an occasion, and walked onto the private screened balcony. I gazed at the lake as it peeked through a veil of late summer leaves and breathed in the crisp evening air. I lay on the lounger, nursing my drink, letting the silence of nature wash away the tension that built when I thought of Kat and the feelings I'd buried long ago.

I needed the escape into solitude to get my unruly emotions under control. Despite my best efforts to ignore them, I was losing the battle. Under no circumstances could I allow that to happen. Getting hurt was something I avoided at all costs.

Hell, I avoided every emotion except perhaps those of anger or rage. When I'd lost Meredith, my heart broke. Yes, there'd been a moment of weakness when I'd believed Kat might be the one to heal the deep wound left when Meredith died. But she'd judged me emotionally unavailable, leaving her open to falling head over heels with that bastard, Tim. Not that he was a bad guy, but he'd stolen my Kat away from me. When she'd left unexpectedly, I was shattered for the second time in my life. I was so sure I'd covered that door with a layer of steel no one could penetrate. Never again. All had been right in my world, except . . . Kat was back in my life, and it scared me to death.

———

I spent the next few days taking long walks in the woods, searching for answers. As much as I craved Kat sexually, I needed a barrier against the emotions she evoked. The glimmer of an idea formed as I walked away the tension, and I grabbed hold of the thought and formed a plan.

When I was ready to return to reality, I turned on my cell and checked my messages. Along with the usual business-related calls, there were five phone and two text messages from Kat. I picked up her first phone message dated the day I'd left. Her voice demanded curtly, "What stupid game are you playing at now, Connor? Call me." Just the sound of her voice created an overwhelming desire, and I called her immediately.

"Connor," she said. "What the hell is going on?"

"Hello to you, too. Calm down, and tell me what this is about."

"As if you don't know. It's about the cute text message I got from that bimbo of yours. It said to ask you who else you're fucking. What game are you playing with me, Connor?"

I frowned. "I have no idea what you're talking about, Kat. Start from the beginning, and tell me what this is about. Please."

There was a beat of silence followed by a loud sigh.

"Don't you Kat me, Connor. I'm going to give you the benefit of the doubt here, but not for one fucking second do I believe you don't know what I'm talking about. The morning after the last night we spent together at the hotel—you know the one when you walked out on me yet again—I turned on my phone and found a text message sent from Tim's phone asking if I knew who else you were fucking.

"Tim told me he just happened to get a blowjob from— guess who. Oh, but you already know that because you had her blow both of us. Obviously you set me up, and I can't believe you told her about me. That's what this is all about."

Connor's frown deepened. "Back up a minute. What do you mean the text said I was fucking someone else? Tell me exactly what the text message said."

"It said: Do you know who else Connor is fucking, Kitty Kat?"

That bitch. Fucking Cecile. If she fucks this up for me, I'm going to kill her.

"You have my word that you're the only person I've been with since our first meeting at Magnum, even though there's no commitment on either of our parts. And I'm not playing any game with you, Kat. I had nothing to do with this Liz giving Tim a blowjob. Is that what he told you?"

"Connor, if you're trying to insinuate something here—"

"I'm not trying to insinuate anything. Give me some time to investigate this, okay?"

"Well, it had to come from Liz. Tim says no one else had access to his cell. But why would one of your subs play a trick like that? And how would she know—"

"Katherine." My tone took on a hard edge. "Leave it with me."

"Okay, Connor, okay. Don't get pissy with me. I'm sure you can understand why this is so upsetting. I'm not into being fucked around with. I'm not a naïve twenty-year-old anymore."

I softened my tone. "I do understand, and I'll get to the bottom of it. You have my word."

I pushed my midnight-gray Maserati Quattroporte far in excess of the speed limit as I drove home, my mind whirling with confusion. What would possess Cecile to start playing games at this late date? She'd been privy to many of my adventures before without repercussion. So why now?

I activated my hands-free phone. "Call Cecile." I drummed the steering wheel, waiting for the call to connect.

"Connor." She sounded happy to hear from me. "I wondered when you'd surface. Where have you been?"

"Cut the crap, Cecile. Meet me in my suite in an hour. I have something I want to discuss with you."

"But, I'm in the middle of—"

"One hour," I snapped and disconnected the call. I tapped the hands-free remote and called Kat again.

"Katherine King."

Ouch.

"Kat, it's me again. We need to meet. How soon are you available?"

"Connor, I don't think—"

"Please, Kat, just hear me out. That's all I'm asking."

Several very long seconds passed before she sighed deeply.

"Okay. I'm due in a meeting in ten minutes, expected to last several hours. How about six o'clock at the Library Bar?"

"That works for me. See you there." I rang off.

Cecile would pay for this.

10

CONNOR

The hour it took me to drive to the Amber Star did little to ease my anger. It must have shown as the friendly attendant looked like a deer caught in the headlights as I threw him the keys to the Maserati.

"Park it," I growled.

"Yes, Mr. McClane, right away."

By the time I entered my suite, I was in a controlled rage. The lights were dimmed, and the room reflected the soft warmth from the flames in the fireplace. Not what I expected. The floor-to-ceiling windows giving a view of the Toronto skyline were electronically shaded, obscuring the view.

The woman most referred to as Liz sat on the plush sofa, languishing in her usual entitled pose, martini in hand. As angry as I was, it was hard to deny the sculpted beauty of Cecile DePoulignac. She had those come-hither violet eyes most men got lost in, and they were in full bloom. Yet, she didn't come close to radiating Kat's beauty, whose imperfections made her even more perfect.

A sheer peignoir hugged Cecile's voluptuous curves,

doing little to hide the shaved mound between her legs or the contrast of her nipples on her alabaster skin. There was a time when I couldn't resist her coy little games, but that time had long passed, and I was too angry to care.

"What the hell is wrong with you? Do you really think you could send that text to Katherine and I wouldn't find out about it?"

"Connor, Connor. Come sit down, and I'll pour you a martini." She patted the leather cushion beside her.

"Keep your fucking drink and answer the question."

Her lips transformed into a petulant pout. "Now you've gone and hurt my feelings."

"Get off it, Cecile. Remember who you're talking to. The last time you had your so-called feelings hurt, you threatened to cut the man's balls off and feed them to him. This isn't about your feelings even if you had any."

"Oh, Connor, how can you say that? You know I have always had feelings for you. Besides, he had it coming. If you thought about it, you'd realize we are very much alike in so many ways. That's why we work so well together.

"You see, I know who you are. If anyone dares to play you, retribution comes swift and furious. Wasn't it you who told me payback's a bitch?"

Cecile swung her legs off the couch and glided over to stand in front of me.

Too close. The smell of her cloying perfume turned my stomach. It took every ounce of my willpower not to back up a step.

"Don't get me wrong, Connor. It's one of the things I love about you. Save me from the indecisive lemmings in this world. You really need to get a grip on your own emotions before you lecture me on mine." Cecile jabbed my chest with a long, blood-red fingernail.

I stood in front of her, rigid, saying nothing. Every fiber

of my being strained to control an irrational urge to strangle her. But, of course, I would never have the pleasure of feeling my hands squeezing her throat for two reasons—one, I never strike women unless it's consensual and desired by the women who embrace the role of a submissive, and two, Cecile was right. I had very little to no use for people who let their emotions override rationality.

And here I was becoming one of them.

I focused back on Cecile, who wasn't about to end her little tirade any time soon. She paced the length of the room. I moved to the safety of the bar.

"Think about it. You're rich, the enigmatic and powerful owner of the world's elite Masquerade Clubs, and damn fine in the looks department. You could and do have your way with any woman you want.

"My God, Connor, they beg me to tell them how they can get you into bed. And the things they would like to do with you might even be a surprise to you."

She picked up the pitcher from the bar and poured herself another drink.

"You say you don't have the time or inclination to give a damn about love, yet look at you. Totally losing it over a harmless text-tease. If your beloved Katherine is truly that naïve to think you don't sleep around, somebody should tell her."

"I—"

"Think about it, Connor. For crying out loud, I manage our sex clubs—and very well, I might add. We are not hormone-driven adolescents desperately looking for the back seat of a car. I know you've been around the block more than a couple of times. Has she? And you know I'll do anything, *anything* you want. Will she?"

She resumed her place on her throne. I couldn't help but marvel that it was me who was supposed to be angry, yet she turned everything into my fault. She was good at managing people, which was why I'd connected with her in the first place.

Right from the beginning, she'd helped me create the perfect fantasy atmosphere at the Masquerade Clubs so I was never left wanting in my life as a dominant. No one would deny she was beautiful, smart, manipulative, and very ruthless. I always found Cecile to be a great fuck, but she never made love.

She patted the sofa with her hand, evoking the dramatic panache of an actor.

"Sit down here, Connor, and have a drink. I know what you need. I always have. You know we're perfect for each other, and it's time you accept that. I am everything you ever desired. You don't believe that little fluff Katherine can ever come close to someone like me, do you?"

She was tempting, but she couldn't leave it alone. She had to bring Katherine into it. Her mistake reminded me of why I was there in the first place.

"I'm only going to say this once. If you ever interfere in my life again, I'll dissolve our partnership. There'll be no discussion."

This time, I was calm and controlled. The words were as cold as ice.

"I can't believe you're serious," Cecile whined.

My eyes, unblinking, never left hers. I stared at her until she looked away, and then I turned and walked out of the suite. I went to the parking garage to retrieve my keys. The attendant was at his desk, reading. When he saw me, he jumped up and managed to grab the keys off the rack, but he fumbled them, and they fell out of his hand and landed at his feet.

"I'm sorry, Mr. McClane. I didn't mean to drop them. I'm sorry. I'm so sorry."

For the first time in too many years, I recognized myself in the self-conscious young man. More memories I had so carefully locked away came rushing back. If I had to explain what happened next, I couldn't. I put my hand on the attendant's shoulder.

"No son, it's me who should be sorry."

I drove to Magnum Enterprises, walked into Brian's office, and fell onto the nearest chair.

Brian Patrick Farrell was head of security for my holdings. He was also my personal bodyguard, when needed, and my confidante and friend since childhood. Ours was an unbreakable bond. Unlike me, Brian was a free spirit who'd never be caught in a suit and tie, preferred muscle cars, and thought boardroom politics should be spelled b-o-r-e-d.

Street smarts and four years of special ops service made him well suited for his role, and he loved it. If it hadn't been for him, I might not have made it through after Meredith was killed. The only time we were separated for any length of time was when Brian did his stint in the Armed Forces. He finished his tour alive but broken and haunted by the experience. I took him in and helped put him back together again. He never looked back. Such was the strength of our friendship.

"You look like hell, my friend," Brian said.

I expected no less. Brian never minced words with anyone as he frequently reminded people. If you want sympathy, he would say, find the door marked exit and keep on going. The only other person I'd seen face off with Brian was his lovely wife, Asha. Just the thought of Asha and her spunky wit brought a brief smile to my face.

"Nice to see you too, Bri."

He gave his usual chuckle. "Spill it, Connor. You want someone to disappear?"

"I wish it were that simple."

"Sounds serious. Why don't you start from the beginning?"

"No, no. It's not like that. It's just Cecile."

Brian sat straight up and looked me in the eyes.

"Cecile? You're kidding, right? Since when can't you handle her? You know what I think of that woman. Hell, I'll take her out for free. Just say the word."

I told him my side of the confrontation with Cecile, and he looked puzzled.

"Okay, college boy, tell me if I've got this right." Brian's voice was full of affection, reminding me he cared about me as a person and not my success.

"Elite corporate boards around the world are afraid to make a decision before consulting you. You have—how should I put this—entertained so many women over the years you put George Clooney to shame, and yet you come to my office distraught over a text message to—what was her name? Oh yeah, Katherine.

"Let me be even blunter, Con. You've spent so long hiding from a broken heart, you don't even recognize what having one feels like anymore."

"Okay, Brian, that's—"

"I know this is not something you want to hear, and as impossible as it is to believe, I think this Katherine means more to you than you know. I also think your feelings for her scare you to death, and making Cecile a scapegoat is easier than admitting it. Tell me I'm wrong, Con."

As usual, Brian unerringly sent the arrow of truth, penetrating my veil of self-delusion. I turned my head and stared blankly out of the office window. The sun slipped closer to the horizon before I whispered, more to myself than Brian, "The real question is, what if you're right?"

I stood up, walked to the door, and opened it. Then I hesitated, not wanting to leave on a sour note.

"Asha mentioned it's been a while since you've been over for a decent meal. She thinks you're eating too many foreign dishes with strange French names to make them sound good, but they're just grubs in a shell."

I smiled. "Tell your lovely wife I'll make a point of it."

As I drove away, I imagined Brian shaking his head.

11

CONNOR

I arrived early at the Library Bar. The server recognized me and seated me at my favorite table.

"It's Stewart, isn't it?"

"Indeed it is, sir. What a good memory. What may I get for you this evening?"

"Bring me a glass of Glenlivet 12 over ice, please. Oh, and bring me a glass of your best Baco Noir blend."

"Right away, Mr. McClane."

Much as I tried to calm my agitation, I kept catching myself alternately drumming my fingers and running my hand through my hair. I usually relaxed and enjoyed the ambiance at the bar, but the only thing I could focus on were the tendrils of fear wrapping around my spine. I could face down the most intimidating business rival without batting an eye, but this chat with Kat had a grip on me I couldn't shake. This might be one of the most important conversations in my life, yet I avoided looking at why that would be true. Maybe I was afraid of what I might find.

The air stood still when she walked through the large brass door. Even from a distance, her brown eyes shone with intensity. The knee-length black-silk sheath accentuated her trim curves. Her slim legs and ballet slippers reminded me of the dancer she'd once dreamed of being. Something about her drew every male eye in the place, but she was oblivious to it. She marched toward me with single-minded purpose.

"Hi." I started to stand up as she neared the table.

"So now you start being a gentleman? Isn't it a little late?

Her sarcasm was a cover so I wouldn't see her upset, but it still stung. I sat back as she sat.

"And what is this?" She gestured toward the wineglass. "Did it ever occur to you to wait and find out what I wanted?

"I feel like we're in a war zone here. Can we start over, Kat?"

"For today, let's make it Katherine. I'm not feeling very cuddly right now."

"I wasn't thinking of the cuddly side of a cat, but as you wish, Katherine."

I enunciated each syllable of her name while I struggled to get a grip on my reappearing temper. This would end in disaster if I lost it with my Alley Kat. She had a real thing about confrontation with loud or aggressive men, remnants from the abusive childhood she was so secretive about.

Her hand shook as she gripped the stem of the glass and took a swig.

"Okay," she said, "I'm sorry. I'm a little stressed right now. What did you want to talk about?"

"I want to clear the air about that text message and address any concerns you have. What would you like to know first?"

"Have you been having sex with Liz?"

That's none of your business. I took a beat to collect my thoughts and let my initial reaction to her question roll through me. If I jumped on her for breaking our agreement to enjoy our sex without the entanglement of commitment,

I'd probably ruin any chance I had of seeing her again. Obviously, the rules of engagement were changing.

"If you're asking if I've had sex with Cecile since I've been back with you, the answer is no. If you're asking if I've ever had sex with her, the answer is yes."

"Cecile? Who's Cecile?"

"The woman you call Liz. Her name is not Liz, it's Cecile."

"Oh, really, so you've been lying to me all along?"

A flush rushed up my neck, and I hoped my tan hid the color. She really was trying to push my buttons.

"Katherine, you have my word I'll be honest with you. Now what's the issue here? I've never hidden my sexual proclivities from you. I ran you through a test with Cecile. Is there something about my behavior that left you with the impression I was a practicing celibate? We both came into this with a history and agreed our only commitment was to explore our sexuality. Has something changed?"

She stared through me as if looking at a thought that existed on the other side of another universe. Was she examining her feelings or searching for a way to blow me off? After what seemed like forever, she came back to me.

"Yes, I think something has changed, but I don't know what. I know I have no right to be jealous of any other women in your life, but I am, and I can't figure out why."

Joy sang through my heart as I kept what I hoped was a mask of inscrutability over my face.

"So are you saying you're developing feelings for me?"

She gave me a wan smile.

"I've always cared for you, C, but I can't get emotionally entangled with you again. You confuse me. One minute you're warm, loving, and make me feel like I'm the most cherished woman in the world, and the next minute you're distant and act as if I don't exist. I don't know how much of this hot and cold I can take. I never know what to expect.

What exactly do you feel for me, if anything?" She took a sip of her wine. "Or am I just another notch to you?

Our future hinged on my answer. Yet how could I tell her what I felt when I had no idea myself?

"One thing I can tell you with absolute certainty is you're definitely not another notch as you call it. As for how I feel?"

I took a drink of my scotch for fortification.

"I don't know how I feel about you. I do know you're a remarkable woman, and I want to spend time with you. We both went into this with our eyes wide open. We agreed to explore the depths of our sexual depravity."

I gave her a wan smile, but my attempt at humor fell flat.

"And now feelings seem to be getting tangled up with our sexual exploration."

I took another drink and swirled the amber liquid. Finally, I looked up into the bottomless well of her eyes and took the plunge.

"I'm afraid of what I may be feeling for you, especially knowing you have feelings for another man. What are those feelings? What is up with you and Tim?"

I wasn't sure I wanted to hear the answer, but I've always been one to face the truth.

"I guess you could say we were friends with benefits. After I left you, I met Tim, and he was wonderful and affectionate and attentive. He was just what I needed, and I agreed to move in with him. We've never lived a committed relationship. He did his thing, and I did mine. It was comfortable and companionable. That's probably why I wasn't jealous when he went off on his sabbatical."

I could breathe again. Obviously, some entity possessed me for these emotions to govern the logic that was central to my existence. And yet, I had to know.

"And do you want a committed relationship with me?"

My voice had the deceptively mild tone I used in business before I went in for the kill, but I couldn't help myself.

"I don't know what the hell I want with you, C, but a committed relationship isn't on the list." A huge grin shone through her eyes and lit up her face.

"Unless you count being committed to sexual ecstasy."

At that moment, I longed to give her the world. Never had I met a woman so in tune with my needs. I relaxed and sat back in my chair. Unlike most women I'd known, Kat never pushed me for more than I had to give.

"So let's get back to our reason for being together. Tell me more about how you felt about your first test now that you've had some time to think about it. From what Cecile told me when she reported back, you found it exciting."

"It was exciting and terrifying. It opened a whole host of feelings I didn't know I had."

"Like?"

"Like the feeling it's just not right to have sex with a woman."

I could feel the frown form on my face and tried to wipe it away.

"Do you mean to tell me you're still letting those fanatical religious rules you grew up with affect you? That's hard to believe."

Kat laughed. "It takes time to change a lifetime of habit. What else do you want to know?"

"Are you sleeping with Tim now?"

She studied me for a moment, and my stomach dropped to my feet. Her answer held an importance that shouldn't exist for me given my insistence about my feelings.

"No, I'm not. It's been well over a year since Tim and I have made love. Would it matter to you?"

It was my turn to be put on the spot, but she deserved an honest answer.

"I guess I'm just discovering it would matter."

"Why?"

Dammit, Kat. "Maybe it's because I want to be the one controlling who you're with. I seem to be feeling rather possessive about you."

"Is that a new experience for you?"

"Well, it's one I haven't felt for a very long time."

We sat sipping our drinks for a few minutes, eyes locked, each searching for answers to the complexities of our Scorpio natures.

"So where do we go from here?

"I guess that ball's in your court, Katherine. The rules haven't changed for me. So I'll ask you—where do we go from here?"

A mischievous smile lit her face. "You can call me Kat now. Let's get some dinner, shall we? I've always wanted to eat here."

Kat took obvious delight in looking around the Library Bar. One might argue the only thing she loved as much as great sex and food was a good book. And here she was surrounded by floor-to-ceiling cases of leather-bound antique tomes. I loved the excitement she exuded now that she was relaxed, and I let her take the lead. She ordered a veritable feast of her favorites and sampled every dish, happily reaching over to take food from my plate.

After we'd settled into our after-dinner coffee, I suggested we take a break from our daily lives and focus on us.

"What did you have in mind?" Kat asked.

"Nothing in particular. Let's just spend some time together without distractions. Any chance you can take a little time off? I know you're starting the new job, but it would be great if we could get away for a few days."

"That shouldn't be a problem. I have some vacation time owed to me, and I may be able to get approval from one of the bigwigs at Magnum, don't you think?" she teased. "Where are we going?"

"Leave that with me. How soon can you get away?"

"I could take a day or two off next week. But I don't have the time to plan a trip right now."

I normally left travel arrangements to my executive assistant, Stella, however, this time I yearned to surprise Kat with a holiday I'd planned. I wanted to take her far away from the day-to-day routine so she could delve into her emerging sexual submissiveness without distraction.

"Seriously, Kat, just leave it to me. Plan on going somewhere warm. I'll take care of the details. Just let me know the exact days you can get away."

"How about a week from Thursday? I'll take Thursday, Friday, and Monday off. Will that be enough time?"

"Yes, that'll do nicely," I said.

I called my travel agent, and she suggested an exotic vacation at a five-star all-inclusive resort in the Bahamas. I checked it out online and liked what I saw, so booked four nights at the rather secluded Great Exuma resort. The Butler Suites looked splendid, just what we needed to focus on each other and explore deeper layers of Kat's psyche.

A nagging voice kept whispering, *You'd better be prepared to disclose your innermost thoughts, too,* and I was committed to doing just that—*I think.*

We arrived at the airport on Thursday morning and found the company jet idling on the tarmac. Without prompting and much to my surprise, Kat chose to leave her smart phone at home.

"I don't want anything to detract from our time. Besides, I need a break. It's been quite the whirlwind tying up loose ends at Magnum."

The flight was uneventful. We alternated between watching in-flight movies and reading. Kat bought me an e-reader and loaded it with books even though she knew I preferred the printed page.

"I can't believe you're so old-fashioned. Just give it a try."

The resort shuttle whisked us away once we'd cleared customs. With each layer of clothing she shed, Kat seemed to lose a layer of the stress and tension radiating from her since she'd found out about Liz, a.k.a. Cecile.

As we settled into our seats for the ride to the resort, I risked reaching for her hand. I wasn't one for public displays of affection and usually avoided her advances, so I wasn't sure how she'd respond to the unexpected gesture. She locked her fingers in mine and snuggled against me. *Thank God.*

A welcoming committee awaited our arrival. Exceptional service was the resort's trademark, and they didn't let us down as they rapidly checked us in, gave us a complimentary glass of champagne, and introduced us to the concierge and our personal butler. We dropped our luggage in our ocean-front suite—the view was breathtaking—and changed into our bathing suits.

We went for a walk along the beach in the hope of finding something to eat. A snack of conch fritters and crab cakes at a beachfront cafe took the edge off, and we continued our walk on the warm white sand. The air was alive with the sounds of the wildlife mixed in with the sharp odor of ripening fruit and the salty ocean. I kept the conversation light, and we enjoyed an afternoon frolicking in the ocean and exploring the resort.

I took a quick shower and went to the front desk to check out dinner options while Kat took one of her long, relaxing baths. Not even the tropical heat deterred her from the soothing warmth, and she chuckled with delight when she found the bath salts and bubble bath waiting on the edge of the Jacuzzi tub.

After making arrangements for a late dinner, I headed back to the suite. I smiled at the sounds of Kat humming as she finished up her bathing routine. A jolt of electricity shot through me as I imagined her massaging her compact body with the fragrant body lotion she loved. I pushed the thought away. Now was not the time for that. I had other plans in mind for the evening.

I grabbed a glass of wine from the well-stocked bar and headed out to the patio to watch the setting sun. Kat interrupted my ruminations by slipping her arms around my waist and hugging me from behind. I turned in her arms and brushed her lips with mine before slipping out of her embrace to pour her a glass of the wine I'd decanted. Together we watched the sun slipping into the ocean as it made its journey, turning day into a dusk full of secrets to reveal. The breeze ruffled the white gauzy material of Kat's long dress, which barely covered the otherwise naked, full bloom of her curvaceous body.

She turned toward me, and the intensity of her gaze tightened my groin. How I loved the way she communicated her need, her body radiating heat, and the gold streaks in her eyes glowing like embers alive with her desire. I kissed her. I enjoyed the way she played my lips with her tongue. I could never quite get over her passion for my lips. She loved the shape and feel of them and often whispered I had the sexiest lips alive.

Her message spoke directly to my cock, and it responded in kind. Plans be damned. Without a word, I took her by the hand and led her inside. Choosing a wide chaise lounge made for the purpose, I lay back, letting the linen of my open shirt drape my chest.

The warm sea breeze drifted through the sheers,

cloaking us. Kat's breath caught as she stood looking at me, head tilted to one side, unaware of the power she had over me. A small smile played over her lips. She swayed her hips just a little as if in time to some Latin music only she could hear while unbuttoning one button, then the next, then the next.

She undid each button of the long dress, bending at a slight angle as she reached the waistband, giving me a vision of the curve of a smooth hip as it peeked through the curtain of fabric. She straightened and looked at me, widening the split edges of the dress just enough so the swell of her breasts peeked through.

Heat and desire coursed through me when her nipples hardened and elongated as she channeled her passion in return. She stood as if waiting for my command, and I let her wait a beat while I got a grip on my cock's urgent requests for attention.

I waited just long enough to assert my control before I motioned her to me with my index finger. She swept the front of the dress wide open and in two strides sat straddled over me. Her small hands massaged my chest, alternately playing with my nipples and gently tugging my sparse chest hairs. The nub of her clitoris peeked through her swollen lips. I couldn't resist slipping a finger into the well of her dripping wet pussy.

This glorious symbol of her womanhood was the canvas and my fingers the pencil as I sketched the outline of the rare orchid it reminded me of. When Kat started to moan and wriggle, I cupped a buttock with my left hand to hold her firm.

For a few moments, her eyes held mine. Her gaze begged me to make her come, but I finished the outline before I worked on shading the nub. She closed her eyes and moaned, and I felt her buttocks tighten as what she called *quivers* of pleasure shot through her. She looked at me again, her eyes bright with need.

"Say it," I whispered. "Tell me what you want."

She moaned, yet didn't say a word. I continued with a motion that kept her orgasm just out of reach. I could feel the internal scream building in her chest.

"Say it."

She shook her head wildly from side to side. She said nothing. Pleading leaped out of her eyes when she fought them open to look at me, and my eyes returned a message of their own. *Say it.*

"Please C, please." Her voice was barely audible.

"Please C, what?"

More silence while I continued the steady rhythm. Then . . .

"Make me come."

It was a whisper, but it was enough. I stroked. I colored the prominent petal of her delicate flower with a firmer and faster motion. For an instant, she froze, and then gushing warmth spread over my hand as the explosion of her orgasm rocketed through her. Without pause, I released my rigid cock, and lifting her hips, I plunged into her.

I almost came that instant. Stifling an internal scream of my own, a low moan matching hers moved through my core. I held her hips with my hands, working hard to control her eagerness as she rode me. She stilled, but every muscle strained to follow her passion.

Fascinated, I watched her struggle. She was relinquishing control, giving me the power to make her submit completely. God, she was perfect.

The dominant aspect of my sexuality was so close to an overwhelming need it shocked me. My thoughts kept repeating over and over what I knew to be true. *Be patient. Be patient. If you go too fast, you'll lose her.* If she was to embrace her submissive nature, she must trust me completely. I kept telling myself to be patient when in truth I just longed to hold her down and ravage that beautiful body.

The rawness of her hunger drove her frenzy. With a groan of resignation, I let her move freely. She rode me hard. An orgasm blasted through me as I felt the grip of another of her powerful orgasms. Spent, we lay together enjoying the warmth of the tropical evening. I'd waited this long, my proposal could wait a little longer . . .

12

CONNOR

The knock came as we finished dressing, and the aroma of a finely cooked meal drifted through the door of our suite. I crossed to answer it.

"Would you like me to set this up for you, sir?" The server pushed in a dining cart laden with covered dishes and linens.

"Certainly, go right ahead and set it up on the patio."

We leaned against the rail, sipping our wine, watching him set the table and decant the Amarone.

"More wine? Why C, one would wonder if you're trying to get me drunk tonight." Her eyes sparkled, and her smile teased as she stood on her toes to deliver a kiss.

"You are perfect just the way you are. Let's eat, I'm starving."

The server finished laying a very elegant table complete with fine linens and a beautifully appointed floral center-piece. He plugged in a warming tray holding several covered dishes from which an array of wonderful smells seeped. Without delay, we sat down and dug in. While eating, we chatted about our pleasure in the suite and our surroundings, taking note of the sounds of the night.

Kat laughed with delight as the deep-throated croaking of the frogs mixed with the scuttle of the sand crabs underneath our deck and the harsh *chewk* call of the mockingbirds mingled with the trilling shrieks of the parrots. It had been a very long time since casual conversation and the uninhibited laugh of a beautiful woman affected me so much.

Once we'd eaten more than our fill including coconut cake and a bread pudding slathered in sweet cream, we rolled our way over to the chaise lounge perched across the edge of the deck. By this time, we were well into the first bottle of Amarone, and I figured the mood was just about right to invite open and candid dialogue.

"Okay, babe, what's on your mind?" Kat asked.

I smiled in recognition of her usual direct and intuitive nature. I handed her a journal before sitting on the lounge chair opposite.

"I wrote this for you, Kat. Please read it, and let me know what you think."

A Double Diary on Tuesday, August 21

Not a new concept, but unique considering the traditional diary is usually a one-person endeavor offering the benefit of personal insight and/or a record for historical reflection. A two-person diary provides the opportunity for so much more.

There is so much I want to say to you, I don't know where to start. In so many ways, I'm afraid to. This in itself is hard for me to admit. Most look at me as strong, decisive, and unaffected by anything getting in the way of the bottom line, and they are right. For so many years, I have pursued success without the slightest interest in how it affected others or even myself. I told myself my emotions would be viewed as a weakness easily exploited by others. Every successful achievement reinforced this fact.

I intentionally kept myself busy with the pursuit of wealth so I could hide in the emotional vacuum I imposed on myself. I can no longer deny that I lay awake at night thinking of you, Kat. Each morning, I wake up wondering when I'll see you again. To be completely honest, I don't know what it means. I know I have more questions than answers.

I am intrigued and excited you have chosen me to explore the nature of your submissiveness. In turn, I may find the courage to look at my life and the effect you have on me.

I prefer to think of this exchange as our double diary—a way to open up to each other. I want to be able to share what we're thinking, how we're feeling, what excites you, when you're ready to take the next step to explore our passions further.

All these things I find easier to communicate in writing. Sex is not by any means the exclusive focus for this diary, but it is the catalyst.

Can we take another step, through this diary, to even more hidden desires and new experiences? Perhaps. This is my way of providing an outlet for fun and insight when other methods of communication just don't work or become awkward for various reasons.

It's a lot to think about, but therein lies the beauty of the process. Take whatever time you need to consider if you're willing to share such intimate detail.

I excitedly await your response. C.

The smile of delight never left her face. After another sip of wine, she grabbed the pen, bit her lip for a moment, and then wrote frantically. I sat mesmerized. She sipped and wrote. I refilled and watched. In a few minutes, she handed me the notebook, grinning. I read.

Double Diary
Katherine on Thursday, August 23

Well, it certainly is a welcome and "stimulating" idea. I like that it's open and affords me the freedom I need, given my life—balancing our time together, life, and work. And, I'm loving anything that moves us in our exploration of our sexuality. I feel ashamed of how I'm reveling in your attention and whatever is growing between us. Sometimes I fear you'll be bored, so this presents a way to add a different dimension to that exploration. :-) Kat

We finished our wine, drinking in the splendor of the full moon as it reflected off the gently lapping waves. Although the fragrant salt sea air and tropical flora tended to overwhelm, it was Kat's scent that penetrated, reminding me of my longing for her.

I stood, took her hand, and led us into our bedroom. Like musicians who have played together so long they have no need of a conductor, we went about our bedtime ritual. I loved just how compatible we were.

As we brushed our teeth, Kat watched me in the bathroom mirror, her caring and desire evident in her gaze. I loved the way she brushed her teeth. Being unashamed to show me an act she considered so personal was yet another gift she gave to me.

I stood behind her and nuzzled her hair with my cheek, letting her warm fragrance envelop me. Minutes passed before she turned in my arms, wrapped hers around my neck, and kissed me deeply. Our lovemaking was long and slow and deep. Eyes the color of chocolate locked with mine as she whispered my name again and again. We explored every inch of our bodies as if for the first time.

I felt the moment of her surrender and knew she was mine. I surrendered to her with equal abandon as our howls of joy drifted out with the ocean tide. We fell asleep naked and wrapped in each other's arms.

The next day, we golfed eighteen holes on a nearby out island at a picturesque private course designed by one of the golf greats. Kat was susceptible to heatstroke, and although she took precautions, she couldn't stave off the headache from the long day in the tropical sun. When we got back to the suite, she took a nap in hopes of recovering for our evening. I took advantage of the time to put more of the feelings overwhelming me in our diary.

I still wasn't sure why this need to show and tell her how much I needed her had surfaced. Briefly I wondered whether it was the threat Tim posed, but he was just one factor making me realize how much deeper my feelings for my Alley Kat ran, deeper than I'd ever allowed myself to acknowledge. I poured a large glass of lemonade and settled on the patio with our diary. Later that evening, we languished over a late-night dinner with a perfect bottle of wine, eventually falling asleep to the hypnotic sound of the ocean.

We woke around nine o'clock on Saturday morning. Kat was back to her old self with an enormous appetite, and we decided to go to one of the resort restaurants for the breakfast buffet. I took generous portions of steaming hot pancakes, scrambled eggs, bacon, and hash browns. Kat chose her favorite breakfast of a poached egg on multi-grain toast and fresh fruit. We sat down at a window table with an ocean view and tucked into our food.

"So, did you write me more in our diary?" Kat asked.

I sighed.

"Wow." Kat laughed. "That sounds heavy. What's the sigh for?"

"I did write more for you, and I'll give it to you later. But first, I have a confession to make."

She laughed. "Wasn't the double diary surprise enough for one vacation, C?"

"This one is serious, Kat, and I don't think you're going to like it." I took a deep breath. "I kind of told you a lie of omission about the sex club. I own it and several others. In fact, I have a partner."

"You do? Who?"

"Cecile."

Katherine stared at me in wide-eyed amazement. She took a sip of her coffee.

"Let me be sure I got this straight. That bitch Cecile is your partner?" Her eyes narrowed, and her lips formed a tight line. "You sleep with her, and you're legally tied to her?"

I sighed again. "It gets worse, Kat. I set Tim up with her in the hopes of distracting his attention from you."

"Anything else?" Her voice seemed to rise an octave with each word she spoke. She gripped her triceps despite the tropical morning heat, her stare unblinking.

"I know this probably pisses you off, but please hear me out. I wasn't trying to hide anything from you. I just needed to figure out my feelings about things before I told you."

"So let me be sure I understand you correctly. You hid the truth about your relationship with this Cecile. You manipulated my friend. And you have a bunch of harems you call *sex clubs*. Have I got that right?"

The chill in her voice cut through me like a knife. I'd never seen Kat this angry.

"Now wait just a minute. I wouldn't call what I have with Cecile a relationship. It's a partnership, strictly business."

"Oh yeah, right. What are you trying to tell me here? Sex to you is business? Listen to me. I can't even speak properly, I'm so mad at you. I can't believe you did this. Wasn't it just a couple of weeks ago we agreed to be honest with each other? How soon we forget."

I put a tight grip on my temper in response to her vitriolic outburst.

"Can the sarcasm and selective memory, Kat. No, *we* didn't agree to be honest with each other until today. *You* agreed to be honest with me about your feelings. We had no reason to discuss my honesty at the time."

"Oh for fuck's sake, Connor. Are you being deliberately obtuse? I can't fucking believe it. You know what—I don't even want to talk to you right now. If we continue with this, I'm afraid I might say something neither of us wants to hear."

She stood and downed the rest of her orange juice.

"Just one more thing, please, Kat. Hear me out."

She glared at me but sat back down.

"I know you're mad at me right now, and you have every right to be. But as you're thinking about this, I want you to know two things. First, remember you didn't tell me about Tim right away—you waited until he came home, which isn't any different from me waiting to tell you this.

"And second, I never meant to hide anything from you. I just needed to get my head on straight before I told you. My life has been anything but predictable, but I've always known what I wanted and exactly how to get it. Seeing you again is nothing that I, and probably you, ever expected. I'm just trying to find my way, Kat."

"Is that it?" She stood.

"Yes, that's it. Where are you going?"

"I have no idea, Connor, but wherever I'm going, I'm going alone. I need some time to think."

I spent most of the day on our patio in the lounge chair, stretched out, sunglasses on, to all appearances just another tourist enjoying the island sun. When I'd had enough sun, I walked the beach, oblivious to the occasional sunbather dotting the wide expanse of sand. My emotions seethed and boiled like a witch's cauldron.

What will I do if she won't forgive me? Surely, this isn't so bad she can't get over it, is it?

I couldn't get my head around this one. I lacked my usual objectivity. The minutes dragged by. It felt like the longest day of my life.

As I sat on the beach watching the sun disappear into the horizon, I realized that part of the rawness in the pit of my stomach came from hunger. I hadn't eaten since breakfast. My step quickened as I headed back to our bungalow—maybe Kat would be there.

She hadn't been back. I tried not to let my heart sink any lower than it already had, but a cloak of dejection wrapped itself around me as I headed for the shower. I tried to push down the thick knot lodged in my throat insistently making breathing a strain.

Had I lost her? I shook my head to rid it of the impression. That wasn't possible.

If she lost trust in you, there's no turning back. This you know for sure, Connor.

The nagging little voice in my head kept nattering away as I cleaned up. In the hopes of pushing it to the background, I cranked up the volume on my favorite Gentle Giant CD and focused on getting ready as if it were any special Saturday date night. A small bead of light radiated through the thick fog—if she hadn't left me, our date night would bring her back. Maybe, just maybe . . .

I checked myself in the mirror before heading off to the

Italian restaurant she'd chosen when seeking comfort food. An average guy with wavy brown hair and gray-green eyes gazed back at me. The white-silk knit shirt accented the long, lean lines of my abdomen, and I'd pushed up the sleeves to display my tanned forearms, just the way she liked to see them. I wasn't muscle bound, but I was in great shape, and Kat loved raking her fingers through the fine hairs outlining those muscles. There were two pieces of clothing that Kat liked me in so much she said they made her wet. This shirt and a pair of black-linen pants that showed off the curves of my buttocks. I was wearing both tonight. I needed all the help I could get.

I don't know what else I can do. I added just a hint of her favorite cologne and headed off.

I asked for a private table for two and settled in to wait with a margarita. After a half hour or so, my despair was complete. She wasn't going to come. Hunger drove me to order a Caesar salad.

"Make that two along with a bottle of a good Ripasso."

She sat in the seat opposite me, stunning in a silky black jumpsuit split in front and back from neck to waist. Damp black curls framed her exquisite face. Everything in me yearned to reach over and run my fingers through them before cupping the softness of her cheeks and kissing her full moist lips.

Stop it, Connor. Don't blow this. I couldn't take my eyes off her.

"Okay, let's talk." She looked into my eyes, her gaze stripping me naked.

"I was hoping you'd come. Am I forgiven?"

"Not so fast, mister. Three things. First, I want to thank you for the wonderful gifts you bought me today including the outfit I'm wearing and the pongee leather jacket that goes with it."

She laughed at the stunned expression I could feel cross my face.

"There are dues to pay, my friend. Second, I want to know if you have any other surprises for me. You have this one window of opportunity, buster."

"Boy, you are feeling a little punchy tonight, aren't you?" Realization dawned on me. "Have you been drinking, Kat?"

"Maybe just a little, but this isn't punchy, Connor. This is adamant. I don't want any more surprises. So?"

Now was not the time to hedge my bets. I squirmed in my chair a little. *Oh shit. We were almost there. Shit. Oh well . . .*

"There is one more thing, Kat, and you may not like it, either. I want to take you to one of my clubs. I want you to see the lifestyle I'm part of firsthand. Now before you get pissed off—"

"I can't fucking believe it. We just survive one big issue, and now you bring up another? Well let's get one thing straight. I'm not into harems or orgies. One man is more than enough, thank you, and I'd better be enough for him."

I could feel myself getting a little irritated at her smugness. She sure could be an aggravation when she wanted to. Yet I loved her bull-headedness. This little woman was no pushover. I took a deep breath and sent a silent prayer to the universe for patience and wisdom.

"Look, I'm not asking you to take part in any sex play with others, unless, of course, you want to. Why are you being so defensive about this?"

"Defensive? Like it's been my lifelong dream to go to a sex club?"

"Okay, let's cut the sarcasm. You just don't get it, do you? You're important to me, and I want to be able to satisfy your needs. Not only that, but I want to be the one who experiences your complete surrender. And another thing, being a dominant is who I am, and I've discovered that I really like sexually dominating you. I think you're a sexual submissive and that there's a lot you'd like to explore if you'd throw away your inhibitions."

I filled my cheeks with air and blew out a breath, shaking my head.

What do I have to do to make you understand? For God's sake, Kat.

We were silent a beat while we stared at each other across the table. Just when I was sure she was going to get up and leave again, a big smile lit her face. Beauty radiated from her whenever she smiled like that. Relief flooded through me.

"What?"

"Thank you. I would like to think that if I hadn't been so pissed off, I would have considered that. I think one of my problems is that, deep down, I don't know how far I'd go."

Her eyes shone as she looked at me for another beat. "Let's order our meal and talk about it. That should help us get ready for number three."

"Yes, you did say there were three things. What is number three?"

"You're going to wine and dine me, then treat me to the best makeup sex of our lives."

She laughed again and reached for our double diary.

"Is this some light reading you brought me to set the mood?"

Double Diary
Connor on Friday, August 24

As this is my first installment, I'll keep it easy. Just a simple comment, no response required . . .

I'm hopeful that if you're reading this, you've forgiven me for my foolish blunders. I so love the feeling of wanting you. It's like a drug or more likely an endorphin release I need to maintain. The

147

longer the foreplay, the greater the sexual hit will be. Understand it's self-serving at best, to pump those endorphins.

Here I pause as I'm not used to revealing myself this way. However, I want you to know how I love thinking of you, seeing you when you're aroused. What an enthusiastic hedonist I've become. Where is the stoicism I've been so devoted to? I blame you, of course. C.

13

CECILE

Fuck Connor, and fuck that little bitch, Katherine.

Cecile seethed as she remembered the conversation she'd had with Connor. He had been livid about the text message she'd sent Katherine from Tim's phone. She should have known the little bitch would run straight to Connor with the news.

He'd had the colossal gall to order her to meet with him as if she were one of his minions. Then he'd berated her. *Her!* And then he'd had the nerve to tell her to get out of his sight. She conveniently ignored the fact she'd tried to push every button he had.

Even worse, he'd threatened to dissolve their partnership, as if it were a gift he'd bestowed on a mistress whom he could and would remove on a whim. Well, she'd just have to see about that. And who the fuck did he think he was, anyway? She owned him, and it looked like the time had come to show him just who was boss. It was long past time for her to coast along on his favor; now she needed to look out for number one.

Be careful, Cec. Better not to show your hand too soon.

From the moment Cecile had set eyes on Connor in graduate school, she'd pursued him with single-minded ambition —he would be hers. He was the most stunning specimen of a man she'd ever seen, the only man who was a match for her outstanding beauty. At the time, rumor had it he'd had eyes for that little bitch, Katherine. That had to change.

Then, miraculously, Katherine disappeared from the scene. Cecile moved in with the speed of a viper taking hold of its prey. At first, Connor desired nothing but a woman who could meet his bizarre sexual needs when, where, and how he wanted. She'd presented herself as the simpering little submissive willing to be completely under his control.

It took some doing, but eventually she'd inserted herself into his life and convinced him she was the woman who would help him build his empire. When she'd suggested marriage, Connor made it clear that he was interested only in having his sexual needs satisfied. She agreed to his terms, and their relationship led to a partnership as Connor built his Masquerade Clubs. As time went on, Cecile convinced herself he loved her.

Everything was perfect until Katherine reappeared on the scene. She pushed these memories out of her mind. The lunch meeting with Tim's coworker, Sophia Drake, needed to be handled with skill if she was going to get rid of Katherine once and for all.

A smile of satisfaction lit Cecile's face as she pulled up in front of Sassafraz. She was fairly certain Connor's anger was a barometer of the amount of trouble the message caused between him and Katherine. Cecile touched up her makeup while the top closed on her Jaguar XKR convertible, got out, and flipped her keys to the valet.

"There'd better not be a scratch on her when I come back."

"No sir, I mean, yes, sir, uh, ma'am."

The valet continued to stutter as Cecile rolled her eyes and walked into the restaurant. Although she found the reaction to her incredible beauty somewhat flattering, she also believed that most people, especially service workers, were incredibly stupid and hardly worth her consideration.

She brushed past the people standing in the entrance begging for a seat on the patio in the hopes of catching a glimpse of someone famous. Sassafraz was the restaurant of choice for anyone who wanted to see anybody and anyone who craved being seen.

Sassafraz catered to the who's who of the Toronto and international business, fashion, and entertainment worlds. Their presence made Cecile aware of the way her curvaceous body, accented by a tight sundress, and her stunning beauty caused their heads to turn while she walked by. They honored her beauty as if she were a princess—no, a queen. She had arrived. This was where she belonged.

She swept through the room, oblivious to the clean, stark lines of the ultra-modern interior. Cecile rarely took note of her surroundings; beauty outside her own mattered only if there was some way she could make use of it for one of her plans.

As the hostess neared the private corner table she'd reserved, Cecile gestured for her to leave before taking a moment to watch Sophia from behind a nearby pillar. A living wall framed the vertical waterfall with a row of candles shedding soft light that played over Sophia's face as she studied the menu. She was a stunning woman in her own right, and although she didn't come close to the breathtaking appeal Cecile herself had, she could see why most considered Sophia attractive. At five feet, nine inches, her willowy frame was the perfect backdrop for a pair of large breasts. Real? Finding out gave her something to look forward to.

Cecile knew from her private investigator's report that all

Sophia needed to do was throw her long blond hair over her shoulder, wink one of those ice-blue eyes, wiggle that tight ass, and she could twist any man of her choosing to do her will. That should come in handy.

She strolled to her seat, allowing time for the server to rush over, pull out her chair, and place a linen napkin across her lap. She loved the impeccable service Sassafraz offered almost as much as she liked being the center of attention.

Cecile sat and favored Sophia with a brief smile before studying her menu. She excelled at playing the game of cat and mouse, and this woman, who thought of herself as all that and more, would prove to be an exciting plaything. Cecile could feel Sophia's cool gaze looking her over. She let a few minutes go by before raising her eyes to meet Sophia's and throwing her a wink to ensure that Sophia got the full impact of her brilliant violet eyes. As expected, Sophia's eyes widened, and she licked her lips. Cecile smiled inwardly at the awe and wonder that lit people's faces when they realized the full extent of her beauty.

"So," Sophia said.

"So?" Cecile put the menu down and fixed her attention on Sophia.

"So, I'm assuming you're the mysterious Cecile DePoulignac who called and introduced herself as one of the university's wealthiest benefactors. You said you had a business proposition for me that could improve my standard of living. So, what's this about?"

"Let's order before we get into this. Lunch is on me, so feel free to pick whatever you'd like. I'm going to have a glass of wine. Will you join me?"

"Sure." Sophia picked up the menu and glanced through it. "What's good here?"

"Everything's good. I'm having the beef tenderloin appetizer."

"That's it? That's not near enough food for me. I think I'll try the mushroom risotto and the green salad."

As if on cue, the server came and took their orders.

"Let's get down to business," Cecile said.

"I take it you want to talk about your donations to the university? I'm not the right person for that. You should be talking to our Provost, Tim Bancroft."

"Oh, I've already chatted with your Dr. Bancroft. Don't you worry. No, I want to talk to you about your career and how I can help you get where you want to be. How does that sound?"

"That sounds great, but I'm a little unclear about how and why you'd want to do that. I'm a complete stranger to you."

"Oh, you're not a complete stranger to me, Sophia. I've been following your career for quite some time now. What I want to know is, if you had your choice, what position would you hold at the university?"

Sophia snorted. "As good as that pipe dream sounds, the post I want is already taken, and the person in it is very good at his job."

"Sounds like you're a little smitten with this person. Maybe it's him you want instead?"

"Me, want Tim? Even if I did, he's already taken, and I'm not sure he's worth the trouble. I'd prefer the job."

"Believe me, sweetheart, I'm sure he's not worth the trouble. But I can get you his job." Cecile paused as the server brought their lunch.

"Before we go any further, I need to know that this conversation will be kept in the strictest confidence."

"Of course it will. You have my word. So how could you get me Tim's job?"

"With your help, I could damage or ruin Tim's career. I think that once he's faced with the threat of exposure, he'll choose to move on. Then, a little nudge and a push in the right direction and the job will be yours."

"What could you do to Tim that could be that bad? You don't know him. By reputation, he's not the type to tuck in his tail and run. He'll fight you and dare you to expose him."

"I'm not ready to disclose that yet, but trust me, he'll cave. I think he'll do anything to protect his bitch of a live-in trophy." Cecile's voice dripped venom as she spat the words out.

"Katherine? What have you got against Katherine?"

"Nothing besides the fact that she's fucking my Connor, and nobody fucks my man without my blessing."

Sophia stared at Cecile, stunned speechless. She took a gulp of wine, and then another before setting the wineglass down on the starched linen tablecloth.

"Oh my God, I don't know what to say. Our precious Katherine is stepping out on Tim? He'll be devastated when he finds out." Sophia smiled.

"I can see the wheels turning in that pretty little head of yours, and you'd better get those dreams of Tim falling gratefully into your waiting arms right out of your head. Tim already knows that she's fucking Connor. They both want her."

"What exactly do these men see in her anyway? Tim is absolutely smitten with her. It's not like she's drop-dead gorgeous like we are. She's not even very pretty."

"Why thank you. Aren't you sweet. As for her, I think it's the exotic thing she's got going that's so attractive to them. My Connor seems to think most breeds are beautiful, and he's particularly vulnerable to those Creole types like her, French blood and all."

"Tim says not only is she beautiful, he loves her honesty and directness. He says she always calls a spade a spade, and you always know where you stand with her. He raves about her, so it's more than just looks we're competing with."

"Isn't that precious. Well, we're just going to have to knock her down a peg or two. What do you say, Sophia? Have I made the right choice here? Are you with me on this? When you do your homework, you'll find I have the power to make this happen if you work with me."

"Let's be honest here, Cecile. My becoming provost is more than a stretch, it's impossible. Provost is an academic position, and only professors are considered. I have an accounting designation, not a doctorate."

"Nothing's impossible if you have enough money, and as you know, your university is crying for money. For example, I'm willing to make sure they have the funds they need to build the new library in exchange for your promotion to provost."

Sophia was quiet while she continued eating her risotto. Cecile sipped her wine, trying not to show her impatience. *Take it easy. Don't scare her off now.*

"I have a lot of questions. How do I know you have that kind of money and clout? I couldn't find a donor named DePoulignac in my files. And what do you want me to do? I have a lot to lose if word of this gets out. What guarantee do I have that this won't come back to bite me in the ass?"

Cecile signaled the server to bring her another glass of wine. She was taking a chance driving after drinking that much alcohol, but she tossed the thought aside. After all, she hadn't met a cop, male or female, that she hadn't been able to sweet talk.

"My fiancé is Connor McClane," Cecile said.

Sophia's eyes widened and she took a quick breath, but she said nothing. Cecile took another sip of wine and smiled.

"As for what I want you to do, it's simple. I want you to find out everything you can about Doctor Tim Bancroft and his precious little Katherine. Not the kind of stuff I can find out from a private investigator but the personal stuff, like how he feels about things. I'll arrange it so that he'll have to work closely with you on a project. And at some point, I may want you to pass along some information to our Doctor Bancroft, kind of like a go-between. If you do a good job, I'll throw in some perks like another week or two at your favorite plastic surgery spa."

Sophia choked as she finished off her wine. "You had *me* investigated?"

"Of course I did, dear. I know about your sordid little affairs and how you, let's say, cleverly used your accounting designation for the benefit of more than just the university. Don't look so shocked. I admire someone who knows what she wants and is not afraid to get it. Besides, it's not you I'm after. So, relax."

Cecile took another sip of her wine. "Oh yes, before I forget, I'll want you to make sure I receive an invitation to any functions Connor is invited to attend."

"Would you stop using that patronizing tone with me, Cecile? I don't like it."

"Let's get one thing straight here. I'm in charge, and your rather large ass is mine, any way I want it. What I've already found out about you is enough to ruin you, but I'd rather do this the friendly way. We can work very well as partners as long as you always remember I'm the controlling partner. Think about it. You get what you want and so do I. Agreed?"

Cecile reached her hand across the table. Sophia paused before she shook it slowly.

"You're not giving me much choice, so let's see how this all plays out. Agreed."

Cecile paid for the meal using her black American Express card. Sophia gathered her purse and rose to go.

"I've got to run. I have a meeting."

"Just a minute, Sophia. There's one other thing."

"Oh, and what's that?"

"This conversation shall remain one of our many little secrets. And, just in case you have second thoughts and think you'll get more mileage out of telling Tim, or anyone else for that matter, about our little chat, remember two words—Justin Roberts."

Sophia sank back in her chair.

"I can't believe you had me followed. You really are a complete and utter bitch."

"Why thank you, my dear. How sweet of you to say so."

Cecile smiled; one she'd perfected—the one that would have frightened Cruella de Vil.

"As the cliché goes, it takes one to know one."

Cecile stood up, blew Sophia a kiss, and strolled out of the restaurant. Cecile barely gave the valet time to get out of her car before she jumped in and roared off toward the west end of Toronto. In about twenty minutes, she pulled up in front of a building in one of those seedy areas that often bordered the homes of the wealthy.

Her nose wrinkled in distaste as she climbed the steps to a small neighborhood mall that had seen better days. She ignored the homeless man sleeping on the subway grate and sidestepped the detritus left by people who refused to clean up after themselves or their pets. Two security guards flanked the entrance to the bank, hands on holsters, ready to shoot anyone who looked at them the wrong way.

Folks who probably couldn't afford their next meal lined up at a lottery kiosk to buy a ticket offering a one-in-ten-million chance of realizing their dream of freedom. Cecile turned down a dimly lit hall lined with several doors and opened one marked Joe Carlino, PI.

The stench of cheap perfume stung her eyes as she crossed the small space between the door and the chipped wooden desk that sat in the middle of what Joe had the nerve to call his reception area. Cecile always felt as if she'd stepped into a low-budget detective movie when the bleached-blond, gum-chewing bimbo, large breasts bursting out of a cheap knit top, greeted her. Ignoring this sad excuse for a receptionist, she walked by her and straight through the open office door.

Joe Carlino was a caricature of the hard-edged private investigator he fancied himself to be. Each time Cecile saw his pockmarked face and greasy black hair, she threw up a little in her mouth, yet she could count on his discretion and ability to get her dirty work done. She despised the way he continuously sniffed through his nose like a coke addict who'd snorted too many lines.

"Ah Cece, sweetie, good to see you. What can I do for you today?" Joe turned from his state-of-the art computer, leaped to his feet, and ran around his desk. He pulled out the stained wooden chair in front of his desk and brushed the seat with his hand.

"Here you go, dearie."

"Joe, I've told you never to call me anything but *Ms.* DePoulignac."

Cecile's voice was severe as she gingerly took the chair that he offered. It had been years since Connor had called her Cece, something best forgotten for now.

"I know, I know. I'm sorry. I just forgot, ya know. I don't mean no harm."

Joe returned to his seat behind the huge, battered secretary's desk that took up most of the floor space in the tiny office. His voice reminded Cecile of the high-pitched whine of a bloodthirsty mosquito and made her want to squish him.

"I have a job for you that needs to be handled with complete discretion and the utmost confidentiality, and I'm willing to double your usual fee for this one."

The leer Joe gave her brought another rush of bile into her mouth, and she had to work at maintaining a semblance of pleasantry toward him.

"Double the fee, eh. Well, dear—I mean, Miss *Dee-Pool-in-yack*, it must be something very special, and I'm just the man for the job. Of course, there's my usual expenses." He sniffed a few more times.

Cecile winced as he murdered her name. She crossed her legs and inched back a bit more in the chair.

"Of course, Joe. That goes without saying."

"It's always best to say things, Miss. Keeps the air clear, ya know." Sniff, sniff. "Would you like coffee, Miss D? Of course you would." He got up and opened the office door.

"Sally, honey, get Miss D here a cup of coffee." He yelled even though the bimbo was sitting less than five feet from the door. "She takes it black." He turned to Cecile. "That's right isn't it, Miss D?"

Cecile nodded rather than waste the energy reminding him that she didn't drink coffee.

"We ain't got any, Joe, so I'm gonna have to go get some," Sally said.

"Okay, so go."

"I'm gonna need some money." She snapped her gum. "You want one too?"

"Yeah, get two for us and whatever you'd like."

Joe threw a twenty her way and then closed the door and sat back down.

"So, what's the job, Miss D?"

He took a wrinkled writing pad from a desk drawer and looked around for a pen.

"No notes this time, Joe. You'll have to keep this in your head. Think you can manage that?"

"Are you makin' fun of me, Miss D? I don't like it when people make fun of me, ya know."

"Of course not, Joe. I'm just making sure that you'll be able to work that way."

"Oh ya, sure, no problem."

He put the pad back in the drawer. He looked up at her and beamed.

"So, what's the job?"

"You know the man I had you investigate—"

"Which one?"

Cecile stifled her impatience. "The doctor at the university, Tim Bancroft."

"Ya, I remember him. He and his little roommate were clean as a whistle and just as solid. It's going to be tough getting something on him."

"Very soon, they'll find him in a compromising position, and I'll need you to help set it up."

"Huh, say what?"

"Let me spell it out for you, Joe. Dr. Bancroft is going to be having sex with a sleazy woman, and you'll help me record them having sex. I want you to be sure the woman sounds like she's in distress, and I want to be sure that there's no doubt that the man and woman are having sex. Is that clear?"

"That's going to cost a lot of money, Miss. I'm gonna need—"

Cecile took an envelope from her purse, leaned forward, and slapped it down on the desk.

"Here's five thousand to get you started. I'll want this done in the next few weeks, and I want it done properly. Wait for my call, and Joe . . ."

Joe snapped to attention. "Yes Miss?

Cecile stood up. "Don't fuck this up or it will be the sorriest day of your life. Do it right and there'll be a bonus in it for you."

Without another word, Cecile left the office.

She left the hallway that housed the office and stepped into the main part of the mall. She strode past a man who stood looking in the window of the dollar store and wore a light gray sweater over a button-down shirt and blue suit pants ...

Double Diary
Katherine on Sunday, August 26 @ 8:00 a.m.

It's the morning after the best makeup sex ever. Good morning, C.

I do want to hear some of your fantasies and thoughts. It's in my nature to ask to hear them—as you've demanded of me. I'm trying to mediate my desires, though. This will be fun. Kat

PS: The double diary is pure genius. I love sharing my thoughts and desires without having to wait for the right moment that is too often lost or forgotten. It's so much easier to share my thoughts without fumbling or searching for the right words in a face-to-face encounter.

14

KATHERINE

I shut the diary and took a sip of my grapefruit juice. Everything was just perfect. Here I was in paradise with my prince charming. I sighed at having to leave this little bit of nirvana where Connor introduced the ideal way to explore our relationship. Things with this splendid man just kept getting better and better. When he let his guard down, he was oh so funny, and something about the way he looked at me made me want to spread my legs wide open. What was he turning me into?

But it wasn't just about the sex—the absolutely great sex. It was about him. Gorgeous, sexy him. Something about him drew me to him, always had. When he wasn't off in one of his moods and he focused on me, he made me feel as if I were the only one who existed for him, as if he'd choose to be with me over anyone else in the world. Oh yes, I know I said he runs hot and cold, and he does. But when he was hot, he sizzled. And when we forgot ourselves, we were a thing of absolute beauty.

He also was becoming a great friend. We teased, we laughed, we debated. It didn't seem to matter what I did or said as long as I was being myself. Most of all, he challenged me with no expectations. Except when it came to sex. But I digress . . . *Mind back on track, please.*

The ocean breeze beckoned, and I stepped through the sliders. I closed my eyes and took deep breaths, letting the flower-fragrant air add another layer to the cocoon this trip had wrapped around me. The imprint of this perfect place and time in our lives joined my special memories of Connor deep inside where no one could ever touch them. There was just one more thing I had to do, and I licked my lips in anticipation.

I slid the thick cotton bathrobe off my shoulders as I walked toward the bed where Connor was just stirring and slid in beside him. He moaned as his cock leaped to life in my mouth, and I gave him the gift of my desire. He really was delicious.

I smoothed lotion onto skin still warm from the shower. A billow of steam greeted Connor as he drew up behind me and ran his hands down my back and over my buttocks and thighs. I felt his hardness as he leaned into me.

I did that.

I turned into his arms and kissed him with a passion that took both our breaths away. I wrapped myself around him, all that control and security and heat and power that I'd run away from twenty years ago fixed on me. We panted as we came up for air.

"This is insane," Connor said. "We've got to stop this, or we'll kill ourselves."

"Not a bad way to go." I leaned toward him for another kiss.

"Stop that." He laughed and smacked my butt.

I loved playful Connor. It was as if, every once in a while, he let the charming little boy he hid away come out. He dropped the towel around his waist and stepped into the shower, giving me yet another chance to marvel over his spectacular body. No, I don't usually go on like this, but he really was something.

While Connor got cleaned up, I read his latest snippet. With a happy sigh, I put the diary on the bedside table and got dressed. It was time to grab some lunch and enjoy our last afternoon of fun in the Bahamian sun—that is if I could keep my hands off his gorgeous body for that long.

We ate a delicious Italian meal on the patio, watching the sun disappear into the emerald-green of the ocean horizon. Connor ordered a feast with a selection of my favorite dishes, skillfully prepared. There was a baguette with not one, but two dipping sauces: one a delicious peppery olive oil with a garlicky pesto and the other a rich, green olive oil surrounding a fifteen-year old balsamic vinegar. *Heaven.* The small Caesar salad was perfect in its simplicity.

A few ounces of grilled salmon were just the right teaser for the richness of the pasta course. Four of my favorite pasta dishes greeted me. I found it difficult to make a choice, so helped myself to some of each. Connor laughed as he watched me stuff and sigh my way through ricotta gnocchi, spaghetti *aglio e olio*, ravioli stuffed with butternut squash swimming in a whiskey-sage cream sauce, and tetrazzini. I even managed to tuck in a bite of his striploin steak, sneaking in a few extra mushrooms before sinking back and sighing with pleasure, sated.

In celebration of our last night, Connor ordered a bottle

of Veuve Clicquot Grande Dame. Normally, I didn't like the taste of champagne, but he asked me to try a taste.

"My God, that's good. This must be expensive. Are you sure you can afford this? I'm happy to split this trip with you."

"It was a great all-inclusive package. I couldn't believe it myself, but the travel agent confirmed it was a last minute sell-off." Connor paused a beat and then sighed. "I don't talk about it, but the truth is money is not an issue for me."

"That includes champagne like this? This stuff has to be over the top."

"The champagne is my gift to you, Kat. Perfection deserves perfection."

Connor raised his glass in salute. He said nothing else, but admiration shone from his eyes, drifting over me like the fine mist of a gentle rain.

"Let's have dessert."

I rose, took Connor by the hand, and led him into the bedroom where we shed our clothes.

Connor lit two candles and placed them on the coffee table that sat in the seating area at the other end of the large bedroom. As my eyes adjusted to the soft glow that illuminated the large room, I took in the arrangement of sofas, tables, and the massive bed. I could see what looked like a large triangular wedge covered with a satiny material sitting close to the headboard. Before I had time to wonder how it got there, Connor bent his head, his soft, sensuous mouth brushing my lips.

His tongue darted and dabbed across the contours of my mouth, reminding me of the care an artist took when preparing a canvas to receive the beauty that unfolded from his mind. Now I was that canvas. Slowly Connor brought the dew to the petals of the rare orchid as he shaped and molded it with his desire.

I caught my breath as his teeth nipped at my lips. I strained to catch his tongue between them. Being the tricky devil he was, he adroitly avoided my efforts, returning to stroking his tongue around mine. I reached down and let the weight of his heavy cock rest in my small hands. *Oh yeah.* How I loved the feel of him in my hands, in my mouth, in my cunt. If there's a heaven on earth, this was it.

He used the soft pads of his thumbs to trace light circles around my nipples. My excitement grew as I mirrored his thumbs with mine around the head of his penis. When my flower fully opened to reach for the sun, he lay me across the end of the bed and parted my legs.

Connor stood behind my head. I gazed up. Blood engorged my labia at the carnal need that covered his handsome face, yet I knew he would take his time. Each time we made love was like the first for me—exciting, fresh, and unpredictable. He took a long admiring look down my body, lingering on the plumpness of my vulva as my clitoral bud peeked out. I sighed and closed my eyes as he blew softly in my ear. More dew leaked from the core of my sex as my excitement built.

"You are so very beautiful," he whispered.

His fingers reached down to make the slow, deliberate strokes that formed the outline of my sex.

"I'm going to play with you until you beg me to come, and then I'll play with you some more. I won't let you come until you're ready to release yourself completely to me."

An eternity seemed to pass as he took deliberate care to draw every little crease and crevice as he crafted the outline of my outer lips as if they were the corolla of a rare flower. Only when he was satisfied with the shading and shadows that made up the canvas of my womanhood did he move on to sketch the detail of the bud of my clitoris.

I almost screamed as Connor executed a series of tiny

strokes, but stopped short of letting the excitement build to a climax. With infinite patience and variety of techniques, he alternated tiny and broad strokes, taking care to draw each to perfection. My clitoris swelled to the point of rupture, and still I couldn't find release. I understood that Connor, like all true artists pursuing perfection, would not stop until he was satisfied he'd captured the inner beauty of his subject.

A shudder ran through me as I freed my mind. Nothing else existed but the smell of Connor's maleness, the sound of his breath in my ear, and the burning that started to radiate through my core. I stiffened as I reached for the elusive eruption that seemed just beyond my grasp. I held my breath. Connor continued his steady rhythm, expertly exerting just the right amount of pressure. Everything ceased to exist.

I begged and I pleaded. As promised, he played for what seemed like several long, torturous hours. Then my climax exploded with such force that violent spasms shook the bed. Connor continued stroking, and my body continued through a series of endless contractions before he finally stopped.

"Now would you like to have a taste of me?"

I moaned out something that sounded like yes. In one swift movement, he switched places and knelt me on the floor between his spread knees. With the eagerness of a child discovering her first lollipop, I sucked and nuzzled his engorged cock. I flicked my tongue in circles around the head, paying particular attention to the heart shape that nestled on the underside.

I slipped him into my mouth, relishing the feel as his fullness slid across my tongue. I drew my own designs on the underside. I slid him out using my fingers and teeth in every way I could imagine. I cupped his balls and gently squeezed. I tickled the root of his now twitching member. I nibbled, sucked, nuzzled, nipped, licked, and gobbled until I was gasping for air. Connor watched, his breathing measured.

The only sign his excitement was building was the arch of his back when his cock pulsed. I continued without pause, my hunger for him insatiable, determined to break through his rigid control.

In another rapid movement, he grabbed my shoulders and lifted me upright. I stood there panting as he slid his hands down my sides across my belly to between my legs. He stepped aside, motioning to the wedge shape on the bed.

"Kneel for me. It's time to continue your training."

The rasp in his voice triggered a series of butterflies that danced their way up my vagina, flitting through my womb before making their way up through my abdomen. Connor brought about the advent of a series of post-orgasmic quivers, like nothing I'd ever experienced before. *Incredible.*

I climbed on the bed and settled myself on the wedge. It was positioned at just the right height, allowing me to rest comfortably, facedown, while giving Connor maximum access to my protruding buttocks. I heard a sound I couldn't identify seconds before feeling a drizzle of liquid slide between my buttocks. Connor's fingers followed, spreading the fluid along the crack of my ass.

I shivered and instinctively clenched my butt cheeks. Adrenaline coursed through my body, increasing my heart rate. I took short, quick breaths. My ass was virgin territory, and I wasn't sure I was ready for this new invasion.

I gasped when Connor slid the head of a hard object through the lubricant that anointed my crack. My butt clenched even harder.

Oh my God, oh my God. He's going to stick a dildo in me. Oh my God. I'm not ready for this.

"Relax, babe. Relax. It's just a tiny little butt plug. It will be easier for you if you relax."

I whimpered. I was so excited I almost jumped out of my skin. I wasn't sure if it was welcome anticipation or dread fueling the river of adrenaline that continued to flow through me.

Connor slid the head of the plug a little way into the opening to my anus. I tensed. He spent a few minutes letting me relax into the sensation. Without warning, he drove the plug in to the hilt, and I arched my back as a warm burning sensation followed the initiation. I whimpered again. My anus contracted as I tried to rid myself of the foreign object. It wasn't so much that it was unpleasant, as it was that I wasn't used to having something *there*.

"Shhh," Connor said. "Relax, Kat. Relax. Don't think. Just feel. Let me fuck you."

He spread me wide with both hands and drove his magnificent member deep inside. He worked me with a slow, steady rhythm that matched the way I'd sucked his cock. The warmth that radiated from my anus seemed to spread through to my vagina, inflaming the sensitive tissues his cock teased. The warmth built to a fire and spread throughout my belly. The power of the first wave of orgasm forced the plug to slide out, yet Connor continued his relentless pounding until I climaxed again.

I panted from exhaustion, and sweat slid down my back. And still Connor continued to pump, his rock-hard cock bringing me to the brink of another orgasm. He tightened his grip on my buttocks and let out a long, low moan. He drove harder and faster for several more thrusts, and then he tightened. That was all it took to push me over the final edge, and our bodies contracted and pulsed in harmony.

As I lay panting, Connor moved me off the wedge and pushed it to the floor. Gathering me in his arms, he held and stroked me until the shudders dissipated.

"My God, you're good," he whispered. "You were made for me. You are so good."

Connor sighed and held me tighter.

"I'm only good because of you. It's all because of you. I wish this feeling would never end."

"There's more where that came from." Connor laughed. "And next time, if you don't relax when I tell you, I'll spank you. Understood?"

Pleasure replaced surprise as I lay running my fingers through the soft hair on his chest.

"Understood."

"Pardon? I couldn't hear you."

"Understood," I said in a louder voice. *Something to look forward to.*

We rose early, dressed, finished packing, and ate a light breakfast before boarding the airport shuttle. With mixed feelings, we took a last look around, trying to imprint the magic of our island paradise before heading into the airport. Boarding and takeoff went smoothly, and we settled in the first-class cabin for the three-and-a-half-hour flight. I looked at Connor, bent over our double diary, writing furiously. My heart melted once again at the depth of my growing feelings for this man. I know that sounds rather clichéd, but the good lord wouldn't have given us clichés if she didn't intend for us to use them, would she? Just another one of life's little blessings.

Connor was the most beautiful creation I'd ever seen, and he was perfect for me in every way. Understand, it wasn't just my bias we're talking about here; he truly was remarkable. Everywhere we went, women watched him, some blatantly, some surreptitiously, and he was oblivious to the attention. He never believed the remarks I passed on about his good looks. I was never sure whether his disbelief was a form of self-deprecation or an intentional humility due to his aversion to the spotlight.

I was starting to love this man, and as I'd written to him, I gave him my friendship and my trust. Trust was something I'd never given to a man before, and I shook off the fear this trust might be misplaced. I still had absolutely no idea whether our relationship was anything more than a sexual tryst for either of us, but something in me was starting to yearn for more. Could I possibly break through that arms-length facade he desperately clung to?

Yet, in a different way, I loved Tim. There was a time after my very fucked-up teen years and that first experience with Connor when what others thought of me was of paramount importance to me. But with Tim's friendship and support, I learned independence and to live comfortably in my skin. I would be eternally grateful to him for that.

Learning to love myself helped heal the wounds that childhood abuse etched in my soul. And now Connor was back in my life, seemingly willing to accept that friendship was what I had to give him. I shushed the voice in my head that started to chant, *Liar, liar, pants on fire.* I knew what I needed, and Connor understood my need for independence. Then again, were we so different? Didn't I hide from a deep-seated longing I was afraid to admit to?

The flight attendant came by, offering drinks and snacks. Connor ordered his usual Pepsi and returned to his scribbles. I opted for a ginger ale before returning my gaze to the view of the endless horizon.

Tim and Connor shared as many similarities as they had differences. Both had a sardonic wit and could make anyone who was deliberately obtuse feel like an inchworm in less than twenty-five words. Both were exceptionally good looking with perfectly molded bodies, although Connor was lean where Tim bordered on muscular. Unlike Connor, Tim was hyperaware of his good looks and how they affected women.

Both had a bottomless depth of compassion for the helpless and the underdog; although they showed it in different ways. Tim took every opportunity to spend time with those lost souls to make them feel as if they'd contributed something special to his day.

As I caught up with what happened in Connor's life during our twenty years apart, I'd found that he'd helped raise extensive funds for causes that supported worthwhile charities. He was so much more than the hardcore businessman he portrayed to everyone, even himself.

Both men cared for me in very different ways. Connor hadn't said so, but I could tell by the way he treated me, he treasured my friendship. But was friendship enough? It was driving me crazy, and I couldn't make up my own fucking mind about how I felt.

You love him.

No, I do not.

Yes, you DO.

Real love is reciprocal, and I can't love someone who doesn't love me.

Bullshit.

Go away.

With Tim, I shared a friendship that was cultivated like a cherished Bonsai with the branches that lacked acceptance and understanding trimmed away as our mutual acceptance bound us together. Connor cared for me as much as he could while shielding himself behind a secret wall of grief and hurt; yet, for some inexplicable reason, he'd chosen to take his relationship with me to the next level.

His decision to share intimacy with me had, in turn, exposed an inner core of sexual desire that frightened and excited me. Once again, I needed to face my fear—how far was I willing to go with this man? Would his feeling for me change if he knew I probably couldn't resist anything he wanted to do with me, and I mean anything? For that matter, could I accept what my tortured desires really said about me? I looked over at Connor and caught him as he looked up from his writing. A smile touched my face; I couldn't help it. Maybe, if I was very, very lucky, we could have it all.

Cecile picked up the ringing phone. "This better be good."

"Cecile, hi, it's Holly. Did you know that Connor was down here with some babe? They've been up close and personal all weekend."

Cecile sprang to attention.

"Some babe? Where are you? Did you get her name? What did she look like?"

"Calm down. I'll tell you everything I know. I'm working at a resort in the Bahamas, remember?" Holly asked. "She's no beauty, not like you, but I guess she's kind of pretty in that exotic kind of way. I was their server at dinner last night. I think I heard him call her cat. What kind of nickname is that, for Christ's sake?"

"Did he recognize you?"

"He didn't seem to, which is kind of insulting. But I've changed my hair color, and he only had eyes for her, as they say in the song."

"I won't forget this, Holly." Without further ado, Cecile hung up the phone.

That bastard. I'll make him and that little bitch pay.

Double Diary
Connor on August 28 @ 11:30 p.m.

Missing you. Needing you. All I can think about is you being with me in the Bahamas. Are you ready to take the next step in our mutual adventure? This weekend I want you to accompany me to one of my clubs so you can experience firsthand the D/s (Dominant/submissive) lifestyle you're so eager to explore. You've had a little taste of it with me so far, but that's just been the appetizer. Don't worry, I won't ask you to participate unless you wish to, but I do think it's time you see what it's like to be a submissive. Are you game? C.

15

CONNOR

When Brian looked this serious, you ignored him at your own peril.

"Someone's been digging into your background."

The arch in my eyebrow spoke the word *"Someone?"* louder than if I'd vocalized it. Occasionally, journalists probed my background because of my executive position at Magnum, but mainly I was able to fly under the radar by keeping my life simple and secretive. I took great pains to ensure no one who had access to my private life would ever disclose what they knew, or the consequences would be dire. Once I needed to teach someone who threatened me a lesson, and anyone who knew me was very much aware that I wouldn't hesitate to take them down.

"That's what I'm here to tell you. I believe it's that PI Cecile hired. As you instructed, Con, I've had her under surveillance twenty-four seven, and you were right to be suspicious. Two things are of note. Cecile had lunch with Sophia Drake, the VP of Development who works with Tim Bancroft, and she went to see this PI named Joe Carlino.

"He reminds me of that TV cop. He's clever in a street-wise kind of way, but he's very unsophisticated in his approach. He's building a portfolio on you. He seems interested in uncovering your net worth."

Brian handed me three files before walking over to the bar and helping himself to a can of Pepsi. I rifled through the files on Joe Carlino and Sophia Drake. I put the file on Kevin Jordan aside to study later. He was Kat's boss and an annoying worker bee who buzzed around from time to time. I was after the queen bee.

"Interesting. Why not hire an upscale firm?"

"I think there is more to it, and I'll find out tomorrow. I have a lunch date with his receptionist if you can call her that."

"Well, Cecile's certainly got my attention. She's up to something, I can feel it. Let me know everything you find out, no matter how trivial."

"Don't I always?"

As usual, I ignored the jab. "I will not let her fuck up the lives of anyone that I care about."

"Oh, so you do care for Katherine." It wasn't a question.

"Fuck off, Brian. I'm not in the mood for this. I'm taking her to the Masquerade Club on Friday."

"Really?" Brian stared at me with brown eyes devoid of moral judgment or emotion. "Isn't that a little sudden?"

"It's no big deal. If she's going to continue to hang out with me, she needs to see what she's getting into."

"*Really*? Are you sure that's wise? Didn't you tell me that this sort of thing scared her off last time? I'm not sure this is a good idea, Con."

I looked at Brian for a long moment. Brian had the best gut instincts, even better than my own, although I'd never admit that to anyone.

"What's on your mind, Bri? Is there something you're not telling me about Tim?"

"No, that's just the thing. He's really good people, and he cares for your Katherine." Brian paused a beat, his eyes examining a thought somewhere within him. "I don't think you want to fuck her up with one of your little games."

"Concern noted. Make sure the club is ready for us. Let's put Kat in the Regency Suite. This is her first visit to a sex club, and I don't want any surprises. I want you to be there when we arrive."

"Absolutely, Con." Without another word, Brian got up and left the room.

On Wednesday, I called Kat. "Are you set for our little adventure?"

"As ready as I'll ever be, I guess. You haven't actually said what—"

"We'll discuss that when we meet. My driver will pick you up at seven p.m. sharp on Friday. Will that work for you?"

"That's fine. What should I bring?"

"Dress is casual. I'll have everything else we need. See you Friday."

I hung up the phone. It was a little abrupt but hearing her voice without being able to see her was absolute torture. No matter how hard I tried to put her out of my mind, there she was—that mixture of innocence and carnality that continued to baffle me.

I swiveled in my chair and looked out of my office window, my eyes seeing nothing but the inner workings of my own mind. The sensual energy of the Toronto underbelly vibrated through me. This was Kat's city, and I'd come to love it as much as she did.

Get real, Connor. The sensual energy had little to do with the city and everything to do with the fact that Kat lived here.

Was Brian right? Did Kat mean more to me than even I knew? More importantly, was I ready to open my heart to the life I had so long denied? My confusion grew the more I thought about it. How did you explain matters of the heart? I knew two things for sure: I trusted Kat implicitly, and I would never do anything to hurt her.

At seven o'clock sharp on Friday evening, the Bentley slid to a stop in front of Kat as she stood waiting in front of the office building. My driver, Dennis Wheeler, held the back door open before stowing her suitcase somewhere in the rear of the cavernous car. Kat slid in the seat opposite me, and I watched her with wry amusement as she surveyed the interior of the limo with wide-eyed amazement.

The interior was massive with a long, leather couch lining each of the sidewalls and two large comfy-looking armchairs clustered around a coffee table nestled at the rear. Recessed lights shone dimly from various strategic points throughout, and wood paneling covered the walls. The luxurious space smelled of burnished leather and something faintly reminiscent of the fragrant smoke from a fine cigar intermingled with an exotic perfume.

"So, this is how the other half lives," Kat said. "Do you own this?"

"Just one of the perks of working for a large corporation." I took a deep breath. Only three other people knew the extent of my holdings, and it was a longtime habit for me to protect my identity.

"I guess you could say I own it, since I'm the major shareholder, but that isn't common knowledge. Anyway, the ride will give us some time to discuss your training. Would you like a drink?" I touched a button and a panel slid open revealing a fully stocked bar. "What's your pleasure?"

Kat eyed the bar skeptically. "Do you have any wine?"

"Of course. Do you have a preference?

"You choose since this weekend is about trying something new."

She reached for the crystal goblet I held out. "Thank you."

"My, my, you are the polite one."

"I'm just really nervous."

I poured myself two fingers of Glenlivet and sat back, swirling the amber liquid around the base of the crystal glass. *What would make her relax?*

"Why does Tim call you Katie?"

"He's a fan of classic movies, especially those with Spencer Tracy and Katharine Hepburn. It's rumored that Spencer called Katharine, Kate, presumably because she was so feisty. He also likes the character Kate in *The Taming of the Shrew*. When he met me, he thought I was a feisty little thing, out to prove myself and battling to make sure no one ever controlled or took advantage of me again. He said I was definitely my own person as I'm sure you'll agree."

She took a sip of her wine and looked at me expectantly.

"You're nothing like either Kate character. Tell me your favorite sexual fantasy."

I kept any hint of anticipation from my voice. A slight frown flitted across her face before it returned to her usual pleasant mask. She studied the flat screen recessed in the back wall while she took a couple more sips of wine. Then she stared directly into my penetrating eyes with an intensity that made me feel as if I'd been stripped of all pretense and exposed for the player I was.

"Geez, C. My head's swimming trying to keep up with these subject changes. You first."

It was my turn to look away and examine the interior of the limousine. What was it about her ability to unsettle me?

"Sounds like we're not quite ready for that level of self-exposure," I said. "I hope you'll be able to tell me more in the diary. Why don't you tell me what you'd like to see at the club instead?"

She ran the tip of her tongue around those beautiful, full lips.

"I don't really know. I don't know what to expect. Let's see."

Her forehead creased. I started to drum my fingers impatiently and willed myself into stillness. After a moment that stretched into eternity, she focused on me again.

"I guess I want to see how a submissive acts. I know you say that I'm a submissive, but I don't feel like the submissives they described when I looked it up online."

"I'm not convinced that you are truly a submissive either. So far, from what I see, yours is more a need to surrender so that you can relinquish control, rather than a need to submit. I think you'd rather choke than call me sir, for example.

"But I do think you have a curiosity about discipline and punishment if it's used strictly in a sexual context. Of course, I'm not into the punishment or discipline aspect of domination. Those are central traits to the personality of a dominant, and it's something I've explored, but I don't gravitate to it. It's more the control aspect for me. Let's see how you feel after our weekend."

"What are we doing this weekend that would make a difference?"

"The Masquerade is an exclusive D/s club. You'll be able to see what true Doms and subs are like."

"Will I have to—"

"No, you don't have to participate. Actually, it should be quite appealing to your voyeuristic tendencies. It's very confidential, and security is tight. Everyone except some security staff wears a mask, so you don't need to worry about being recognized or seeing anyone you know. I'm offering you the chance to explore the world of bondage, discipline, domination, and submission firsthand. Our members don't get into serious sadomasochism. There are other clubs for those interested in participating in that world. Of course, if you're not ready for this, we can turn around right now. Just say the word."

"I do want to see. I'm just nervous. More wine, please." She held out her glass for a refill.

I laughed and poured more wine. "Lucky for you we won't be participating in the activities at the club. Participants don't drink at the club."

"Why is that?"

"Too much danger of it clouding the judgment of the subs or boosting the egos of the Doms, so alcohol is strictly *verboten* for anyone participating in a scene as we call them. I assume you have other questions?"

"Oh, I have a lot of questions. Like where is it? Why would your members let a complete stranger watch them? How do I know there won't be pressure for me to participate? Like—"

"Whoa, whoa." I laughed. "You are quick. One question at a time, please. The one we're visiting is in upstate New York. Members agree to take personal responsibility for any guests they bring. But to ensure our safety and security, we never disclose the location. I'm sure you noticed that there are no windows in this limo."

"Yes. Pretty cloak and dagger."

"It's not foolproof, but it does deter intruders from invading our privacy. Every member is thoroughly vetted by our security firm. A member can gain access with a finger-print, retinal, and voice scan.

"As for why members would let a complete stranger watch them, that's an easy one. As part of our extensive vetting process, the applicant specifies what particular activi-ties they're inclined toward, including voyeurism and exhibi-tionism. There are viewing rooms for the voyeurs, play rooms for the exhibitionists, and private rooms for those who prefer privacy."

I poured myself another two fingers of scotch without taking my eyes off Kat.

"Huh. I'm surprised that you limit yourselves to the confines of one location, or do you?"

"How perceptive of you. There are several clubs around the world. Members recognize each other with this ring, which enables them to take part in their particular hobby without disruption to their vanilla home lives."

I held out my right hand, and she fingered the ring I wore.

"A scorpion? Why a scorpion?"

"Because it's the astrological sign that rules the genitals, and the founding members liked the symbolism it represents."

"And we're both Scorpios." She spoke as if murmuring to herself.

"Yes, we are, which is one of the reasons why I think you may be better suited to this lifestyle than you think."

"And what about the InterContinental? Is that a club?"

"No. That's a suite I set up for my own personal enter-tainment. Canadian law enforcement isn't as accepting of sex clubs as many other cultures so most are membership based."

The limousine slid to a stop, and a few seconds later, Dennis held open the door. Kat followed me through the lobby of what looked like a very luxurious hotel and into the elevator that stood waiting for us. I motioned her inside before stepping up to a gold-toned panel with a small red light about eye level just above the buttons indicating the numbers of the floors.

Kat seemed fascinated as I pressed a small dark pad that rested beside the top button, and the red light shone brightly for a few seconds before winking off.

I hummed a few bars of a song and chuckled.

"What's that about?" Kat asked.

"It's nothing. I was just thinking of one of my favorite songs."

"Oh, what song is that?"

"'Spanked' by Van Halen."

"Huh. I'm not familiar with that one."

"I'll play it for you on the way home. Ah, here we are."

The doors slid open, and we stepped back in time.

Double Diary

Katherine on August 29 @ 9:05 a.m.

Your proposal is intriguing and scary. My pulse increases exponentially as I consider the consequences. However, I'll take the leap. So yes, I'll accept under one condition (I know, I know; you hate conditions . . . Oh well, suck it up, buttercup. :p). It's actually a request more than a condition—please don't leave me while we're there. I'm having this vision of you going off with one of your playthings . . . Kat

Double Diary

Connor on August 29 @ 12:35 p.m

Not to worry. You're the only plaything I'm interested in. C.

Double Diary

Katherine on August 29 @ 3:15 p.m.

You do know how to flatter a woman, but I love that you said it. I know I've said this before, but I love the way our double diary allows us to explore our feelings. It has opened the door to so many things that too often go unsaid. Kat

16

KATHERINE

I gasped at the opulence as we stepped out of the elevator into a vestibule resplendent with wide burnished walnut and alternating gold paneled walls, a cathedral ceiling crowned with a crystal chandelier, and gold- and black-veined marble flooring. It was like stepping back into another era. I needed a long flowing gown with one of those low-cut bodices and a dainty piece of lace covering lots of cleavage—in my dreams —to fit in.

"Wow!"

Connor smiled. "You haven't seen the half of it. Wait until you get inside. One of our guides will be here shortly to show you around the facility while I grab a shower. But first, you'll have to check in with our security chief. He'll give you a safety deposit box where you will leave your phone and any other electronic devices you have.

"You'll step through a body scan before your guide shows you to your room. You may want to change into the lounging pants and robe that are there for you, but you're welcome to stay dressed as you are, whatever makes you more comfortable. As I mentioned before, we ask guests and members to wear masks to protect their anonymity."

"This sounds very James Bond. Why would you need to do a body scan? Are you expecting a terrorist attack?"

Connor grinned. He seemed delighted by my questions, or maybe he just found me humorous. I was never quite sure whether he was laughing with me or at me. *Oh boy, the insecurity queen surfaces again . . .*

"I think I'd call it more *Mission Impossible*. We take our privacy very seriously, and we're committed to ensuring that all who are admitted to the premises are safe and secure. That means no devices, no weapons, no drugs, no anything is brought into the facility. You'll see that everything we could want is provided for us. Why, do you object to the body scan?"

"Not really."

I didn't object. Actually, this cloak and dagger stuff fascinated me. It just seemed so surreal. However, I'd promised myself I would *try* to suspend my usual analytical nature and go with whatever flow Connor had in mind.

He was much more of a go-with-the-flow kind of guy than I was. I was pretty much a planner who liked to know what was ahead for me. As far as I was concerned, going with the flow was best left to someone taking a leisurely canoe ride down the Humber River. Anyway, I figured I could leave if I wished to, although with all of this talk of security, I wasn't even sure of that.

"You are free to go at any time, Kat. Just say the word. Security will give you a call button in case we get separated, and if you press it, I'll come right away."

And now he's a mind reader.

"I'm sure I'll be fine. I'm more curious than anything else at the moment. Let's get the show on the road."

"Okay. Let's go." As if on cue, one of the wood panels slid

open and a stunning brunette walked over to us. Everything about her reeked sex. She wore a blue silk dress in the fashion of a Greek tunic. The inner globes of full, firm breasts peeked through the slit that ran to the waist. The skirt skimmed her ass, and I would have bet my paycheck it was bare.

As she bowed her head, the faint scent of something floral and very expensive drifted over to us. My insecurities came on full force, and I glanced over to see how this intimidating creature affected Connor. *Sheath those claws, Kat.* I'd have to have been staring into his eyes to see any hint of a reaction; he was the master of the impassive face.

"Good evening, Master C. How may I be of service?"

She kept her head down, avoiding eye contact as if inviting us to enjoy her enticing body without feeling the usual awkward inhibitions against staring. I was struck by the realization that the insignificant gesture of avoiding eye contact engendered a feeling of power and control over her.

"I'd like you to take my guest through the security check while I grab a shower." He looked at me and extended a palm-up hand toward the woman. "K, this is O."

"O?" *You're kidding me, right?*

"All of our submissives read *The Story of O,* hence the moniker. She'll take care of you for a short while until I catch up with you. You can do whatever you like in the meantime. Make use of our spa services, grab a drink, or both. I'll come get you in an hour, and we'll grab a bite to eat."

Without another word and before I could protest, he strode toward the door O had come through. As he neared it, the door slid open as if by magic. Had he forgotten his promise?

This way Miss K," O said. She held her hand toward the wall opposite the one that Connor disappeared through. Her eyes remained demurely cast down.

As I neared the wall, another door slid open, and I stepped onto an incredibly thick burgundy carpet. A dark-haired man rose from behind a carved desk that housed a large computer monitor, a phone, and a slim metal box similar to a safety deposit box.

Like Connor, he was dressed in black, but that's where the likeness ended. Where Connor's knit shirt draped over the well-defined muscles on his slender form, this man's T-shirt stretched across his bulk. He circled the desk and walked toward me with his hand outstretched.

"Good evening, K. My name is Brian, and I'm your security for the evening. Welcome."

He grasped my hand and shook it firmly. I could have sworn he winked at me although his face remained stern. *Interesting.*

Apart from his muscle-bound appearance, I had the impression this Brian possessed great inner strength. The look in his glacial eyes told me he was someone I wouldn't want to be on the wrong side of. He released my hand and gestured toward the desk. O stood near the opposite wall. Her head remained bowed, yet I was sure she didn't miss a thing.

"If you'll step this way, we'll finish these formalities so that you can relax and enjoy your evening. Master C wants you to feel right at home."

I took the few steps to the desk and waited for his instructions. Brian slid the box toward me and flipped open the lid.

"We ask our guests to let us store valuables for safe keeping, including all electronic devices. I suggest you leave your jewelry as well because it could identify you, but I'll leave that to your discretion."

I put my purse, keys, and change in the box before taking my cell phone out of my jacket pocket. My rings, earrings, necklace, and bracelet stayed put. They were part of my identity, and I took them off only if necessary. *They aren't going anywhere, thank you very much.*

"I'll need this to call home," I hung onto the phone. "Oh, and I'll need my bag. It's in the car."

"Not to worry. There's a phone in your private suite, and you can call anywhere you wish as part of your guest privileges. Your bag is already there."

I put the phone in the box. He flipped the lid closed, locked it, and handed me the key fob. There were two buttons on the fob.

"The button with the key on it is for your suite, and the button with the alarm symbol is for calling security, should you ever feel the need."

He certainly was efficient.

"Why do you keep saying *my* suite? I'm staying with C— um, Master C."

I worked hard at keeping the hysterical edge from my voice. *At least I sure as fuck hope I'm staying with Connor. He promised.*

"Actually, he insisted we give you your own suite so you could have personal space if you chose. You and he can work out any other arrangements later."

Brian picked up a beautiful black lace mask and held it out to me. "Here's a mask that we'd like you to wear at all times when you're outside your suite."

I grimaced but slipped the mask over my head. It fit as if made for me and was very comfortable.

"Now, if you'll step through this door, we'll get your body scan out of the way so you can begin your evening. O will meet you on the other side and show you to your room," Brian said.

I stepped into a cubicle that reminded me of a shower stall, fervently hoping it wasn't some kind of transporter sending me to visit an alien planet. *Get a grip, girl.* Nervousness was getting the best of me. This was all so strange.

The door slid shut behind me. There was a faint humming noise, and light shone through the circular walls for a few seconds. Come to think of it, things here were so surreal that it might as well be an alien planet. When the lights dimmed, I stood for another few seconds before the panel in front of me slid open. I stepped out, and sure enough, O stood waiting for me with her head still inclined to avoid eye contact.

"Please come this way, Miss K." She led the way down a hallway.

A series of recessed pot lights lit framed painted and sketched nudes hanging on hunter-green walls. I paused to take a look at them.

"They are exquisite, aren't they? They are part of the owner's private collection. The entire facility is filled with artwork of all kinds. You'll no doubt have plenty of time to see it if you're so inclined," O said.

"Who is in charge?" *Please don't let that bitch Cecile be here.*

"Discussing personal information about any of the staff, members, or guests is strictly forbidden," O said quietly. She stopped in front of an ebony wood door. "This is your room. Master C will join you shortly. Is there anything else I can do for you? Anything at all?"

"No, that will be all, thanks."

Was it just my imagination, or did O look a little disappointed as she turned away? I pressed the button on the fob, and the door silently opened inward. The suite was as opulent as the entrance and the hall. I took the mask off and laid it on the bed. It stood on a dais. I had a sneaky feeling it rotated, although I couldn't see the controls for it.

The enormous room held a large, round copper Jacuzzi with a freestanding fireplace on one side. *Awesome.* I was quite content with my humble abode back in Toronto, but it didn't hold a candle to the comfort real luxury brought along with it.

Careful Kat, you could get very used to this lifestyle.

I explored the rest of the suite before I took my travel case from my overnight bag. The marble bathroom housed a double shower and a sauna. I found several outfits in my size in the adjoining dressing room. They were made of fine materials with loose, comfortable cuts.

Since I was here and it would please Connor, I might as well dive in and experience the opulence in all of its forms. Who knew if I'd ever have the opportunity again to wear silks and linens that looked as if they were one-of-a-kind designs. I took a shower and luxuriated in the subtle fragrance of the shampoo and Cor Silver Soap I found in a gift box sitting on a shelf in the shower.

I toweled off with the ultra-thick, large cotton towel. Sitting on the vanity was a selection of my favorite creams, lotions, and perfume. *How on earth had C. known?* Some people thought food was the way into a woman's pants. For me, it was being surrounded by my favorite things. Okay, so I liked a good meal as much as anyone—okay, maybe more, I admit it—but this pampering was making me feel very receptive to whatever Connor had in store for me.

Hopefully, it's a ride on that magnificent specimen of his.

It occurred to me that every accommodation was a prelude to sex, and it was certainly leading my thoughts. I slipped into a bathrobe that felt like the Egyptian cotton I'd drooled over at the Sandal's resort. He really didn't miss a trick.

After applying a little makeup, I poured myself a drink for fortification from the fully stocked bar and explored the rest of the suite. By the looks of things, someone had more money than God. How did Connor and Cecile play into this?

It reminded me of how little I knew of Connor's world. In so many ways, Connor was still very much a mystery.

I couldn't think of one thing missing from the perfection greeting me. The furnished covered terrace overlooked what appeared to be a large lake, although it was difficult to see in the moonless night. There was an enormous cherry wood desk and table, a large suspended plasma television screen, and a lounger that looked designed for sex. *Or maybe you just can't get your mind off sex, Kat.*

Then again, given the surroundings and the reason I was here, why would I? I looked at the bedside clock. Just enough time to dress before Connor came. *Before Connor came—too funny.* Yup, my mind was on the runaway train to Smutsville.

I chose a pair of loose, black-linen pants with a draw-string waist and a cream-colored knit shirt. It was just the kind of shirt Connor would approve of. He loved to run his hands over my knit shirts while he exclaimed about how they showed off my magnificent form—his words, not mine. Although I must admit I thought his eyes needed examining, it was an absolute turn-on to hear the rich tenor of his voice washing over me with his words of approval. I'd just finished my drink when I heard a tap on the door. I opened it to find Connor dressed in similar attire to mine except his shirt was black. I tried not to stare like an immature schoolgirl, but he did take my breath away.

"Are you ready to go?"

"I am indeed. I'm starving. Lead the way."

"Remember your mask." Connor's tone was mild but brooked no argument.

He took me on a tour of the club before leading me into a large private dining room, complete with one of those chaise lounges made for fucking.

O-M-G—how many women had he screwed on there?

The decor matched the opulence of my suite. To say I was

impressed is an understatement, but I tried hard to act as if I were used to this kind of living. No big deal, right? I could play Nicole Kidman or Audrey Hepburn with the best of them.

Yeah, right, Kat. Who are you kidding?

The meal was the epitome of fine dining. Connor spent most of dinner describing the food and wine before telling me about the roles the serving staff played. I spent the time sipping—okay gulping—my wine to hide my nervousness while trying to get my head around how things functioned at this "club."

It seemed that none of the "staff" at the Masquerade were paid. Most were subs doing penance either as punishment or discipline, which was part of the nature of their need and desire to be controlled by their Dom or Domme.

Connor explained that some people call Doms "Tops" and subs "Bottoms," but he preferred to refer to them as sub and Dom. He said subs selected their Dom or Domme for the visit in a large bar that was the focal point of the Masquerade. As we finished our coffee, Connor suggested that experiencing my first viewing would help me start to understand just how things worked.

After touring another series of hallways adorned with more enticing art, we entered a salon much like the viewing rooms I'd seen in the movies, except the room they looked into was much larger. Connor gestured for me to take a seat with a view of a floor-to-ceiling window overlooking a large oval container that looked like a basin with elevated sides so that it could hold water. It was sitting on a dais in the middle of the room much like the one in my suite, and this one was indeed revolving.

A petite woman with flawless skin the color of coffee with double cream lay facedown and spread-eagled over a large wedge-shaped cushion placed in the center of the dais, her buttocks lifted over the wide edge. The cheek of her blindfolded face rested on the narrow part of the wedge, and her cuffed arms and legs were extended and clipped into rings fastened near the edge of the dais.

My heart raced for a moment. She looked like my twin, lying on display in front of us. *Had Connor chosen her on purpose?*

I didn't know whether to be flattered or—well, quite frankly I didn't know what I felt. After all, how would you feel if your doppelganger was lying naked and bound in front of you?

She had an intriguing scorpion tattooed on the small of her back. A tall masked woman dressed in high heels and a red leather bustier stood over her with a showerhead in her left hand and what looked like a small leather strap in her right.

The sub's engorged nether lips, just like her legs, were spread wide to accommodate her Domme. The Domme directed a stream of water on the squirming sub's enlarged clitoris, which was standing out long and hard.

I could feel the lick of the water, like a soft tongue, caressing her clit, urging her to want more. As the sub's pleasure mounted, she struggled against the restraints, and with each movement, the Domme rewarded her with a swift stroke of the strap across the fleshy part of her buttocks.

My clit sprang to attention with each stroke of the strap. I was barely aware of taking the glass put in my hand, so fixed was my attention on the spectacle before me.

The dais rotated very slowly, and the sub panted with excitement. I could feel the waves of sensation emanating from her core and spreading up her abdomen to her breasts. Her hips moved uncontrollably as if reaching for every sensation possible each time the strap made contact with her buttocks. She didn't seem to care that her body and the raw essence of her sexuality were exposed for view.

It was as if her emotions were part of me, and I could feel what she was feeling. Even if she wanted to, she could no longer stop. Her need to orgasm became too overwhelming to hold back. She was far beyond any sense of modesty or shame she may have had at being so exposed. Each moan sent a jolt of electricity from my nipples straight through the tip of my throbbing cunt.

The sub's body went rigid. She arched her back. The movement was small because of the restraints, yet I could see the tension in her muscles. Her orgasm started in slow motion and then intensified, building to a climax so strong, I wouldn't have thought it possible had I not experienced similar with Connor. Shock waves surged through her lithe body. When they began to subside, the sub seemed to recognize the gasping and tortured moaning emanated from deep within her. I could sense her reluctance to let go of the feelings. She relaxed on the wedge and smiled. A drape slid across the wall darkening the window. Every muscle in my body longed for release.

In contrast, Connor, always controlled, sat calmly at my side, watching me. Suddenly self-conscious, I strove to show the external calm I displayed for the world to see and took a large gulp of the soft drink in my hand. *How the hell did that get there?* I shook my head and took another drink, feeling the cool, crisp tingle calm the fire in my throat.

It took everything in my power to control my breathing when I ached to feel Connor's rock-hard cock plunge into my dripping wet pussy. It was going to be a long night; hell, a long weekend.

"Did you see how much pleasure the sub enjoyed even though she was tied down and feeling some measure of pain?

How did you feel watching? How would you feel about being treated like that?"

"I don't know."

I wasn't ready to let him know just how much the idea of being restrained excited me. It was not a new feeling for me, but one I needed to explore in private and with Connor.

"Have you ever fantasized about being spanked?"

Connor was like a dog with a bone when he wanted to know how I was feeling, and he wouldn't let this go. *Yes, all the time.*

"Sometimes." I could barely get the word out. Connor looked at me for a long beat.

"But?"

"But as you know, my life has been predicated on being in control. When I think about my sexuality, my world is turned upside down. It frightens me to realize how much I think about being dominated by you. Part of me wants to explore this world of bondage and submission, and part of me is scared to death and wants to run and hide."

Okay, at least I'm trying to be open.

"You're safe with me, you know. I won't push you farther than you want to go."

"I know. It's not you I'm afraid of, it's me."

I was relieved the dim room hid the blush that warmed my ears. It was hard even admitting to myself that I would beg him to spank me and more.

Connor gazed at me and waited. Then, he ran a finger through the goose bumps that sprang up on my arm.

"I need to know what's driving you, what's motivating you, what's at the bottom of this need of yours to explore the world of bondage and submission, and so do you. Only then will we have a better handle on where this is heading and how best to handle your needs.

"As for why now, well I think that I may have awakened a

sleeping dragon. When we were together years ago, I was new to life as a Dom and somewhat unsophisticated in my technique. Yes, I pushed too hard, too fast, but deep down we both knew you wanted it. I think that's part of what scared you away, although you blamed it all on my my emotional unavailability."

"Maybe." *Damn his insight.*

"Well, we're going to need to delve into those things now. As your Dom, it's imperative that I find out what motivates you to surrender. I need to know how to please you." Connor stood holding a hand out to me. "Now, are you ready for the next voyeuristic pleasure?"

Everything was happening so fast, words escaped me. He was right, and I knew it. *Time to stop hiding, Kat.* With tentative resolve, I took his hand, and he led the way out of the room.

17

KATHERINE

Connor held my hand as he led me to the next viewing room. The stage was set up like a prison cell with the open bars set close to the glass wall of the viewing room. This sub was a voluptuous woman wearing a prisoner's uniform, and she lay on the low single bed positioned on her left side. A bare light recessed in the ceiling and covered by wire mesh illuminated the stark gray prison cell. Three masked female prison guards stood staring at her, smiling with obvious intent.

The head guard was not a large woman, but the strength of her presence and the well-defined musculature that was obvious through her uniform commanded attention. Below her mask, her mouth was fixed in a cold, sinister smile that didn't reach her eyes.

The two assistant guards were what you'd think of as cute with the soft curves expected on the female body. They stood quietly, awaiting orders from the head guard. She stood at ease with her hands clasped behind her back and posture so rigid I wondered whether she had military training.

"Get up and stand beside the bed," she said.

The sub opened her mouth as if to say something and

then snapped it shut, but she didn't move, as if in defiance. The head guard's smile widened, and she brought her hands from behind her back. In her right hand was a long, thin riding crop that was slightly larger in circumference than a teacher's pointer. The sub wisely stood.

"You are a prisoner," the head guard said. "If you wish your stay here to be pleasant, at least from our perspective, you will comply with the rules."

She paused and snapped the crop a few times against the pant leg on her tight thigh.

"I make the rules. You may not agree with my rules, but I don't give a damn."

The tension seemed to ease from her body as she walked around the sub. Her assistants stood motionless in the background.

"You're what I like to refer to as my pretty, pampered little Italian princess." Her voice took on a husky male sensuousness. "Take off your shirt."

Before the sub could comply, the guard swept the crop across the cheeks of her buttocks. She flinched.

"Don't make me wait," the guard hissed with that husky voice. The sub quickly took off her shirt, still gasping. The guard continued her slow walk around the sub, who stood in rigid silence.

"You have beautiful skin."

Using her riding crop, she lifted each of the exposed breasts then pulled the crop away and watched the large breasts shudder and fall back to their resting position. With the end of the crop, she prodded her nipples.

"I love your big red nipples. I bet they'll get even bigger if I play with them, and you do like having them played with, don't you?"

The sub said nothing, and the guard lifted the riding crop

and delivered another stinging blow across her firm, round buttocks.

The sub winced. "Please don't hurt me." She sounded as if she would sob.

I turned to Connor, but before I could voice my concerns, he put his index finger against his mouth. "We'll talk later." He turned his attention back to the drama unfolding before us.

The head guard said, "When I ask a question, I expect an answer. You like your nipples played with, don't you?"

The sub nodded. The guard placed yet another sharp stroke across her buttocks and continued her slow circle around the sub. She stopped from time to time to run the tip of the crop across the sub's chest and back. "I didn't hear you," she said.

"Yes," the sub sobbed. "Yes."

I didn't know what to do. The woman seemed genuinely distressed, but whenever I looked at Connor, he sat there watching and smiling. Surely, he wouldn't let anything happen to her against her will. The logical part of my brain was telling me she wouldn't be here if she wasn't willing, but her fear looked so *real*.

The sub seemed frozen in place. The guard wedged the crop into the waistband of her loose prison pants and pushed them over her hips. They came to rest on her thighs just below her naked vulva. The guard put the crop between her legs and drew the long shaft through the crease of the sub's labia as it buried itself between the folds. The crop grew slick with her juices. The guard smiled as she looked at the glistening wetness that coated the shaft of the crop.

"How easily my pampered little princess shows the nature of her sexuality. Although you've spent your life desperately living up to societal standards of a repressed morality, in here, those standards have little meaning.

"You've known it all along. You might as well face up to it. You're just like the rest of us. If you're honest with yourself, you know you have the same needs, but you hide them, fearing that to recognize them makes you a salacious little slut, which you are."

What kind of prison guard talks like that? Who writes these lines, anyway?

I was getting excited. I leaned forward in my chair, mesmerized by the play unfolding before me. It was like the guard gave the sub permission to embrace her sexual reality even if it was no longer hers to control. A sudden gush of wetness flowed down the inside of the sub's thighs.

The head guard turned to her assistants. "Strip my little princess. Force her onto the bed and hold her down on her hands and knees with her legs spread. I want to see her pussy lips, full and inviting, protruding between the cheeks of her pretty, round ass."

The assistants put the sub in position. The guard's strong hands molded her ass in firm manipulations and occasionally slid between the sub's legs and pulled on her engorged clitoris in a milking motion. She spread the wetness that covered her hands onto the sub's ass, kneading the soft flesh. The sub moaned, and the guard delivered a slap to her right cheek.

"That's not good enough. I want to hear you scream like the little bitch in heat you are." She slapped the wet ass even harder. The sub screamed as if the stinging shock surpassed her control.

"That's it. Let it go." The guard shoved two and then three fingers deep into the dripping cunt. "Be my squirming little slut."

Now that's more like it.

I took a drink from the glass that magically appeared at my elbow. By this time, I was squirming with the heat of arousal, and the cold fizz did little to extinguish it. I looked around to see what Connor was doing.

He was fixated on the action unfolding before us. Maybe he wouldn't notice what I was doing. I slid my hand under the waistband of my pants, slipped two fingers between my own slick lips, and pressed down on the throbbing ache growing in my clit. As I submerged in the fantasy, I felt the pain of the slaps and the pleasure of the guard's thrusting fingers. They blended into a peak of sensation that took the sub beyond any dignity she may have hoped for. I couldn't wait to see what happened next.

The sub's loud moans of abandon echoed off the cell walls. She thrust her ass in the air, reaching for her orgasm. The guard stopped and stood back. The sub turned her head, and I could see the tears in her eyes. "Please," she begged.

The guard bent down to her ear. "Relax. I'll let you come for me when I'm ready. I like to watch you squirm when I shove my fingers into your cunt. But that's not enough for my little slut. You deserve to be properly fucked."

Her two assistants stood beside the sub on either side of the bed. As if on cue, each put a hand on her shoulders and pushed her head down to the mattress. With their other hands, they encircled her legs just above the knees, pulling her ass higher and her legs farther apart. The guard cupped one hand and slid it between her legs.

"Now my wet little princess, relax your pussy and fill my palm with your sweet pussy juice."

The sub must have tightened, perhaps overcome by her humiliation, because the guard said, "Do I have to remind you where you are? Do I have to remind you that your only role in here is to be my little bitch slave?"

She continued to hold her cupped hand between the sub's legs and, with the other, repeatedly slapped the cheeks of her ass until a rush of fluid gushed from her cunt into the guard's hand. The assistants pulled each cheek of her ass farther apart, opening her anus like a small, dark cave. The guard poured the captured fluid into the opening.

She turned to the small table in the cell and picked up two dildos, one larger than the other. She handed the smaller one to the assistant on the sub's left and hefted the larger one in her right hand, positioning herself behind the sub.

"Now I want to watch you come for us while we fuck you. My guess is that you've never really let yourself go enough to know how to satisfy that sweet little pussy. You will give it to me, princess."

The assistant eased the lifelike phallus into the sub's anus while the guard penetrated her cunt with one long slow even motion until the hilt of the dildo caressed her buttocks. The sub groaned. The assistant matched the head guard's rhythmic penetration as she increased the intensity of each stroke.

Her hard, deep thrusting brought the sub to an explosive orgasm causing her to scream and shake uncontrollably. She collapsed on the bed, but the guard wasn't done with her yet. The assistants held her arms and sat her on the side of the bed. The guard stood in front of her, naked from the waist down, legs spread, with her hips at the sub's eye level.

"My turn, princess." She grabbed the sub's head and pushed her clitoris into her mouth. She went into a wild frenzy, grinding her hips into the sub's face, screaming, "Suck me! Suck me! Suck me!" After her orgasm, she held the sub's head inches from her wet cunt and ordered her to lick her come.

"Something to remember me by." She pulled on her pants and buckled her belt. Without another word, the guard and her assistants left. The cell went dark.

I sat frozen in place, my fingers still buried between my legs.

"Are you okay?" Connor asked.

"Did you know that I have a prison fantasy?" *I'm so horny I could burst.*

"Huh. No, I didn't know. That's something new we can explore in our double diary."

"I'll try. That's kind of private. I can't believe I just told you."

"So what did you think about the scenario?"

I blurted out the first thing that came to mind about the sub seeming humiliated by the whole thing. "I wonder if she knew what she was in for."

"Actually, the sub wrote that particular scenario and could have used the safe word at any time if she wanted it to stop. I know it sounds rather complicated, but either the dominant or submissive can suggest a fantasy they want to play. They post these on a secure intranet we have set up, and when they find one they like, they agree on a date to meet up at the Masquerade."

"And what if they don't like how they look when they meet?"

"Babe, not everyone is as picky as you are about looks. Everyone is well groomed, and their air of sexuality makes them quite attractive. Anyway, I wanted to know how you'd react if that was your fantasy, and now you tell me you have a prison fantasy. Are your guards male or female?"

I was silent for a beat and then sighed.

"I've fantasized about both at one time or another." My voice was soft and a little throaty.

"Together?"

"No, it's usually one or the other. I fantasize about you being a prison warden commanding me. Sometimes you command me to be with a woman."

I paused for another beat. It was difficult for me to over-come my rigid puritanical upbringing where anything to do with sex was disgusting and evil. Talking about it was just not done.

"And?"

"And you watch." My voice was barely a whisper.

"Are you wet?"

I didn't respond.

"Kat, are you wet right now?" Connor's voice took on a commanding tone.

My fingers were saturated, and my juices ran down between my butt cheeks.

"Yes, but I think you know that already."

"Here's what I want you to do, Kat. Go to your room and make yourself come. Enjoy the privacy of your room and give yourself the opportunity to explore what you really feel about what you saw here today. Look at it as the first step in knowing who you really are. I know I'll enjoy thinking about you touching yourself. Did you bring the double diary with you?"

"Yes."

"Write me about your prison fantasies, and don't hold anything back."

"But you promised not to leave me."

"I'll be right next door. You need some time for yourself. Enjoy the amenities of your suite. Free up your mind while you touch yourself. It might be interesting for you to see where your imagination will take you with nothing to influence or distract you. The only way to truly know yourself is to let go."

He walked me back to my suite and planted a light kiss on the top of my head.

"Good night."

He turned and walked away. I stared after his retreating back. I locked the door and tore off my clothes as I rushed to the bed. The next thing I remember is writhing against the hand I'd thrust between my legs.

For you, C, for you.

Double Diary
Katherine on Saturday, September 1 @ 8:35 a.m.

In my prison fantasies, I'm often taken to the warden's office to pleasure and "feed" her. I never touch her. She always has me strip. Sometimes she has me lie on her desk and sucks me when she needs to "eat." Sometimes she then fucks me with a phallus. Sometimes she has me kneel on the desk and probes my anus. So you can see why the prison scene turned me on.

In a different version, she gives me to the guards because I've been bad or need training. Sometimes the guards come into the isolation cell I'm in, one by one. Sometimes they sit around me as I lie on a high bed that converts to different positions. They take turns while the others watch. I know what I said about one person at a time, so this is hard to admit.

As hard as it is, I love that you asked me to write my fantasies. I'm hopeful that we'll act out some of them, at least to some degree (you can skip the riding crop). When it comes to the BDSM-type fantasies, I have some trepidation as I've said, but I want to—no, I need to explore it. It's time to stop hiding from the things I've been secretly thinking about for years.

I'll carry this fantasy with me all day. I'm smiling and thinking wet thoughts. God, you excite me. Intimately yours forever. Kat

18

CECILE

"What have you got for me, Joe?"

"Cece, hon—"

"Don't even think it, Joe. I need a well-built man tonight. Can you arrange that?"

"No problem, Miss D." Joe snickered. "You just tell me when and where, and I'll make sure he's there. Any particular hair color suit your fancy?"

"This isn't for me, you stupid man. Get someone who looks like this." Cecile slid a photo across the desk. "I'll tape the action, and I'll need you to find someone who can do a good job of editing the tape. I'll need it done by Monday."

"No problem, Miss D. I'm your man."

"I'll call you back with the place and time." She hung up without another word.

Cecile dialed Sophia's number. She picked up on the first ring.

"What have you got for me?"

"I met with Tim on Thursday night and taped our conversation just like you asked. Oh, and I found out the name of the company where Katherine starts work on Tuesday, and I found out where Tim went this weekend."

Sophia sounded like an eager little lap dog waiting for her cookie. Cecile took a great deal of pleasure in the eagerness of the vacuous little twit.

"So that makes Tim's office free for the evening, right?"

"Um, I guess so. What did you have in mind?"

"I'll let you know when I get there. Meet me at the back entrance at nine tonight, and I'll explain everything."

"I don't know about this, Cecile. What if someone sees us?"

"Don't you worry your pretty little head about that. Now where will Katherine be working?"

"She's taken a job as Editor in Chief at Harvard University Press, and she'll be working for a man named David Thompson."

"That's excellent, Sophia. Well done. Now I want you to go and treat yourself to whatever you like at the Lotus Spa. It's on me. I'll see you later tonight."

Cecile smiled as she hung up the phone. David owed her big time. Things were falling into place quite nicely. This was going to be easier than she thought. She'd show that little bitch Katherine and show her good. She'd make sure she found out what the world of BDSM was really like. As for Sophia, tonight Cecile would teach her what it was like to play in the big leagues.

She scrolled through her address book until she found the number. She was just about to hang up when someone picked up the phone.

"Hello. Thompson here."

"Davy, how lovely to hear your voice again." Cecile made sure her voice dripped with sarcasm.

"Who is this?"

"This is Cecile DePoulignac, sweetheart. Remember me?"

Cecile heard a sharp intake of breath before the line went quiet.

"I know you're there, Davy, and it's time for that favor you owe me. Just sit tight, and I'll be there in an hour or so."

"What kind of favor, Cecile? I'm very busy right now, and I was just leaving."

She could imagine him shifting the weight of his huge stomach as he tried for the bullying bluster he used to assert his authority.

"I'll explain when we meet, Davy. You don't want to piss me off, now do you? Or would you rather I send a few of those pictures of you trussed up like a Christmas turkey to the press?"

"No, no, that's okay. I didn't mean to give the impression that I wasn't willing."

His wheedling tone made her want to vomit.

"I was just heading out for some lunch. How about meeting at The 41? We can share a meal and have a nice long chat."

Cecile would rather walk over cut glass than be seen in public with him. He reminded her of an enormous doughboy with the spine of a jellyfish.

"I said we'd meet in your office, and that's where we'll meet, you fat fuck. Be there."

"Okay, okay, you don't have to get mean."

She slammed the phone down. She detested him with every fiber of her being but seeing him was a necessary evil in her plan to humiliate Katherine and get her out of Connor's life.

Cecile left a message for Joe Carlino with the time and place for the evening's meeting before heading off to the offices of Harvard University Press.

As she drove to David's office, she flashed back to the party he'd invited her to all those years ago. She'd wondered why she was the only woman there but had readily believed him when he said the others would be arriving later. The drinks and drugs had flowed freely, and she'd been more than happy to match them drink for drink, snort for snort.

She'd been so drunk and stoned she'd enthusiastically complied when they hooted at her to strip. She had a knock-'em-dead body and was more than happy to show it off. The dog collar was a bit weird, but she was having a good time, so she went along.

The rest of the drunken debauchery was a blur. She remembered David sitting on her chest and ramming his pitiful penis down her throat. He'd wrapped her hair around both fists and yanked at it as he thrust. She had a vague recall of flashbulbs going off somewhere in the background. But it had all been in fun.

That was until the next day, when she'd had to endure the embarrassment and humiliation of David showing her the pictures they'd taken of her in every degrading position possible. He'd threatened to publish them unless she helped him get the goods on Connor. If Connor had caught her doing that, he would have dropped her like a hot potato. Never before had Cecile been at someone else's mercy, and she vowed it would never happen again. She'd have her revenge. David would learn what it meant to mess with Cecile DePoulignac.

That had been back in the days before she could afford to hire a private investigator. With single-minded detachment, Cecile spent every spare waking minute finding out everything she could about David Thompson. They'd been living in New York where he and Connor both worked at Longfellow Publishing, and it had been relatively easy to get the gossip on him from the admin assistants. Word was that he liked rough play, including with his poor wife, and he was one to avoid.

She'd watched him and followed him whenever possible. For months, nothing of interest happened, and she'd almost given up. But Cecile never forgave and never forgot, so she'd kept on, certain that her diligence would pay off. And one night it had.

She'd followed him to the Thriftway Motor Lodge on Eighth Avenue in Manhattan. The asshole went to a room in the back of the motel and was stupid enough to leave the window partially open. The drapes were the kind with cracked rubber on the back and were not wide enough to close, so there was more than enough room for a good view. Thanking her luck that it was dark back there, she'd crawled beneath the window and listened.

A female was talking as if to a small child. "Come here, you bad boy. Momma is going to give you a good spanking. Now you take your clothes off and lie down on the bed, Junior."

Cecile put her fingers on the ledge and pulled herself up inch by inch to take a look. When she could see over the edge, she saw a woman dressed in what looked like cheap black vinyl and spandex wearing eight-inch spike heels. She was holding a paddle and watching as David eagerly took his clothes off and sprawled facedown on the bed.

David's ass was fire-engine red by the time the hooker stopped spanking him, and he was begging her to let him suck her. The woman sat on a stained, moth-eaten chair with her hips thrust forward and her legs in the air. David got off the bed and crawled over. Cecile watched in fascination as he sucked the woman while she said things like, "That's it. That's my baby boy" and "Come on, Davy. Suck Momma good."

After a while, she said, "Okay, Davy, now let Momma suck her little boy."

David crawled back to the bed and pulled his bulk into a

sitting position on the edge. The woman knelt and sucked him off.

David had rested for a few minutes while he caught his breath. Then, he'd gotten up, dressed, and taken out his wallet. He held out what looked to be two one-hundred-dollar bills.

"That was great, Dolly. Same time next month?"

"Sure, Davy." She took the money and lit a cigarette. She propped herself on the pillows resting against the headboard and blew a stream of smoke.

"What game do you want to play next time?"

"You know I like you to surprise me. I wish you'd quit asking me that. You should know by now."

"Sure, Davy, whatever you say. You take care of that sweet little ass now. Momma will have a great surprise for you next time."

Cecile hurried to the side of the building as David drove away. She'd waited a few minutes to be sure he wouldn't come back before going to the room and knocking on the door.

"Yeah?"

The hooker held open the door. A fresh cigarette stuck out of the corner of her thin painted lips.

"May I come in? I have a proposition for you."

"Yeah?" The hooker looked her up and down. "And why should I want to listen to anything from you, Miss Designer Label?"

"Because I'll make it well worth your while."

Cecile flashed a fifty-dollar bill and suggested there was more to come. The hooker stood aside and let her in.

Cecile was seated comfortably on a stool in the closet when David arrived for his next assignation. She'd instructed the hooker to blindfold him and tie him to the bed before administering his "punishment."

"Momma has a very special surprise for you, Davy," the hooker said.

He'd been eager to play along. The radio playing in the background hid the sounds of the shutter as Cecile took her photos. It was the best five hundred dollars she'd ever spent.

Now all she had to do was get her pictures back. She'd figured it was highly unlikely that he kept them at home where his wife could find them and bided her time until she had a chance to search his office. As she'd suspected, he had them in his desk drawer, and they looked well used. She shuddered in disgust at the thought of him jerking off with visions of her dancing before his eyes.

It was with great satisfaction that she'd sent the note along with a couple of the worst photos of him showing his fat, trussed-up ass being whipped. She wished she could have been there to see his face when he read her note.

You fucked with the wrong person, Davy, and you owe me big time. One day, I'll come calling for a "favor," one that you'll do without question unless you want these photos released to the press. Stay tuned. C.D.

PS: I took my pictures back. Nobody fucks with me. Payback is a bitch.

David held open the door as Cecile walked toward the entrance to the Harvard U Press head office. Maybe the little fuck had learned a thing or two since she last saw him.

"Hello—"

"I'm not interested in making small talk with you. Where is your office?"

David pointed up the staircase that stood in the center of the wood-paneled reception area. Cecile mounted the stairs and strode through the office door that stood open before them. As she crossed the large room, she barely noticed the floor-to-ceiling bookcases and stained glass windows that lined the walls. Instead, she homed in on the oak partner's desk and sat in David's oversized leather chair where she glared, daring him to ask her to move. He stood, hands in the pockets of his ill-fitting jeans, jiggling the loose change.

"For fuck's sake, sit down. I'm not going to eat you." Cecile laughed mirthlessly at her play on words. "I'm here to give you a gift, so sit down and take a load off."

David pulled out the matching secretary's chair and gingerly sat down. "Gift? What kind of gift?"

"Oh, you'll like this one. Now listen up because I'm going to say this once. I'm going to tell you a little story about your new employee, Katherine King, and just what you'll do with her to help her get off to a good start here at Harvard U Press. I met Kitty Kat—that's what we call her—at one of the BDSM clubs that I own."

"I didn't know you owned BDSM—"

It was best to keep the lies to a minimum.

"Interrupt me again, and I'll make this one of the sorriest days of your life. Now, as I was saying, I met Kitty Kat at the club, and during one of our girly chats, she told me how much she longs to explore her need to feel pain and humiliation for sexual release. Her boyfriend is one of those vanilla men who's as boring as snot and just as adventurous. She also told me about starting her new job here and how attractive her new boss is. Imagine my surprise when she mentioned that you were the hunk."

David preened as Cecile went on to fabricate some of the things that Katherine had said about him.

"I can't fathom what she sees in you."

"Some women find me very handsome, you know. I've met many women who've complimented my good looks."

"Huh. It must be the power of the office. Well, there's no accounting for taste. Now, here's what I want you to do."

She instructed David on just how she expected him to welcome Katherine to her new job the following week.

"No way I'm doing this. What are you, crazy? I'd be ruined."

"You'll be ruined anyway. Think about it, doughboy. If you don't play ball with me, I'll make sure you lose everything with single-minded devotion."

"I'll lose everything anyway if I'm in prison."

"Don't worry. She won't call the cops. She's into this. If you're worried, set up an airtight alibi. Or are you too slow to figure that out? It will be your word against hers. It's not as if you haven't done this before. Just have fun with her like you did with me. Have a few drinks and get your rocks off. And, of course, if you ever mention my name in connection with this or anything else, I'll destroy you and this little empire you've built. Are we clear on this?"

Cecile focused on his collection of Visconti fountain pens. She picked up one from its gold holder and started tapping it on the desk. David winced and leaned over to take the pen. Cecile held it out of his reach.

"Uh, uh, uh." She shook her head while waving the pen in the air. "You haven't answered my question, Davy. Are we clear?"

"Crystal clear. Now, can I have my pen back?"

"You mean, may I have my pen back, don't you? That's pretty appalling grammar for someone who's the president of one of the world's most prestigious publishing houses."

Cecile rose from the chair, tossed the pen in David's direction, and headed out the door. She laughed as he scrambled after the pen as it rolled across the floor.

At nine o'clock sharp, Cecile arrived behind the executive building at Royal University and parked beside Sophia's waiting car. Her Jaguar XKR was invisible in the darkness, and only the soft purr of the engine announced her arrival. She silenced the automatic lock mechanism before joining Sophia and entering the building.

"Hi Cecile. Thanks so much for sending me to your spa. I had a great time. Why are you wearing that hat?"

"Let's go to your office, and I'll explain everything."

Sophia led the way to the elevator and hit the button to the eleventh floor.

"Where's Tim Bancroft's office?"

"Oh, it's right down there beside the president's office." Sophia pointed down a hallway to where two office doors were barely visible in the ambient light.

"My office is this way." She led them down the left branch of the connecting hall.

Sophia unlocked the door and flipped the light switch before setting her oversized purse on the conference table. She sat in one of the plush upholstered chairs and gestured for Cecile to have a seat. Cecile sat, placed both hands on the table, and turned her penetrating violet eyes on Sophia.

"Who knows about your meeting with Tim on Thursday night?"

"I called Tim's executive assistant when the president's assistant was covering her lunch and confirmed the appointment, so I imagine half the office knows about it by now."

"Good. And do you have the recordings of the team meetings that I asked you to get?"

"Yes, I do."

Sophia rose from her chair and crossed to her desk. She removed a USB key from her desk drawer and handed it to Cecile.

"Excellent. So here's what I want you to do tonight. Very

shortly, a man I hired for you will be arriving, and you're going to have sex with him right here in your office. You'll pretend that it's Tim forcing himself on you against your will, so you're going to protest and make it sound like you're resisting him."

"You're not serious."

"I'm dead serious, Sophia. You're going to take one for the team. Call it a little test for the position."

"Oh no. There's no way I'm going to do that. No way in hell. It would be the end of my career."

"Oh really? Well let me show you a few reasons why I'm certain that you'll cooperate."

Sophia's face drained of color as Cecile slowly and deliberately placed one photo after another of her and Justin Roberts, the teenaged lover she'd taken during a secret vacation of drunken debauchery in Cuba. Cecile watched the emotions play across her fair features and saw them turn from mortification to consideration to certainty. She could hear Sophia thinking: *That's not so bad. Most would envy me.*

"And just in case these haven't convinced you, there's these."

She placed five new photos beside the ones of Sophia and Justin. There could be no doubt from those photos about the levels Sophia was willing to sink to in satisfying her sexual predilections. Although Cecile had confirmed that the young girl in the photos was of age, she looked prepubescent. If these photos were published, Sophia would never work in North America again.

Sophia rested her head in her hands. "Wh-wh-when will he be here?" Her shoulders shook with the force of her sobs.

"Cheer up, darling. You have to resist only long enough for me to get it on tape. After that, I'll leave you two alone, and you can do whatever you like with him." Cecile's cell phone rang. "Ah, here he is now. Time for you to get ready,

Sophia. Panties off and facedown on the desk. While you do that, I'll go and get him. She lowered the veil on her hat and left without waiting for an answer.

When she returned with the man and PI in tow, Sophia lay with her chest across the desk and her face turned toward the back wall. She'd removed her panties and hitched her skirt up around her waist.

"John-Boy, this lady is your date for the evening, although as I told you, she'll be calling you Tim to fulfill her fantasy. Sophia, meet John-Boy. John-Boy, that's a good one." Cecile rubbed the ridge that rose in John-Boy's tight jeans and laughed as if entertained by a good joke. She gestured toward Joe Carlino. "Set up over there and keep your mouth shut."

"Hi," said John-Boy.

Sophia said nothing.

"Okay, let's get this show on the road," Cecile said. "Remember my instructions."

John-Boy nodded, removed his jeans and rolled a condom over the hard-on that sprang free.

Cecile walked over and slapped Sophia on the butt. "Now, spread your legs wider. That's it."

Sophia inched her legs farther apart.

"Are you wet, or will we need a little prep?" Cecile put her hand between Sophia's legs. Oh goodness, I can see you're going to enjoy this after all."

Cecile moved aside, and John-Boy moved into place. The muscles stood out on his back as he flexed before grasping his enormous cock. Sophia grunted as he slid his long, thick phallus into her glistening cunt.

"Oh, nice and big and wet, just how I like them," John-Boy said. "Hang on, baby. I'm going to give you the ride of your life."

He grasped Sophia's buttocks with each of his large hands and buried his cock to the hilt.

"Let's hear it, Sophia," Cecile said. She activated the recorder on her phone and placed it in front of Sophia's face. Then she leaned forward and brushed the hair from Sophia's cheek. She smiled as the humiliation crossed Sophia's face. "Convince me."

"Oh no, Tim, no. Please don't. I'm begging you. Stop it, Tim."

As instructed, John-Boy took it slow and easy while Sophia made her protestations. Her cunt made wet sucking sounds as he repeatedly buried his massive length. He leaned forward and shoved his hands under her chest and grabbed her full breasts. Sophia started to thrust back eagerly, and John-Boy matched her rhythm.

"Not yet, my sweeties," Cecile cut in. "I haven't got what I need yet. I'm not convinced."

John-Boy slowed. Sophia let out a sobbing sound.

"Please stop, Tim. Why are you doing this? Why are you forcing yourself on me?"

"That's better." Cecile waited a few minutes more before clicking off the recorder and heading out the door. Joe grabbed his tripod and scrambled after her.

"Have a blast." Cecile smiled.

"Come on, baby. Let John-Boy show you a good time."

Cecile closed the door behind them and marched out of the building before speaking to Joe.

"You know what to do. Make it good."

She gave him Sophia's USB key that now included a little something she'd just recorded. Joe nodded his head and drove away.

Cecile crossed to her car and started it, feeling the dampness that saturated her pants. She headed in the direction of the Collars & Cuffs Club. She'd need more than one or two of the boys and girls to satisfy the burning need between her legs.

19

CONNOR

The late summer breeze blew a wisp of my thick brown hair across my forehead as I stepped onto my private terrace on the rooftop of the Masquerade Club. I poured two fingers of Glenlivet and hoped that a few minutes of solitude before my dinner with Kat would calm the nagging feeling in the pit of my gut.

What if last night was too much for her? What if she wants to end things? I didn't want to think about that.

"What's up, Bri?"

"Good to see that your Spidey Sense is still working, Con." Brian stepped from the shadows cast by the shrubbery.

"I've told you before that the molecules arrange themselves into a maelstrom whenever you're around. Care for a drink?"

"Not right now. I think you'd better hear what I have to say first. Cecile's up to something."

"Cecile's always up to something." I sighed and took a sip of my drink. "So what's she done?"

"Frankly, I'm not sure what she's doing, and that's what

bothers me. That and the fact that she met with David Thompson earlier today."

"That asshole? I'd heard that he'd ousted the president at Harvard University Press. What could she possibly want with that slime bucket?"

"I don't know, but I'm afraid it means trouble for Katherine. On top of that, she's set up a meeting with her PI and Sophia Drake tonight at the university. Two connections with Katherine are just too many coincidences. My man didn't find out much else. Cecile's very careful about what she says on the phone or in her email."

I put my drink on the wrought-aluminum table and walked over to the edge of the garden that formed part of the rooftop jungle. I stared into the light shining through the flowers framing a reflecting pool. Brian sat quietly. He knew better than to interrupt when I was in one of these moods. Several minutes passed before I retrieved my drink and took a seat opposite Brian.

"Until we know more, we need to be on high alert. Step up the surveillance. Is there any way your man can record this meeting tonight?"

"That might be tough. A better plan would be to see if we can find out what's going on from this Sophia."

"Good idea. Meanwhile, make sure that your man never lets Kat out of his sight." I started pacing around the patio. "Better yet, you do it. I don't trust that asshole Thompson, and if he's met with Cecile, something's up. You'll have to find a way to track Kat when she starts work on Tuesday."

"She's gotten under your skin, hasn't she? I can see why. She's stunning and looks like she has some spunk. Don't you think it's about time you admit you have feelings for her, that you may even love her, Con? I haven't seen you like this since Meredith died, and I'm worried about you. If you don't let some of this out, you're going to implode."

I went rigid. I opened and closed my fists and took several deep breaths. When I spoke, each word was like a series of right hooks from a heavy-weight prize fighter. "How. Dare. You?"

I strode over to where Brian sat, placed my fists on the cold metal of the table, and leaned forward until I was nose to nose with him. "I told you never to mention her to me again."

Brian sat unperturbed. He simply stared into the icy depths of my eyes.

"I asked you a question, and I expect an answer." My anger increased the harshness of my tone.

"I dare because I'm your friend." Brian leaned forward until he was less than a hair's width from my face. "And because I'm not one of your lackeys you can order around, and because we vowed that we'd always tell each other the truth, no matter what.

"I was there for you when she died. I watched a carefree young man turn into a hard, calculating entrepreneur who became rich and powerful. I watched you turn into someone who believes a profit margin is a substitute for anything that requires you to give a damn.

"I've never said anything before out of respect for your feelings, but it hurts me to see you like this. For the first time in years, I see a light in your eyes that reminds me of the old Connor. I don't know if your Katherine has anything to do with that, but I think it's time you take a hard look at yourself and find out."

The contest of wills continued, I rigid with tension and Brian relaxed yet vigilant. After several more minutes, I found myself at the railing surrounding the terrace, staring at nothing, lost in thought.

Brian broke through the silence. "Do you still want me to have Lucy set up in the Ebony Room? Are you sure your

Katherine is ready for that? Maybe you should find a way to work off some of this instead."

"Some of this? Is that what we're calling my feelings for Kat? *This?*"

"No, we're calling your feelings for Kat, your anger toward Cecile, and your fear of the unknown *this*. You and I both know that if you don't work off some of your inner turmoil, you'll explode, and we both know what happens then."

"Nothing good," I muttered.

"That's right, nothing good." Brian paused a beat. "Okay, you win. I hope you know what you're doing. Shall I have Lucy ready for around nine?"

"Yes, and make sure she's ready for what I need. I want Kat to see a little more than the usual rope and whip play."

Brian stood and flexed each of his sculpted back muscles in turn. "Did you want to meet with Cecile when you get back?"

"No, not this time. I warned her last time that if she fucked with Kat again, I'd cut her off. I reminded her of the double-cross clause in our partnership agreement. There's nothing more to say."

"Maybe she thinks this is one of your games. You know how competitive she gets. I warned you years ago these games with Cecile were a stupid fucking idea that would leave you vulnerable."

"I told her in no uncertain terms that Kat was not part of any game. I told her Kat had never been and would never be part of one of our games. In fact, I told her the games were over when I confronted her about the text message she sent to Tim."

"Oh shit. Cecile won't take that lying down."

After a moment, I smiled. "Oh shit, indeed. Now I'd better go and meet Kat." I stood and briefly clasped Brian's bicep. "Thank you, my friend. You've given me a lot to think about."

I joined Kat in my private dining room. She seemed a little distant, so we exchanged a few pleasantries and settled in to enjoy a splendid meal of grilled Porterhouse steak, vegetables, and Caesar salad. The sommelier opened the bottle of the 2007 Sassicaia I ordered and poured a taste. I checked the legs, aroma, and bouquet of the red wine and pronounced it suitable.

Kat took a sip from the glass the sommelier set before her.

"I never thought I'd call a wine delicious, but this one certainly is. You really know your wines, Connor."

"It's a hobby of mine. Actually, it was you who got me started drinking and savoring red wine."

"Me? Really?" She seemed pleased. "I still like my wine, as you know, but I'm no expert."

I sat back in my chair, holding my glass by the stem and swirling the deep ruby-colored liquid.

"I missed you, Kat."

At my words, her position softened imperceptibly as if I'd loosened the tension on an overtight violin string.

"I missed you back, C." She took another bite, her eyes never leaving mine. I waited.

"You could have stayed with me in my room, you know."

"I was right next door. You needed time to think about what you'd seen, and I refuse to influence your feelings. Now you've had the day to think. Have you seen anything here that you'd like to try?"

"There's a lot here that's piqued my interest, but I'm not too sure how much of it I would be interested in. It gives us a lot to talk and think about. I checked out some of the whip-ping rooms today. I think I'd like to see one of those scenes. But what happens if the participants or whatever you call them have had enough?"

"We have very specific rules about the use of safe words. If one of our clients wants the activity to stop, he or she says 'red' or 'red light' and all activity stops immediately. When the intensity has reached the level that the patron can tolerate but she or he wants the activity to continue, the signal is 'yellow' or 'yellow light'. 'Green' or 'green light' signifies that it's full speed ahead. Same as you and me do.

"If any patron breaks the rules, they're barred from the premises. Everyone's rights must be respected here, and we have no tolerance for those who don't show that respect."

"But I notice that some of them wear gags. How do they give the signal then?"

"They use a simple hand signal—thumbs-up for green, thumbs-down for red and thumbs-to-the-side for yellow. The subs puts their complete trust in the Doms or Dommes they've chosen, and it's the responsibility of that dominant to ensure their limits are respected and they're well cared for.

"As an added safety measure, there are safe buttons on every piece of equipment and within the sub's reach, so they can call for help if needed. Why don't I give you a tour of one of the whipping rooms."

"I don't think I'm ready to see the action up close and personal yet."

I smiled as I rose and reached for her hand.

"Oh, the room is unoccupied. I know you're not ready to dive in with both feet—yet."

I led the way through one of the panel doors and down a hallway. Like the other halls, the art was exquisite and provocative. I stopped in front of a mahogany door and extracted a key card from my pocket. Opening the door, I gestured to Kat. She stepped into the large room, stopped abruptly, and rotated her head from side to side.

The room looked something like a medieval torture chamber with a large bed at one end. I strode to a large X shape that stood beside a large display case full of whips and paddles.

"Why don't we start here?"

I waited for Kat to join me and managed to suppress the laugh that threatened to erupt at the stunned expression on her face. This room was equipped with BDSM apparatus unlike what she'd seen in the viewing rooms.

"What is all this stuff? It looks like a person could get seriously hurt here."

"And that's why we have safe buttons installed. In truth, Kat, it's not about being hurt. It provides the client an opportunity to explore and enjoy their specialized tastes. Have a look at this whipping post. It won't bite."

Kat skirted around a sawhorse-like contraption that sat in the middle of the floor and joined me in front of the post.

"This is called a St. Andrew's cross." I ran my fingers over the wood and around the restraining bolts.

"It's made of specially treated ebony so that it doesn't splinter. This is one of my favorite pieces of equipment because it can be used for flogging, bondage, or sexual teasing. The spread-eagle position gives lots of options."

"How would you use this for sexual teasing? Isn't that just foreplay?"

"In the D/s world, sexual teasing is the term we use for orgasm denial or orgasm control. I think this is a toy we could make good use of."

"Really?"

"I know you say you aren't into spanking or whipping." *Although I have my doubts about that.* "But I do think orgasm denial or control might be a great way for me to discipline you."

A gleam of interest lit the gold flecks in her eyes. "And where's the safe button you told me about?"

"It's right here." I pointed to a spot on the back of the top cross bar. "The sub is restrained in such a way that he or she can reach around and press the button if needed."

"So why not just put it on the front?"

"Because in the throes of pleasure, the sub often thrashes around, and if it's on the front, it can be hit by mistake."

"Huh." Kat pointed to the sawhorse. "What is that for?"

"That's another device for spanking or whipping. It's called a spanking bench or spanking horse. It's the piece most newbies start with because it's so easy to build. The sawhorse type like that one is the most common, but there are other styles as well."

Kat turned to the display case and ran her fingers over some of the whips and crops.

"Aren't you afraid of people going too far when they first start using these?"

I smirked. "That's the point."

Kat gave me her don't-fuck-with-me look, and I laughed.

"Sorry, Kat. I'm just playing with you a bit. Our members go through an intensive training program to learn how to safely use the equipment. If done properly, flogging is not particularly painful although it definitely stings. Our patrons must learn how to wield the whip so it lands on its chosen location with just the right degree of force."

Kat strolled around the room for a few more minutes, pausing to examine a chair with padded and curved armrests.

"What's this for?"

"That chair is designed for rope play. The armrests are designed so the sub can comfortably rest their legs when tied in the spread-eagle position. And on that note, I'm going to bring this tour to an end. I've got a little surprise for your viewing pleasure tonight."

"Surprise? Am I going to like this surprise?"

"I certainly hope so. Come this way, babe."

I opened the carved door and led Kat into the adjoining room. A large sofa sat in front of a wall of glass that was a mirror on the other side. I sat and pulled Kat into my arms.

"Make yourself comfortable, and enjoy the show. Lucy and Jim will be here shortly."

A well-formed man led a tall naked woman with smooth olive skin into the adjoining room and restrained her facing the cross. Lucy's long black hair was pinned above a lapis-blue blindfold giving full access to her flawless back and buttocks. Jim strode over to the display case and made his selection.

"Can they see us?"

"No, they can't. Remember the mirror in the other room? Well, this is the other side of it. We can see and hear them, but they have no idea that we're here although they're both exhibitionists and like to think someone is watching. That's their choice."

"What's that?" Kat pointed to the whip in Jim's hand.

"He chose a deerskin flogger as his warm-up tool because it'll caress her skin and bring her to the pitch of arousal she needs to enjoy the whipping that will follow."

I rolled my thumb over the fabric covering Kat's nipple, and it sprang to attention. Her eyes were fixed on the scene in the next room.

"Hello, Lucy," Jim said.

He trailed the handle of the flogger down the length of

her spine and through the crack in her buttocks. His cock twitched to attention inside the silk pajama pants he wore.

"I hear you're ready for a hard workout today. I hear you need a lesson in control."

"Yes, Master," Lucy said. Her butt twitched in anticipation. "I broke the rules, and I need to be punished."

Jim tucked the flogger under his arm and ran his hands up and down her sides, brushing the soft curve of her breasts. Like Kat's, Lucy's breasts were on the small side, forming a firm mound that fit perfectly in the palms of Jim's hands. As he hefted their weight, she wiggled her ass against him. When he stepped back, his cock was rock hard.

"That will cost you ten strokes, Lucy. Count."

Lucy moaned as Jim expertly laid the lash across the fleshy part of her buttocks. He increased the intensity a notch as he placed the next stroke above the first.

"Count."

This time his voice held a distinct edge of command. Kat sat forward, watching intently.

"Two," Lucy moaned but continued to count the next seven lashes.

"Nine. Please, Master. Please," she said, her voice tight and pleading.

Jim paused a minute, giving her time to cool down. He flexed his muscles and looked at the dusty pink of Lucy's buttocks. Without warning, he cracked the flogger, letting some of the tails slide between her ass cheeks.

"Ten. Oh, thank you, Master, thank you."

Jim rubbed his hand over the pink strokes on her ass before he unclipped the wrist and ankle restraints.

"We're not even near ready for you to come yet, Lucy. Stop begging, or I'll gag you. Do you understand?"

"Yes, Master."

Jim guided Lucy to the armchair where he tied her in

such a way that her legs were spread wide with her glistening vulva exposed and waiting for his touch. He pulled up a stool before pressing a button that raised the chair to eye level.

Jim took a few moments surveying the splendor that lay before him. The lips of Lucy's vulva, full and plump, spread to reveal her clitoris throbbing with the magnitude of her longing. The essence of her desire flowed from her inviting vagina, which was a gorgeous shade of deep red.

I rubbed the silk of my pants against my throbbing cock while I slipped the other hand under Kat's shift and played with her ripe clit. Her legs parted invitingly. I painted her vulva with her flowing juices before brushing the pad of my thumb over the nub that was engorged almost to the point of bursting.

I took my time; this was my favorite part. I loved taking Kat to the edge of the cliff only to pull her back when she started to fall into the abyss.

Kat writhed and moaned as I played between her legs. Flick the clit, now rub the nub. How I yearned to lean down for a long lick and a taste of her succulent female juices. *Delicious.* That would have to wait.

I circled the pads of two fingers just inside the lip of her vagina. Then I sucked on them loudly enough so that Kat could hear over the noises coming from the next room. Her breath caught, and I knew she was mine.

I continued playing with her until a fine sheen of sweat covered her body. When I was content with watching her need, I leaned over and pinched the hard purple nub of her clit. Kat's body shook violently, and she screamed as the contractions of her orgasm rippled through her. I thrust three fingers deep inside her. She shook and bucked as wave after wave of pleasure ripped through her.

"More, Master, more," Lucy begged, drawing our attention back to the action. Jim withdrew the dildo he had buried in her and stood up.

"I warned you, Lucy, but I'm going to give you a choice. Gag or silken lash?"

"Lash," she panted. "Lash, please, Master."

Jim untied the ropes and led her to the spanking bench. He spread her over it facedown and adjusted the restraints. Lucy wiggled her ass in anticipation.

"How many strokes, Lucy?"

"Ten more, Master, then fuck me hard and make me come."

"Uh, uh, uh, Lucy. No topping from the bottom. Let's make that fifteen strokes, and I'll fuck you when and if I'm ready. Now what's a safe word if you want me to stop the whipping but continue the session?"

"Yellow, Master."

"And where are we now?"

"Green, Master."

Jim picked up the silken lash and ran his fingers over the braided tail. His muscles worked in concert while he methodically and accurately placed each stroke where it would give Lucy the maximum pleasure without causing her to orgasm. He paused between each one giving her a chance to use the safe word, but she wiggled her silent appeal for him to continue.

Without a word, Kat lay back against the sofa and spread her legs wide. I slipped out of my pants and positioned myself between her legs. My cock throbbed and threatened to release as I inched my way deep inside her. She sighed with pleasure and thrust back to meet me, causing me to grab each buttock hard to stop the tightening that began in my scrotum.

"Don't move," I hissed. "It's my turn."

I took a few deep breaths, not daring to look down at the

glorious view of her slick opening, and buried my cock deep within. When I'd gained control, I slid my dick out of her cunt, reveling in the way her juices glistened on my bulging purple veins. I eased my way back in to the hilt before reversing the stroke once again.

In and out. In and out. Like a maestro conducting an orchestra, I moved my baton to the music of a symphony only Kat and I could hear. Kat moaned and shook with her need. Her mounting intensity was so beautiful to watch that it took all my strength to stop, but it was time for her second real test. I turned her facedown, kneeling on the sofa. She didn't resist and, in fact, was very compliant as I positioned her. Wasting no time, I slid my hard cock into her wet and inviting cunt. When she pushed back, indicating her need, I slapped her right buttock—hard—with the palm of my hand.

"Don't move."

She went still, and I had her. With each penetration, I slapped the cheeks of her ass just a little bit harder each time.

"More," she pleaded. She moaned louder and louder with each stinging slap.

In and out I slid until my breathing was gasping and ragged. Then, with one loud roar, I plunged inside her and rode her hard. As my orgasm erupted, I wasn't sure whether I heard Kat's screaming or my own. Or both.

I remained deep inside her for several minutes allowing the aftershocks of our orgasms to subside. Then I released her and gathered her in my arms. I caressed and soothed her. I couldn't get enough of her.

Could she be mine?

Wanting her for myself was more than my usual selfish pursuit, and it shook me. For the first time in so many years, it was more important that she want me. Yes, I had my pick of women and frequently indulged in the experience, and that's exactly what it had been—experiencing the excitement of sex. As appealing as that was, Kat was different. She had somehow reached out and touched a part of me.

As much as I was guiding Kat to discover the depth of her sexuality, she was leading me to a part of myself that I lost for so many years. Intimacy.

Brian was right. The door to those hidden feelings had opened, and I struggled to take the first step, knowing there was no turning back. I held her close, desperately hoping this would never end.

20

KATHERINE

Here I am in Connor's bed, satiated from our long weekend and eager to start my first day at Harvard University Press. I woke early, so I lay enjoying the warmth of Connor's body spooning mine, his breath tickling the back of my neck. As I moved to slip out of his embrace without waking him, he let out a tiny snort and tightened his arm around my waist. I smiled and luxuriated in the warmth for a few minutes longer, letting my thoughts drift over the weekend we'd just shared.

The next time I woke, I rolled over and stroked his semi-erect cock—he must have been dreaming of me—

Stop this right this minute, or you'll be late for your first day.

With a sigh, I lifted and placed a gentle kiss on the back of Connor's hand before wiggling out from under his arm. He moaned and snuggled into my pillow. He was so very beautiful, and I couldn't believe how lucky I was to be waking up beside him.

I slipped into my dressing gown and hurried downstairs for a cup of the steaming coffee that awaited me. The coffee maker with a timer was one of the best inventions ever, except for the We-Vibe—

Stop that, Katherine. Get a grip.

I took my coffee to the table and found the double diary sitting at my spot. Yes, I'd been here so often that I now had *my* own spot. I smiled with pleasure as I flipped it open to Connor's latest entry. It was going to be a very good day.

I fixed a fruit smoothie for breakfast and wrote Connor a quick reply before heading out the door. The vice president of Human Resources was at reception waiting for me when I arrived for work. I spent the morning in HR, completing the relevant paperwork and being advised of the company policies and procedures before meeting my new team. I greeted each of my new staff and spent a few minutes letting each of them know how eager I was to be working with so many well-qualified individuals. After assuring them of my desire to have their input at one-on-one meetings during the remainder of the week, the VP took me to my new office and left me to get settled.

The first thing that drew my attention was the floor-to-ceiling window that made up the back wall of the large room. The view of the Don Valley ravine made me smile. The forest formed a backdrop for the river that cut through the rocky crags. I spent a moment enjoying nature's splendor.

The room was about twelve feet by twenty feet, giving it a spacious feel despite the amount of furniture it housed. A red-oak, L-shaped desk with a bubinga wood inlay sat overlooking the rest of the office a few feet in front of the window wall.

Relaxing into the soft leather chair, I ran my fingers over

the polished surface of the desk before bringing them to rest on a small gift box sitting in the middle of the desk blotter. I pulled the card from beneath the ribbon and read.

Like you, this gift is one of a kind made especially for you. Keep it with you at all times to remind you of what matters most. C.

A grin lit my face. I couldn't have been more pleased, surprised, or touched, unless, of course, Connor had been here to give me the gift himself—naked. I carefully lifted the gold foil wrapping. An exquisite gold retractable pen bearing the Cartier logo nestled inside the velvet-lined box. I drew in my breath. The blue ink matched that of the tiny sapphires that formed my name along the length of the barrel.

It was similar to the EnerGel pen I preferred, right down to the soft, blue finger grip near the bottom of the barrel. The ink flowed smoothly on the pad as I wrote my name with delight. How thoughtful of Connor to remember my first day on the job, and how like him to command my attention even at work.

I picked up the receiver to give Connor a call when David Thompson, my new boss, rolled into the room. I slipped the phone back in its cradle.

"I see you're getting settled in. Go ahead and make your call. Don't let me interrupt you."

"Good morning, David. It can wait. Did you need me?"

"No, I just dropped by to welcome you aboard and see how you're doing. What's that you have there?"

He walked around to the back of my chair and leaned over, covering my hand with his before plucking the pen from my grasp. *Rude.*

"What a beautiful piece of work. It looks custom made. Where did you get this?"

"It is a gift from a friend." I had to work hard at controlling the urge to leap up and snatch it out of his hand. *How dare he?*

"That's a pretty special gift. That must be some friend. I collect pens, you know, and this will make an excellent addition to my collection." He slipped the pen into his shirt pocket.

"It's my pen, David, and I'd like it back." I held out my hand. "This isn't negotiable." The steel in my tone matched my words.

"I'm just kidding." He handed me the pen and then rubbed his hand down my arm, making me flinch.

Kidding, my ass. Even if he was the boss, he was a bit too familiar for my liking.

"I can find out where it was made for you, David."

"Well, only if it wouldn't be too much trouble."

I didn't appreciate the sarcasm in his voice. He headed toward the door.

"I've scheduled a meeting of the division heads in the conference room beside my office in one hour. Don't be late, Katherine." He closed the office door behind him.

I stared after him incredulously. I couldn't believe it; he'd actually been pouting. Maybe I overreacted, although the colossal gall of taking the pen unnerved me. The incident made me very uncomfortable, but I decided David meant no harm. He seemed to think it was funny. Maybe it was just a case of bad manners. I was confident I would be able to get things back on the right track with him.

There was a knock at the door, and I hoped that it was David so we could clear the air.

"Come in."

A statuesque, redheaded woman with a wide grin stuck her head around the door.

"Welcome, Katherine. I'm Trudy, and I head up the school division. Would you like to grab a coffee and get the skinny on the tribe before our meeting?"

Grateful for the warm welcome, I grinned in return.

"I'd love that, Trudy. Can you give me a minute to send this email?"

"Sure thing. Take your time."

Trudy perched on the arm of the overstuffed armchair in front of my desk.

From: Kat@xmail.com
To:Connor@magnum.com
Date: Tuesday, September 4
Subject: A Pleasant Surprise

C, thanks so much for the pen. I love it. As instructed, I'll keep it with me. Who knew you were such a romantic. Talk soon. Kat

"Okay, lead the way."

The rest of Tuesday passed uneventfully. Wednesday proved a stimulating day as I met with each of my staff, learning their individual views of the corporate culture. Although they were guarded when it came to talking about David, each of them seemed forthcoming when it came to their feedback on what needed to happen to move the university press into the digital age.

Exhausted yet content, I headed home, eager to call Connor and tell him about my day. I parked the Beemer beside Tim's car. After dropping my briefcase and purse in the mudroom, I went to Tim's home office, expecting to find him there working away. His office was dark, as was the rest of the house.

Puzzled, I went into the kitchen and turned on the light. Tim sat at the kitchen table, head bowed, a half-empty liquor bottle in his hand.

"Tim, what the hell happened? Are you okay?"

I pulled out the chair opposite him, willing my heart to stop the fox-trot of anxiety beating in my chest.

"I'm ruined." Tim kept his head bowed.

"What do you mean, you're ruined? Are you sick? Talk to me, goddammit, Tim. Look at me."

Tim raised bloodshot eyes to meet mine. His look of despair shot straight through me.

"Look, whatever it is, we'll deal with it together. But I can't help you if you don't tell me what this is about." I stopped myself from wincing at my pleading tone.

"I've been suspended from the university for sexual assault."

"What? Who?"

"Sophia." He took a drink from the bottle of what looked like scotch.

"That's impossible. You detest Sophia. You'd better tell me the story from the beginning."

"There isn't much to tell, Katie. I just can't get my head around this. It happened so fast. The president called me into his office just after lunch and told me that I'd been accused of assaulting someone last Thursday night. I, of course, vehemently denied the allegations and insisted on confronting my accuser. I figured whoever it was couldn't possibly stand by their story if we met face-to-face.

"So the president called Sophia and asked her to join us. I can tell you I was some stunned when he said her name.

"Anyway, she came in and sat on his couch and said, 'I'm sorry, Tim, but I had to tell the truth. Why did you do this to me?' And I said, 'What are you talking about, Sophia?'

"She said that I'd asked her to meet to work on the Redwine project last Thursday night. She'd wondered why I'd asked to meet after hours. According to her, I'd said so we wouldn't be interrupted and could get some solid work done.

I was flabbergasted, Katie, and she sat there with this pitiful little girl look and tears rolling down her face.

"Then I said, 'That's a bald-faced lie, and you know it. Why are you lying about this?' And she turned to the president and said, 'I'm not lying, sir. I have proof.' Then she brought out one of those small tape recorders and played what sounded like a recording of our meeting except that the meeting never happened. In it she says some bullshit like, 'I thought we were here to discuss the Redwine project,' and then she's screaming, 'No, Tim, no,' making it sound like I'm taking her against her will. She said she had a video of my rape."

I sat rigid with concentration. This couldn't be happening.

"Then the president excuses her and tells me that given the serious nature of the allegations, he's going to have to suspend me while an investigation is carried out. He asked me to clear out my office and said that the legal department would be in touch. So I cleared out my office and came home." Tim took another drink.

"And started drinking right from the bottle, I see. What is that, scotch? You don't even like scotch."

I reached over, plucked the bottle from his hand, and took a sniff.

"I just needed to get drunk fast, and I figured this would do it."

"And how's that working for you? Not very well by the looks of things. Why didn't you call me?"

"I knew you were in meetings all day, Katie, and it's not like we've been close recently."

"So, you're just going to sit back and take this, Tim? That isn't like you."

"I don't know what I'm going to do. Whatever I do, it's humiliating. And if I fight it, more people will hear that recording, maybe even see the film, and they'll believe I did it. It sounds just like me."

"Well, I don't believe it, Tim, and I bet anyone who knows you won't believe it either. Let's try and figure out why Sophia would be doing this. What does she have to gain?"

"I've thought of nothing else, and I can't come up with anything."

"Well, who can we go to for help? There must be someone at the university who can help sort this out."

"That's the thing, Katie, there's no one I can approach without putting them in a compromising position. You know how it is when things like this happen. The accused becomes a social pariah."

"Let's get something in your stomach besides scotch, and we'll figure this out together."

We sat up most of the night, trying to hash out the problem and find a solution. I wanted to call Connor for help, but Tim was adamant he would handle the situation on his own. Normally, I'd have chastised him for letting his male ego get in the way, but I held my tongue. Around four a.m., Tim reminded me I needed to get some sleep if I was going to work. I tossed around the idea of calling in sick, but that wouldn't be the prudent course of action on my third day.

The lack of sleep and the enormity of Tim's situation hit me as I drove to the office. I sighed deeply and considered rescheduling some of the back-to-back meetings. But it was best to bite the bullet and get through the day so I could get back to help Tim. It took several strong coffees and my first staff meeting to get into the swing of my day, but after that it was smooth sailing. The phone rang as I packed up to leave.

"This is Katherine."

"Thompson here, Katherine. I'd like you to meet me in my office in an hour. I've blocked some time to do some strategic planning for your division."

I almost said no. I was exhausted and wanted nothing more than to go home. But since I'd already started on the wrong foot over the pen, I thought better of it.

As if sensing my hesitation, David said, "And there's a small matter with your personnel file that we need to clear up."

"I'll be there, David." I disconnected and called Tim to let him know I'd be late.

"That's okay, Katie, take all the time you need. I'm much better today and have a plan of action. We'll talk when you get home."

Tim reminded me to get something to eat, and we disconnected.

Trudy stuck her head in the office and asked me to join her for a drink.

"I wish I could, Trudy, but David's asked me to meet to do some strategic planning. I'll have to take a rain check."

"That's odd," Trudy said. "That little shit never works late. I don't know what's up with that, but I'd watch him if I were you."

We agreed to meet the next day after work.

"Sounds good, ta ta for now." Trudy waved and was gone.

The phone rang, and Connor's number showed on the display.

"Hey."

"Hi. How's it going? Can we meet for a quick drink? I heard there are some rumblings at Royal U."

"I can't tonight, Connor. David's set up a strategic planning meeting tonight, and he says there's some problem with my personnel file. As for Royal U, Tim's handling it."

"Really? And how's he doing that?"

"Listen, I can't talk right now. How about I give you a call later."

"Come over instead. I need to see you tonight."

"I can't, C. Tim needs me. I need to be there for him."

The silence was deafening and Connor's withdrawal like a physical blow.

"I may not be here when you call. I've got to go." He hung up.

Annoyed, I called back, but the call rang through to his voice mail. I barely had time to grab a quick sandwich from the vending machine before it was time to meet with David. As my heels echoed on the marble flooring, I marveled at how quickly the place emptied out in the evening. Was everyone who worked here a clock-watcher? The hallway was dark as I made my way past the executive suites to David's office. David waved me through his open door as I approached. The smell of liquor wafted off him as I walked by.

"I heard you coming," he said with a huge smile. "Come in. Come in. Have a seat."

David motioned toward a couch and two large armchairs that sat in front of a fully stocked bar. I perched on the edge of one of the chairs. He went behind the bar and took two glasses from the shelf.

"You said there's a problem with my personnel file, David?"

"Let's not worry about that right now. Let's have a toast to your success."

"I don't drink and drive. Thanks anyway."

"Are you really such a tight-ass? Come on, it's one drink to celebrate. It will be long worn off by the time we're done."

He came around the bar and handed me a glass with a couple of inches of an amber liquid in it.

"Here's to you. Bottoms up."

He raised his glass and tossed it back. I did the same and grimaced. It tasted bloody awful. I set the glass down on the coffee table.

"Ah, that's better. Now let me tell you about some of the plans that I have for your division."

"I'd rather clear up the problem with my personnel file first if you don't mind."

I took my new pen and notebook from my briefcase and leaned forward.

"I do mind. That little matter can wait a few minutes. Let's start with me giving you some of the history of your division."

He launched into what seemed like a regurgitation of the information I'd studied when they'd recruited me, but I hid my impatience.

Ten minutes or so went by, and I felt a little dizzy. I stood up, and the pen and notebook slipped to the floor. *Something is very wrong.*

"Excuse me." I stumbled toward the door.

"Are you okay, Katherine? You don't look very well."

"I just need a bio break."

I reached the door and grappled with the handle. *Why won't it open?* David came up behind me and put his arms around me.

"Ah, that's better, my pet. Now you're ready for us to talk about that little problem with your personnel file."

"Let go of me."

I tried to shove him, but my limbs turned to jelly. Adrenaline spiked through me, prickling my fingers, and my breath came fast as panic swamped me.

"What have you done to me?" I wasn't sure whether I'd said the words out loud.

"Nothing compared to what I'm going to do to you. Word has it that you like to fuck around, which is fine with me as long as you're willing to share the goods. Don't worry, nobody has to know what a little vixen you are. I like that in a woman. Trust me, this could be mutually beneficial."

I screamed and grabbed the door handle. David slammed me into the door and pulled my arms behind my back. Before I could move, he'd slapped handcuffs on me.

Oh God, please God, don't let this happen again. The rapes that took place in my teen years flashed through my mind.

"Scream again, bitch, and I'll hurt you. You might like that, eh? My sources tell me that you like it rough."

David strong-armed me over to the desk. I tried to get away but couldn't seem to make my limbs work or figure out my surroundings. He shoved my face onto the desk, hard.

"Don't move, bitch, and quit pretending to be such a prude. We both know what you really are."

My ears were ringing, but it sounded as if he undid his belt and slid down his zipper.

"It's not like this hasn't happened before. You act like you're so high and mighty. Well let's see how high and mighty you are with your pants down. He hiked up my skirt and ripped my panties down around my thighs. He leaned over me, and the smell of his liquor-laden breath made me gag. He grabbed my hair and jerked my head back.

"Don't make one sound. Behave, and you'll get away with a good spanking. I know you like that." He laughed.

"Don't . . . do . . . this."

Even though terror coursed through every pore in my body, I managed to squeeze the words out. What was immobilizing me? The memories rushing back or whatever he put in my drink?

"That's it. Pretend you don't like to be humiliated. I like that."

He slipped off his belt and then held me down with one hand. I was frozen with fear.

"Now count, bitch. I hear that's how you like it."

He struck me full force across the thighs with his belt. A

silent scream reverberated through my head, but I said nothing. He hit me again.

"Count."

"I. Will. Not."

Tears coursed down my face, but I managed to force the words out.

"Fine, then don't count, but you're leaving me no choice. I'll just keep strapping you until you do. You've got to learn who's boss here, you little slut."

I tried to keep track of the number of times he hit me but lost count somewhere around thirty.

"Still not ready to count, eh, you little bitch?"

He pulled my head up by the hair and stared into my face. I screamed. He slammed my head back onto the desk and renewed the beating with even more vigor.

"Now count or I'll—"

A loud bang pushed back the descending darkness. Suddenly David's weight lifted off me, and I slid onto the floor.

"What the fuck?" David's panicked voice. Another bang.

Mercifully, blackness descended.

21

CONNOR

Darkness surrounded me as I battled with an inner thought that threatened to elude me. A sliver of ice had pierced my heart when Kat told me she chose to spend time with Tim over me.

Grow up, Connor. You love her compassion.

But logic wouldn't shake the foothold of funk that gripped me. Then it came to me.

I loved her, and *I* wanted to be her first choice.

A fist of fear held my guts in a vise grip. *I can't love her. I can't lose again.*

All the hurt I fought so hard to escape came rushing back, tearing down the self-imposed walls that protected me. Reality stared me straight in the face. No amount of denial would change the fact. I loved her.

The phone display lit up with Brian's cell ID. I punched the speakerphone.

"What?"

"Katherine's been hurt. She's drifting in and out of consciousness, like she's drugged or something. And when she comes to, she starts fighting like a wildcat. I don't think I should drive while she's in this condition," Brian said.

Terror washed over me as Kat's moans came through the speakerphone.

"Goddammit. I'm on my way. Just stay put. Where are you?"

"The parking lot of Harvard U Press."

"Don't move. I'll be right there. I'll call you back from the car."

I raced to the parking garage and jumped into my Bentley SUV. I punched the button on the Bluetooth hands-free device and said, "Call Brian." The disembodied voice replied, "Call Brian Farrell, calling."

"Dial, goddammit. Dial."

Brian answered on the first ring.

"What happened?"

"Thompson attacked her."

"Oh God." I gripped the steering wheel to stop my hands from shaking and fought to control the panic that shot through me. "How is she now?"

"She seems a little more lucid, but she's curled into a fetal position and goes rigid if I touch her. I've told her who I am, but I'm not sure she hears me."

"Are you on speaker?"

"Yes."

"Kat, it's Connor. Hang in there, babe. I'm on my way. It won't be long now."

Kat said something, but I couldn't make out what it was.

"Did she say something, Bri? What did she say?"

"She called your name, Con. That's all I can get her to say."

"How badly hurt is she? Should we take her to the hospital?"

"I don't—"

"Nooooo. No. No."

Kat's screams sent a chill down my spine. "Okay, okay, Kat. No hospital. I'll take you home. I'm almost there. Hang on."

I swore as I dodged in and out of the traffic on the Don Valley Parkway. Even at this hour, the highway was busy. Metro Toronto never slept.

The next ten minutes felt like ten hours as I fought to control my rage and focus on how to help Kat. *That fat bastard. I'll kill him.* I shook my head. Right now, my priority was to help Kat. I pulled into the driveway and stopped beside Brian's vehicle. We met in the space between the two SUVs.

"How is she? Let me see her."

"She seemed to calm down once you told her you would take her home. She's still curled up on the back seat."

"How bad is it? What did that fat fuck do to her?"

"From what I heard over the transmitter in the pen, he beat her. You were right not to trust him. I headed over as soon as she screamed, but it took me a few minutes to break in. He had the place locked up like the Dominion Bank vault.

"He'd handcuffed her and was beating her with his belt. Her forehead is bruised, and she's got welts on her buttocks and thighs. He broke the skin in some areas, but from what I could see, she doesn't need medical attention."

"At least not physically," I murmured. I ran my fingers through my hair.

"She's one determined woman, Con. She could have made it easier on herself. He demanded she count as he strapped her, but she refused."

"Thank God we gave her that pen. I don't even want to think about what could have happened if you hadn't stopped him. Where is he now?"

"I knocked him out and handcuffed him to his desk. Then

I disconnected the landline and took his cell phone. I figured it was poetic justice to use the same handcuffs he used on Katherine."

Brian handed a BlackBerry to Connor. "You might find the last message of interest."

Connor scrolled through the phone until he found the message. It read: *Make it tonight, Davy. Follow my instructions to the letter. Don't screw it up if you know what's good for you.*

"You've got to be fucking kidding me. That's Cecile's cell number. Why that fucking little bitch."

Brian's massive fist closed around my arm before I could throw the phone. "You don't want to do that, Con. It's the only proof we have that she's involved."

"Somehow I think there's more, but that can wait. I've got to take Kat home."

I opened the back door of Brian's SUV and crawled in beside her. I turned on the overhead light and touched her shoulder. She went rigid and squeezed her eyelids tightly shut. I left my hand resting on her shoulder. "Kat, babe, it's Connor. You're okay now. I'm here. Open your eyes and look at me."

I stroked her hair as some of the tension left her body. "That's it, Kat. Now look at me."

She opened her eyes and looked at me, those beautiful brown eyes wide with shock and fear. "He beat me, Connor. He beat me just like my father used to. Why would he beat me?"

Great sobs racked her body. I sat back and pulled her head into my lap. I stroked her head and shoulders. I was crippled by frustration and fury at my inability to take away her pain. "It's going to be all right, babe. It's going to be all right." I held her until her sobs died down to sniffles. "Come on. Let's get you home. Can you walk?"

"I think so, but it hurts."

Brian and I helped her into the back seat of my Bentley. She managed to crawl in on her side, wincing as her backside and thighs made contact with the cool leather. I climbed in behind the wheel, and Brian pushed the door closed. I pushed the button that lowered the automatic tinted windows and looked at my friend, the one constant in my life.

"I'll take care of it, Con."

I nodded once and drove away.

I pulled into the driveway of Kat's condominium townhome, got out, and rang the bell. Tim answered, looking unkempt and unshaven. He smelled of scotch.

"What the hell are you doing here?"

"Kat's been hurt."

"What do you mean Katie's been hurt? Is she in the hospital? Let's go. I'll just get my jacket."

"She's not in the hospital. She's in my car. You'll need to pull yourself together, Tim." My tone was ruthless. "Whatever you're dealing with doesn't matter right now. You need to be here for Kat. I need your help. I think she should go to the hospital, but she refuses. I don't want to traumatize her further. I need you to help me convince her."

"Okay, you're right. Let's get her in, and you can tell me what happened."

"I'd better tell you now before we get her. She's sleeping right now. I think she was drugged. I don't know how she'll react if she hears it again."

I quickly explained what had happened before we walked to the SUV. I opened the rear door and Tim climbed in and knelt beside Kat. When he touched her shoulder, her eyes flew open, and she started to scream.

"Katie, it's me. It's Tim. Let's get you to the hospital."

"Tim," Katherine moaned. "No, Tim. No hospital. No police."

"Let's get her in the house and have a look," I said. "Then we can decide whether she needs to go to the hospital."

I got the doors while Tim picked her up and carried her into the house and up into her bedroom. We took her skirt off amidst her groans of pain and protest. I helped her climb onto the bed where we examined her wounds.

"I just want to sleep," she murmured.

I couldn't stand to see her in such pain. I gazed out the window into the inky darkness of the suburban night.

"We'll be right back, babe," Tim said. He draped the comforter over her.

"May I see you downstairs?" he hissed at me.

He marched down the stairs and into the kitchen. He took two glasses from the cupboard, poured from the open bottle on the table, and shoved one glass toward me. We downed our drinks and sat at the table.

"I still think we should take her to the hospital, but I know if I do that she'll never forgive us. She told me once that she'd never allow herself to be the subject of ridicule again."

"What do you mean, again?" I asked.

Tim looked at me in amazement. "You really don't know, do you? She was raped several times when she was a teenager, first by her bastard neighbor. He attacked her with a knife. From the little she told me, the nurses and police treated her like she'd asked for it."

"Bastards."

Tim stared at me, and then put his head in his hands. I reached for the bottle and poured myself another drink. We sat in silence for a few moments.

"I don't know what to do here, Connor. I'm afraid this is going to ruin Katie. It took her years of therapy to get over those assaults. *I* don't even know the details. She's never been able to talk much about it. And then there's the mess at the university."

"Tell me about what happened at the university."

I sat while Tim told me about Sophia's accusations and his suspension.

"The worst of it is that I can't get my head around why she'd do this to me. And now this. I'm going to get the bastard who did this to Katie." Tim was full of bravado. "But first, I've got to get her out of here and take her someplace where she feels safe and can heal from this."

He got up and paced the floor. "Fuck, I wish I could think."

I pushed aside the uncharitable thoughts I had in response to his tirade.

"I'll be the one to help her, but first I need to take care of some business here, so I could use your help. I have a place where I can take her where she'll be safe. How long will it take you to pack a few things for her?"

Tim stared at me then shook his head.

"You're full of surprises, aren't you, Connor. Katie's needs come first right now, so I'll help you although I'd be less than honest if I didn't tell you that I wish it were me."

I turned, unsure of where he was going with this.

"What do you mean?"

"It means I surrender. I've been fighting for her love, but I've finally realized that she'll never love me the way she loves you even if she hasn't admitted that to herself yet. Sadly, she'll never look at me the way she looks at you."

"But she chose to be with you last night."

"No, Connor, she chose to help me last night. That's very different. Katie is an incredibly loyal friend, and she'll always leap to help when her loved ones are in need. You should know that about her. If you continue to be this self-absorbed, you'll lose her. Again."

His words stung. He was right. I had been a self-absorbed asshole. I had no idea what to say to this man who loved my Kat as much as I did, so I simply said, "Thank you for this."

"No thanks necessary. I'd do anything for her. If it means losing her to you, so be it. I'm not doing this for you, Connor. Don't ever make me regret it. Katie will always be important to me."

I nodded and downed the last of my drink. I understood.

"Do you have anything to help the bruising?"

"Katie has a whole arsenal of herbal remedies, so I'm sure I'll find something."

"All right, good. Find some and put it on her bruises. Then pack some of her things. I'll be back in a few hours."

"What are you going to do?"

"I'm going to make this all go away."

He followed me back to Kat's bedroom. She lay curled on her side, her face still wet with tears. My anguish at her pain hardened into a certain resolve. Cecile would pay for this.

I leaned down and kissed Kat gently on the forehead.

"You're safe now. No one will ever hurt you again. You'll be okay. I have some business to take care of, so Tim's here to take care of you. I'll be with you just as soon as I can be."

I paused for a beat before brushing my lips against hers.

"I won't be long, Kat."

Kat smiled weakly and reached for my hand.

"Don't get lost."

The next morning, Sophia Drake opened her office and hung her coat on the coat rack in the corner. She dropped her purse and briefcase on the desk and picked up the receiver. She punched in a few numbers and stood with her back to the desk, tapping her foot.

"Okay, I've done everything that you told me to do. Tim's gone, and the campus police took my cell phone and my day planner. Now when do I get the job? Hello, Hello?"

She turned and yelped, dropping the receiver. I stood with my index finger pressing the phone's release button.

"Sit down, Ms. Drake." I sat down in the chair opposite the desk. She stood there, staring at me. "That's not a request. Sit down."

Sophia sat and fidgeted with a lock of her hair. "Mr. McClane. How did you get in here?"

"I'd strongly advise you not to talk until I tell you to. Now, I'm going to give you one opportunity to tell me the truth. I know what went on with Tim and with your creative accounting here at the university. I need to find out who set Tim up."

I got up and stood behind Sophia's chair and pushed it closer to the desk. My voice was deceptively quiet. She melted into the chair, caught between fear and sobbing pitifully. Some might have taken pity on her; after all, she was just a stupid pawn driven by greed. Unfortunately, for her, I wasn't one of them.

"Before you answer, let me give you a piece of advice. Don't lie to me, and don't treat me like an idiot. I know enough about you to make your life a living hell, but I'm not going to do that. You know why? Because you're not worth the effort. You're just a fool who doesn't have the sense to know when you're in over your head.

"I'm not after you. Tell me the truth, and there's a plane ticket, a suitcase with the things you'll need, and more than enough money for you to make a fresh start."

I pointed to a bag sitting on the edge of her conference table. "Now, who set Tim up?"

She hung her head, unable to look at me. "It was your fiancée. It was Cecile," she babbled. "She said Katherine and

Tim were setting you up and were after your money. If they got enough on you, they could screw up your life. She said she needed to get them out of your lives. I'm sorry. I'm sorry." Huge crocodile tears slid down Sophia's face.

"I can't believe you bought into such a crock of shit. What makes you think she's my fiancée?"

"She told me, and she knew so much about you."

I stared at her, cold and hard. "You have exactly one hour. That should give you enough time to write your letter of resignation and get out of town. Be sure to include all details about your pathetic little attempt at framing Dr. Bancroft."

I slid the envelope with the money and a business card across the desk toward her. "I'll arrange to have your house sold and your belongings put in storage. When you decide on your new location, call this number, and they'll ship your stuff to you. Take my advice and find yourself someplace warm to live like South America, and don't ever set foot on this continent again.

"Look at me, and know that I mean what I say. Wherever you are, I'll be watching, and if you ever interfere in my life again, I'll destroy you. That's a promise, Ms. Drake."

I shut the door quietly as I left.

I sat watching the monitors in the surveillance room at the Amber Star Hotel as Cecile tried to gain entry to her suite. She fumbled with her key and then kicked the door. What had I ever seen in her?

She reached in her purse and pulled out her cell phone. "Send someone up here to let me in my suite. The lock isn't working."

She listened for a moment. "No, I said send someone up here."

After another beat of silence, she said, "Oh, for Christ's sake."

She stomped off toward the elevator.

I switched the view to the camera in the reception area of the hotel's security offices. Within moments, Cecile strode off the elevator and up to the young woman sitting at the desk.

"My name is Cecile, and I understand that Brian left a room key here for me."

The young woman looked startled. "I'm sorry, no one left a key here, Miss. Have you tried the front desk?"

"I don't need to try the front desk, you little twit. I own this hotel. Now get Brian for me."

"Connor owns this hotel," Brian said from behind her. "Would you step this way, please, Cecile?"

He pointed toward the door of one of the meeting rooms that opened off the reception area of the hotel's corporate offices. Cecile opened her mouth to speak and then huffed and marched into the room.

Brian followed her and closed the door behind them. "Have a seat."

"I don't want a fucking seat. I want the key to my suite."

"Connor asked me to give you a message."

Brian slid an envelope across the meeting table. Cecile snatched it up and ripped it open. She opened a single page with a highlighted section on it. "What the fuck is this?"

"I believe it's self-explanatory."

It was a page from her partnership agreement with me that detailed what would happen if she broke the nondisclosure agreement or in any way conducted herself in a manner that could bring harm to me or my holdings. The highlighted clause read: "In the event that any part of this agreement is not upheld by Cecile DePoulignac, it is the intent of the parties that all provisions of this agreement shall be null and void. The partner loses access to all properties and forfeits all gifts." A yellow sticky note attached to the page read: "You were warned. Now, you are nothing to me."

I watched her reaction on the monitor at my desk as I zoomed the security camera in on Cecile's face but felt no satisfaction as the color drained from it.

"He can't do this to me."

"He can and has. The money for your shares is in your private account, and he has a jet waiting to take you wherever you'd like to go. I've taken the liberty of cleaning out your suite. Your belongings are on board."

"Let me see him. He's here, isn't he? You wouldn't be doing this if he wasn't nearby." She turned toward the door. "He's not going to get away with this. I know his dirty little secrets. You don't think I played his dirty little games without making sure I protected myself, do you?"

She looked toward the camera in the ceiling. "Do you, Connor, you bastard?"

Brian picked up a newspaper and shoved it toward her. The headline read:

Publishing executive, David Thompson, disappears without a trace. Foul play or misadventure?

I leaned forward, watching the monitor intently. Her knuckles turned white as she gripped the sides of the chair in front of her. A tight little smile flitted across my lips.

"Are you going to go quietly, or do I need to have you escorted out?" Brian's cold brown eyes brooked no argument.

"You tell him he hasn't seen the last of me," Cecile spat. She slammed the door as she left.

A few minutes later, Brian joined me, a look of weary resignation on his face. "Well, that was pleasant. We're going to have to keep a close eye on her, Con. She loves you in her own twisted way, and that means she's even more dangerous. I'm wondering if she's behind the takeover bid that's brewing."

"Bluster and bravado. I have no doubt she'll find some snake pit to settle into. When the word gets out, no one will give her the time of day. You worry too much, Bri. I've got to go. I've left Kat alone for too long as it is. Is the plane ready?"

"It will be by the time you hit the airport. I've called the housekeeper, and the house will be stocked and ready when you land." He turned to go, then turned back. "Oh, and Con?"

I looked up from the papers I was stuffing into my brief-case. *What now?*

"What's up?"

"Don't be afraid to show her your love. I know you, Con, and life is too short. Take the leap. It's time, Connor."

His words reverberated through my head all the way back to Kat's house.

We were on the way to the airport within the hour. I settled Kat in the bedroom at the back of the jet and went to the cockpit. I gave the pilot instructions to take us to my private estate in the south of France and then returned and drew her into my arms.

"Are you okay?"

"I'm better now that you're here. I thought he was going to kill me. I was so scared, C."

She tucked her face into my chest, her tears soaking through my shirt. New anger surged through me. I pulled her closer, careful not to touch her bruises. Kat rarely cried, and the depth of her sobbing wrenched my heart. I leaned my head back against the headboard and closed my eyes.

"I should have been there. I'm so very sorry this happened to you. I'll never let anyone hurt you again."

I held her until the sobs subsided and let the myriad of emotions roll through me—love, fear, excitement, anger, anticipation, and more. *Take the leap. Take the leap.*

"I love you, Kat."

I squeezed my eyes shut even tighter. My heart pounded in my chest. It was new for me to use those words, but it felt so right to say them. Kat stared at me, eyes wide, but said nothing.

"I've never said those words before, not even to Meredith."

Kat rested a small hand on my thigh. Compassion shone behind the hurt in her eyes. "It's okay, C. I know it hurts you to talk about her."

In that instant, I realized that it didn't hurt anymore. All that remained of the pain I'd run so hard from was fond memories of my first love. Meredith had shown me just how beautiful true love could be. With Kat I was learning that the pain was worth the experience.

"She was my first love, and it almost destroyed me when she was killed. I've spent my time running from any real emotion ever since. But I can't run from you." I squeezed my eyes shut as they filled with tears. Where the fuck had that come from?

"I love you, Connor. I think I always have."

I let out the breath I'd been holding. A tear slid down my cheek. Joy joined the mélange of feelings swirling through my heart. I opened my eyes and almost drowned in the pool of love mirrored in hers.

"Stay with me always, Kat. Be mine. I can't promise you I won't be moody anymore or that I won't make mistakes, but with you by my side, everything is possible."

"No regrets, C. I'm yours. Always and forever. I think I've known that from the beginning."

She poked me in the chest. I looked at her through the dampness in my eyes. She grinned through her tears.

"To eternity and beyond."

Cecile instructed the taxi driver to make one stop on the way to the airport. She strode into the Magnum offices, walked past the security guard, and went straight up to the executive offices. The man at the head of the conference table looked up in surprise when she burst into his office.

"Ah, this isn't a good time, Cecile."

Cecile looked at the three other people sitting around the conference table and pointed toward the door. "Get the fuck out."

They scrambled to their feet, grabbed their papers and cases, and ran out the door. The security guard ran in and stopped abruptly.

"It's all right, George. I've got it under control," the man said. "Close the door behind you." After George closed the door, he turned to Cecile. "Now what is this about?"

"I need you to call him right now. He said you'd connect him any time without question if I asked."

"But—"

"Without question. I don't think you want to fuck with me or him right now."

He opened and closed his mouth, then walked over to the desk and picked up the phone. He dialed and listened for a few moments and then said, "It's Cecile DePoulignac calling." He listened for another beat before handing her the receiver. She snatched it.

"I'm ready to help you take Connor down. Bring me in."

Thank you for reading *Tempt Me*! I hope you love Connor and Kat. Find out who tries to steal Kat's heart in *Tame Me*, the final book in the Masquerade Club series...

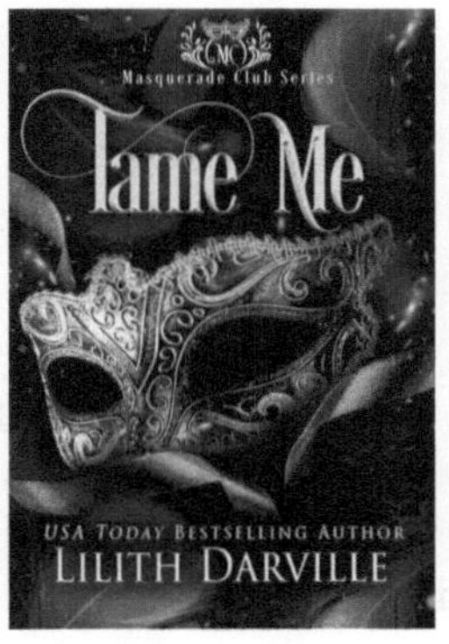

Chapter One
Connor

Life has a way of fooling us into thinking something good is just around the corner. It's like in those feel-good movies Kat loves to watch. You know the ones—where girl meets boy, they fall in love, and live happily ever after. Sure, they have a fight and break up, but that's because they need to have great make-up sex thrown into the mix. Of course, there are all those movies that show the shiny side of living, the bowl of cherries. Like Forrest Gump, who compares life to all the interesting choices in a box of chocolates.

That's the mood I was in as I cruised around the kitchen making dinner for my Kat, who was due back any moment from taking her ex, Tim, to the airport. I'd been on an emergency conference call with Magnum's US Real Estate Division when Kat sashayed into my office pointing wildly at her watch.

"I'm putting you on hold for a moment. I'll be right back." I pressed the hold button and smiled, trying to hide my impatience. Katherine King, the love of my life, wasn't someone you could ignore when she was on a mission, and she wasn't the type to interrupt without a good reason.

"What's up?" I asked.

"You've forgotten, haven't you?"

I looked at her blankly. "Forgotten?"

She walked behind my chair, put her arms around my neck, and kissed the top of my head. "The airport."

"Oh shit." I had forgotten. I'd agreed to drive Kat's ex-turned-friend, Tim, to the airport while she cooked dinner. We were expecting my best friend, Brian Farrell, and his lovely wife, Asha, for dinner and drinks. It was the first time Kat was formally meeting them, and she wanted everything to be perfect.

"I'm sorry, babe, but I can't leave this call. We could get him a cab."

"I'd rather not. How about I take him, and you start dinner?"

And that's how I found myself buzzing around the kitchen, cooking up a storm, with *Led Zeppelin II* cranked to full volume. Oh, and I should really mention that Kat's the cook in the family, but I make a mean kitchen assistant. That's probably the only place where I'm good at following instructions.

I was well into making the perfect marinade when that box of chocolates with questionable outcome reared its head in the form of the beautiful Asha Farrell.

"Hey, you're early. Grab a seat, and I'll get you a glass of wine."

Before I could make good on my offer, Asha walked over and put her arm around me. "Connor . . ."

I planted a quick kiss on the top of her head. "Good to see you, Ash. Where's Brian? Wait a minute. Let me turn this down." I used the remote to lower the volume on "You Shook Me."

"You'd better sit down," Asha said.

I was so engrossed in my cooking it took me several more seconds to realize there was something very wrong about her affect. My heart skipped a beat. *Something's happened to Brian!*

"What's up? Is everything okay with Bri?"

"Brian's at the hospital—"

"What?" Panic surged through me, and my heart was kicking the hell out of my rib cage.

"Brian's fine, but there's been an accident. I'm sorry, Connor, but Kat's been hurt."

"That's not possible. She's taken Tim to the airport. She'll be coming through the door any second. There must be some mistake." I'd always prided myself on my ability to face reality, and here I was babbling my denial just like your average Joe.

"Her car went off the road. Tim was pronounced dead at the scene. By the time we arrived, the ambulance was leaving to take Kat to the hospital in Cannes. Brian went with her."

How I had the presence of mind to shut off the stove and remove my apron, I do not know. A part of me detached and orchestrated my actions without my knowledge. Asha hugged me even tighter. I tried to struggle out of her grasp, but she was like a statue holding me in her clutches. It was amazing someone so small could have so much power.

"So she's okay, right? What is it? A broken arm or something? Please tell me she's all right, Asha!"

"She was unconscious, and she was bleeding—"

"Bleeding?" My voice was strident with horror. "From where? How much? For God's sake, talk to me."

"Her head. Brian says she has a head injury and is unconscious. That's all I know. He'll stay with her until we get there."

I ran to the door, grabbing my set of keys to the Cayenne before I remembered that Kat had taken it to drive Tim to the airport. *Shit!* I was about to throw them across the room when Asha took them gently but firmly from my shaking hand.

"I'll drive you to the hospital, Connor."

I sat slumped in the passenger seat of the Mercedes SUV. Despair enveloped me. It was during moments like this that I understood those people who sit in a corner and rock. I could not and *would not* lose my Kat now that I had her back in my life.

The fifteen-minute drive to the hospital in Cannes took an eternity. I stared out the window, frozen with shock, seeing nothing. Asha remained calm and cool as she navigated the late afternoon traffic.

"How did this happen? How were you even there?"

"We were driving in from the airport when we came across the accident. I have no idea how it happened. We recognized your Cayenne and stopped. Brian talked his way onto the ambulance using his Canadian Special Forces creds. He'll make sure she's well taken care of, Connor. You know that."

I slumped further in my seat, unable to move or even think coherently. How the fuck could this have happened?

"Who hit them?"

"What do you mean?"

"I mean, was there another car involved? Kat is a good driver, so someone must have hit them."

"There was no other vehicle. The car went off the road."

"That's not possible. The road from Miramar to Nice is one of the safest roads in the world."

Asha was quiet for a beat.

"We took the scenic mountain route, and I guess Kat had the same idea. There's a gazillion hairpin turns on that route. You know that, Connor."

"Details, I need details."

"It happened on the hairpin loop just out of Spéracèdes."

"Kat is too careful to lose control of the car. That's just not possible."

"Maybe there was a mechanical failure."

"I don't get it, Ash. The Cayenne is new, and we just had it serviced. If this was mechanics, I'll sue the bastards. And what about guard rails?"

"There's a slight curb of raised brick, but it looked like the Cayenne crashed right through it."

"Kat would never be going fast enough to crash through a curb. Was that asshole Tim driving? If he wasn't dead already, I'd kill him."

Asha remained quiet and let me rant. She pulled up in front of the hospital. I jumped out of the car and rushed to the emergency department where Brian stood.

"Here's her husband now," he said. "Connor, this is Dr. Desmarais, the neurologist assigned to Katherine's case. Doctor, Connor McClane."

Husband? That was my cue to follow his lead.

"Where's my wife?" I demanded.

The doctor ran a hand through a shock of jet-black hair. He looked as if he was ready to drop from exhaustion, which didn't boost my confidence one little bit.

"We've taken her down for an MRI, Mr. McClane. We need to ascertain the extent of the head injury she's sustained. It's a great concern that she's still unconscious." The doctor spoke flawless English with only the touch of an accent.

"When will you know something?"

"In many of these cases, it's a wait and see. We should have the results from the preliminary tests in a few hours."

"Tests? What other tests have you done?" I held back my scream of frustration and rubbed the back of my neck. It was everything I could do to keep from leaping down the man's throat. The logical part of my brain reminded me that to him she was just another patient. Every other part of me wanted to shake him into realizing just how important Kat was.

"We've done an EEG, and it shows plenty of brain activity, so that's a good sign. The X-ray doesn't show significant swelling or bleeding, and her skull is intact. The MRI will give us more detailed information about the extent of her injury. After that, we'll run a CT scan, and that will give us a complete picture."

"So, what's the bottom line here?"

Dr. Desmarais sighed. "As of now, all we know is that she suffered a head injury. She may have a concussion, but symptoms are not immediately apparent. We'll know more after she regains consciousness and we assess the damage."

"What kinds of symptoms can we expect to see?" Brian asked.

Common symptoms after a concussive traumatic brain injury are headache, amnesia, and confusion.

"Amnesia?" I asked, hackles raised.

"Amnesia usually involves the loss of memory regarding anything related to the traumatic incident. However, in some cases, the patient will have impaired ability to recall past events and previously familiar information. The memory loss can extend back decades. The good news is the patient usually always remembers who they are, although they may not recognize people who have been significant in their lives. They—"

"Doctor, how about we deal with one thing at a time,"

Brian said, knowing I was on the brink of losing it. "When will we be able to see Katherine?"

"She should be finished with the testing and admitted in a couple of hours." The doctor looked at his pager as it went off. "You're welcome to wait in the family lounge in the neurology wing. That's where she'll be admitted. I'll look for you there when I know anything else." He turned and hurried off down the hall.

"Fuck! This can't be happening," I said. Fear bubbled through me like lava about to erupt from a volcano. Brian grabbed my elbow and steered me toward the door Asha was entering. She stopped abruptly, turned, and went back out.

"Come on, man. Let's go get something to eat and grab a coffee. Asha will bring the car around."

"I don't feel like eating, and I'm not leaving Kat," I said like the petulant child I wished I could become. That way, I'd have an excuse for the temper tantrum I wanted to throw. I jerked my arm out of his grasp.

"Then don't eat. But we're getting out of here for a bit to clear our heads. There's nothing more we can do at the moment."

"But—"

"We should at least pick up some things Kat will need when she wakes up. You heard what the doctor said. Kat will be having tests for the next couple of hours and pacing up and down the halls isn't going to help. I gave the nurses my cell number, so they can reach us if anything happens."

When we got back to the villa, Brian and Asha insisted I eat something, so I choked down some soup and several quarts of coffee while they each ate something more substantial. I remained in a daze, tormenting myself with a thousand what-if scenarios. One prevailed—what if my Alley Kat died?

After what could have been two minutes or two hours, Asha trundled me off to the car, suitcase in tow. As she pulled out of the drive, it dawned on me that Brian wasn't with us.

"Isn't Bri coming?"

"He's going to check out the Cayenne. He made a couple of calls, and one of his contacts got him access."

I grunted and lay my head back on the headrest. Brian knew his cars, and if anyone could find out what had happened, it was him. There was no one I trusted more.

We checked in at the nurses' station on the neurology ward. A nurse led us to Kat's room, advising that Kat remained unconscious. And there she lay, her tiny form dwarfed by the bed, a single IV trailing from her left arm. A mass of tangled black curls framed her still face. *She needs you.* As my heart tore, the mantle of calm control finally dropped over me. I would not allow myself to wallow in any more pain. I would do whatever it took to bring Kat through this. I brushed a stray curl and ran my fingers down her arm. Her hand seemed so small in mine, reminding me that she needed me strong.

"I don't care what it takes, I want the best neurologist in the world, and I want him here now."

"I'm on it," Asha said. She knew better than to argue with me.

I sat with Kat and began my vigil.

"I'm here, Kat. I don't know if you can hear me, but know that I love you and I'm not going anywhere." I stared at her, numb and silent, as a lone tear ran down my face.

End of Sample

To continue reading, be sure to pick up *Tame Me* at your favorite retailer.

ALSO BY LILITH DARVILLE

Wicked Angels Series

Dark Urban Fantasy Romance

Interconnected Standalones

Follow a team of fallen angels as they fight against human trafficking and navigate the blurred lines between good and evil. Set in Pandemonium, a notorious club where they blend in with humans, this heart-pounding series will leave you breathless. Don't miss out on this intense and spicy journey of redemption and second chances.

.

Rogue Angels Series

Dark Urban Fantasy Romance

Completed Series

Rogue Angels is a twist retelling of the Snow White fairytale. Enjoy an adventure with fated mates, midlife crisis, and evil demons. This story includes themes of love, sacrifice, and self-discovery.

.

Sexy Sins Afterlife Retreat Series

Paranormal Reverse Harem Romance

Completed Series

Warning: This series has one strong woman and four dangerously sexy immortal men. She's been their fated mate in every life they've lived and they refuse to live one without her. Read this series if you like why choose romance with a paranormal twist and hunky guys times four!

.

Masquerade Club Series

Dark Contemporary Romance

Completed Series

A contemporary saga with a side dish of spice and a second chance romance for two people you'll never forget. The Masquerade Club is exclusive and available only for the ultra-rich where all your dreams and fantasies come true. Join the party and fall in love with Connor and Katherine in this angst-ridden suspense-filled series.

.

ABOUT THE AUTHOR

Lilith Darville is a *USA Today* bestselling author of dangerously delicious romance, including sizzling paranormal reverse harem. With over forty years of storytelling experience, her stories are guaranteed to make readers flush and blush.

lilithdarville.com

ACKNOWLEDGMENTS

In writing, as in life, it takes a village, and there are some key people in mine I want to acknowledge. Special thanks go out to my editor, Maggie Morris—I worship at her feet for using her amazing skills and expertise to help me bring this story to you. Huge thanks go to my cover artist, Melanie Card. She's been incredibly enthusiastic, and always considerate of my opinion as the author.

Where would I be without my wonderful critique partner, romance author Hélène Sopher. The moment the universe brought us together, we clicked. Thank you so much for your critical input and prodding. Working with you is a joy, and you're the best conference roomie ever.

Thanks to friends and family who encouraged, supported, and badgered ☺ me to follow my heart and keep writing.

And most of all, thanks to my beloved Neo. For enthusiastically embracing my projects and collaborating with me on them. For more helpful suggestions than I can count. For prodding me and keeping me on track. For helping me research – tee hee. For his unconditional love and acceptance. He makes all things seem possible!

Most of all, my thanks and appreciation to my readers. Your feedback and support help fuel the creative juices that keep me (and Connor) on this journey. Now, enjoy this read and feed your fantasies!